# Earth's Embrace

an Elemental Series Novel

## Alex E. Carey

Alex E. Carey - Greensboro, NC

Copyright © 2014 by Alex E. Carey

Published in the United States of America


Photo Credit: "Cherokee Suntree" ©2010 Bob Hower, used and modified with permission. www.qphoto.com


Alex E. Carey/December 2014
First Printing

Paperback edition ISBN: 978-0-9910291-6-7
Hardcover edition ISBN: 978-0-9910291-5-0
Ebook edition ISBN: 978-0-9910291-4-3

Cover Design by Alex E. Carey and Dee Ferris

Author Contact - ElementalSeries5@gmail.com

# Table of Contents

# About the Author

I majored in English at the University of North Carolina at Greensboro. Kira's story came to me during my first year while waiting for class to start. I began to scribble and the next thing I knew I had the beginnings of a story. I continued to imagine what would happen next and wrote bits and pieces in between classes and during work breaks. Once I typed up all the notes, I realized I had enough for a full novel, and ideas for more, resulting in the Elemental Series.

I enjoy a variety of books, but especially enjoyed the Twilight series by Stephenie Meyer, the Harry Potter series by J. K. Rowling and the Percy Jackson series by Rick Riordan. If you also like those book series, I hope you will enjoy my Elemental Series.

# Acknowledgements

For Dee Ferris, my mother, for helping with editing and publishing; and encouraging me to be my best.

For Randy Ferris, my father, for his encouragement.

For Wil Ferris, my brother, for his support, help and offering ideas for the book.

For Kristen Henderson, my cousin, for offering to be a beta reader and for being one of my biggest fans.

For Daphne Keys, my aunt, for being so supportive and encouraging from the beginning.

For Bryan Coyle and Chris Dies, managers at the Moose Cafe, for supporting me and teaching me skills I can apply in various areas of work and life.

For Bill and Margaret Walker and Will and Michelle Walker, owners of the Moose Cafe restaurant chain, for their constant support, and for allowing me to base the book's restaurant loosely off the Moose Cafe.

For Lisa Poole and Kayla Martinez, for offering (with mild begging) to be the basis for characters in the book. These ladies are very sweet in real life and I'm grateful to know them and count them as friends.

For Bob Hower, photographer, for graciously allowing me to use his picture, "Cherokee Suntree", in the cover design of this book.

For all of my family and friends who I didn't mention specifically, please know that I love you and am thankful for all of you.

For all of my readers who loved my first novel, Fire's Love, thank you for being fans of the Elemental Series. I hope you enjoy Earth's Embrace.

# Chapter 1
# Unpacking Nightmares

*Dear Diary,*

    *Ever since Pyre and I moved in together, things have gone missing or been broken. We're gradually finding everything, and we fixed the broken items. I'm glad the apartment has two bedrooms. I love Pyre, but we've only known each other a few months, and he's the first boyfriend I've ever had. Pyre is still adjusting to living in the apartment instead of the cave, and to being closer to humans. And... I'm paranoid that he'll accidentally squeeze my head off in his sleep.*

    *Every day has been an adventure since I met Pyre and Lowell. It began with Lowell and my discovery that he was a demon, Ulric the wolf thief. I wasn't supposed to find out, but he saved my life. Lowell introduced me to Pyre, a fire demon; and we've been together ever since. My life has also been in constant danger. Soon after Pyre and I got together, my roommate, Melissa, tried to kill me. She used me to get revenge on Pyre and Lowell since she thought they killed her family. Pyre wanted to destroy her when he thought I was dead. The event apparently affected him more than he'll admit. Occasionally, I wake up in the middle of the night because he has called my name. He won't talk about it though, which worries me.*

    *Christmas will be here soon, and I'm nearly done with my Christmas shopping. I still need to find something for Pyre and Lowell. I have an idea for something for*

*Lowell but I'm not sure yet. For Pyre I might—*

CRASH! The commotion came from Pyre's room, followed by a rattle and a thunderous boom. I arose from my desk and ran to his door, imagining all the catastrophes that might be happening in there. Perhaps he dropped a bowl, tripped over a table, or set something on fire. He might have tripped over a table, causing him to drop the bowl, making him so mad he set the table on fire.

"Pyre?" I knocked on the door, praying he wouldn't set the door on fire. I didn't smell anything burning, which was a good sign. He opened the door to reveal a box on his head and stared at me with chagrin.

"Are you okay?" I asked as I took the box off his head.

"Just trying to finish unpacking."

"Tell me if you need any help."

Pyre sighed, nodded and closed the door.

I walked back to my room, sat at my desk and opened my diary to the current entry. I hadn't even clicked my pen to write again when Pyre yelled from frustration.

*I wonder what happened this time.* I cringed and hurried to his door. He opened it before I could knock.

"I hate unpacking!" He exclaimed as he leaned against the door frame.

"Why don't you take a break?" I clasped Pyre's hands and pulled him into the living room. "Do you want something to drink?"

"No, I just want to sit." He sat on the couch and held out his arms. I leaned into them, wrapping my own arms around his neck. "Unpacking sucks. I keep tripping on boxes, dropping things, and crashing into the wall. This has been a terrible day."

"At least you haven't set anything on fire yet." I tried to make him smile, but he just glared at me. "I'm sorry. Do you want me to help?"

"I'd rather put it off." Pyre leaned his head on the back of the couch.

"I understand, but you need to finish." I sat beside him and looked into his eyes.

"I don't want to." He moved around so his head hung off the couch and his feet dangled over the back, resembling a little kid. I noticed his shirt had ridden up, partially revealing his stomach.

"You need to." I poked his stomach.

"No." He swatted at my hand. I smiled mischievously as I poked him again. He looked at me. "Stop it."

"Why?" I poked him while trying to sound clueless and innocent.

"It's annoying." Pyre sat up and raised an eyebrow at me as I poked him again. "Why won't you stop?"

"Because it's fun." I poked him repeatedly.

"It's fun, huh?" My only warning was his wicked leer. The next moment, I was on the floor, laughing from his tickling. "How much fun is it now?"

"Stop! Please! Can't breathe!" I laughed hysterically and tried to get loose.

"I love you." He stopped and pulled me up onto my feet.

"I love you too." I kissed his lips. He rested his head on my shoulder and I stroked his hair. "What's the matter?"

"I'm just tired." He yawned.

"Are you getting enough sleep?"

"No." He groaned as I rubbed his shoulders.

"Why not?"

"I just can't sleep."

"Is something on your mind?" When he didn't answer, I lifted his head to look him in the eyes. "You know you can talk to me about anything, right?"

"Yes, I do. You're the sweetest person I've ever met." He rubbed my face.

"That's not what you said when you first met me." I crossed my arms and squinted at him.

"Only because I didn't understand what had happened. I had already developed a crush on you, but I was anxious about it and tried to fight it. Because of my history of bad relationships, I never wanted to fall in love with anyone else. In fact, I mostly kept to myself. Even Eira didn't know me very well. I guess I wasn't consciously aware I was pushing you away."

"Oh, you were aware, but even though you preferred the solitary life, deep down you wanted to belong, which is the reason you stayed near your friends and Eira. Still, you behaved so mean to me, I thought you hated me and was afraid to be alone with you."

"I was mean to you? That's not how I remember it."

"Allow me to refresh your memory. When we first met, you carried me to an alley and unceremoniously dumped me there, and hurt my side in the process."

"I saved your life from the monster in the park. I had to put you down quickly to hurry back to help the others."

"I'll give you that one, but the whole situation was scary to a mere human. When we met again in Lowell's apartment, at first you only stared at me. The expression on your face alone was enough to make me anxious, and then you started to speak. You asked me why Lowell would be friends with a weak and worthless human."

"There is that, but if I recall correctly, I also said I felt something for you."

"Yes, you did. You said it was something strange, you didn't know what it was, and you didn't like it. Then you and Lowell left to train."

"That's right! Which is when you told me to stay away from you."

"After you said, and I quote, 'The human isn't allowed to go.' You followed up with, 'The human needs to learn to keep her mouth shut.' We met again at Caedmon's apartment. Everyone greeted me, except you, and Caedmon and Eros. They were busy fighting as usual, and you sat next to the window, refusing to look at me. As the conversation in the room progressed, Lowell said he thought he'd found your soul mate in me. You looked at him with thoughts of death in your eyes, so they all locked us in the closet together for seven minutes."

"But you found a way out, through a vent in the wall."

"Once we were in the vent, you asked me what Lowell told me about you. You told me not to ask you any questions and not to get in your way."

"Yep, our first bonding moment."

"Our first bonding moment? When I did ask you a

question, you told me the answer was none of my business. I knew you were anti-social, but I was sure you hated me."

"I could never hate you. Being in the closet and the vent together was our first chance at bonding, because it led to our first real conversation, and to admitting my feelings for you. Besides, you weren't much help or need I remind you of the way you treated me."

"I only acted that way in response to your behavior."

"Whatever. You acted that way because you were frightened of me." He pulled me back into his arms.

"You gave me plenty of reasons to be."

"I gave you numerous reasons to be terrified of me but instead of scaring you off, you fell for me too." He hugged me close and yawned again.

"You should take a nap."

"But I want to spend time with you."

"You can after you get some sleep."

"Fine, Mom, I'm going."

As Pyre walked away, I threw the couch pillow at him and hit him on the head. He turned and stuck out his tongue in response. After convincing myself he was back in his room, I went to my own room and worked on organizing my desk and shelves for the new school semester. I had nearly finished when I heard Pyre calling my name.

"Kira!" Pyre yelled, sounding frantic.

I dropped what I held in my hands and ran to his room. He was still asleep, but he was terribly restless.

"Kira!"

"Pyre, wake up!" I gripped his hand.

"Kira!" He squeezed my hand and growled as he began to transform.

"Pyre." I kissed his forehead. His breathing slowed, and he changed back to his human form. I rubbed his face and kept calling his name to get him awake.

"Kira, what's happening? What's wrong?" He sat up and searched the room in defensive mode.

"I could ask you the same thing."

"What do you mean?"

"You were calling my name and changing into your demon form."

"I was?" He rubbed his face. "I was having a horrible dream. I'll get up now."

"Have the nightmares been happening often?"

"Only the past few days, but it's nothing." I understood he lied because he didn't want to worry me, but it still upset me.

"You promise?" He looked up at me with a guilty expression on his face.

"I promise there's no need to worry. I get nightmares all the time. If it hasn't stopped soon, we'll talk about it."

"Fair enough." *That's all I can ask for now.* "Do you want me to help you unpack now?"

"Aren't you busy working on your room?"

"I'm practically done. You've been asleep awhile."

"In that case, I would appreciate the help."

We got to work unpacking his boxes. I spotted a trunk against the wall that appeared ancient in age. I walked over to it and admired it for a moment. "What's in this?"

"Those are my swords. Each sword belongs in its own case. I store the cases in the trunk. I also use a special wall display for the swords." He opened the trunk for me.

"Swords? You mean more than one?"

I pulled one of the cases out of the trunk. It was ornately carved cherry wood with a brass clasp. A name was carved on the lid, but I couldn't read it. I lifted the lid to reveal a beautiful sword with detailed decorations on the blade and the handle. It rested on a tan satin pad which was molded to fit the shape of the sword. The lid was lined with the same fabric.

"I collect swords. It's kind of like you with your stuffed animals."

"Yes, but stuffed animals can't kill anyone." I scrutinized him and the sword.

"Swords only kill because the wielder kills. A sword can't kill on its own. Let me show you." Pyre picked up the sword and put it in my hands. He stepped behind me and wrapped both of his arms around me, clasping his hands around mine. "A sword and its wielder need to maintain balance. A sword isn't merely used for maiming or killing. It can also be used to defend and protect, an instrument of survival." He moved the sword in precise yet fluid motions. "By itself the sword is only a piece of metal. It's not until a wielder gives it a purpose that it becomes a weapon."

"Wow, this is... powerful." My face grew warm as he spoke and demonstrated his technique. "You know a great deal about swords." I glimpsed back into the trunk. There had to be at least twenty cases in it. "How many swords do you own?"

"That's not important." He took the sword out of my hands and put it back in the case.

"What is the inscription on the lid?"

"It's nothing." He seemed embarrassed.

"Come on, tell me what it is."

"It's the language of fire demons. The word on the lid identifies which sword is in the case. It's... It's the name of the sword."

"Then it is kind of like me with my stuffed animals."

"Don't make fun of me." He tried to turn away from me, but I grabbed his arm.

"Pyre, honey, I'm not. Why are you self-conscious about it?"

"You don't think it's silly?"

"No, not at all. A big wide world of no. I collect and name stuffed animals, remember? So what's this sword's name?"

Pyre seemed relieved and became animated as he told me the name of the sword, why he called it that name, and how he acquired it. He pulled another case from the trunk, which was made of mahogany with a bronze clasp, and opened it for display. This sword was decorated with rubies, nestled in a black velvet padding. I inspected the other cases in the trunk. Each was a different type of wood with different carvings and fixtures. He pulled a few more out and told me about each one. I realized each sword was a unique work of art, and each case was crafted to match the sword it would hold.

As he spoke, I also realized this wasn't simply a collection or a hobby. Like my stuffed animals, each one had its own story and meaning for him, but it was much more than sentiment. Unlike my stuffed animals, these swords were a reflection of his life. They weren't merely hunks of metal which had been heated and shaped into a sword and given a sharp edge. Each one carried the weight of battles fought, whether won or lost; and the blood, sweat and tears shed by the combatants. The swords stood for the lives he had saved or defended, including his own. They also represented the lives lost, whether at his hands, or loved ones he couldn't protect. Each held its own importance, purpose, memories and symbolism. This imbued them with an essence of power so strong I could sense it when holding one in my hands. The sword seemed to vibrate in my grip. The handle warmed at my touch, which in turn warmed my skin, like an energy radiating into my arm. The sword appeared to have become an extension of me, or maybe the opposite. It comforted me oddly enough, like an old trusted friend saying, "I'm here for you."

Pyre stared at me with a peculiar expression, and it was my turn to feel self-conscious.

"At least I know which room to run to if I'm ever under attack and you're not here." He kissed my neck.

"I will make certain I'm close if you're under attack. If I'm not, Lowell will be." He gazed at the ceiling for a minute. "But at a distance."

"Pyre."

"Until he gets someone of his own, I don't trust him alone with you."

"Pyre, Lowell wouldn't do anything to break his friendship with either of us."

"I realize that. I'm just concerned about him. He hasn't been the same since losing Cadel."

"It takes time to get over losing someone you love."

"Lowell's had time; he doesn't want to get over it. He needs to talk about it and put it behind him."

"You need to let him be. If he wants to keep it to himself, who are we to force the issue? We're his friends, and the only family he has. When he's ready, he'll talk to us." Pyre crossed his arms and made a strange face at me. "What?"

"How old are you again?" He studied me as if trying to guess my age.

"What is that supposed to mean?"

"You're too young to be this smart." I punched his arm. "What? It's true."

"You can thank my parents for that. They taught me to be prepared for anything." I walked over to another box.

"Not everything." I looked over at him. He wore a devilish expression on his face.

"No, they didn't prepare me for you; for demons, that is. I'm uncertain if or what my parents knew regarding demons." He appeared confused. "I've shown you my book about demons. I can use it to learn all the information available regarding any demon. The book is how I originally figured out my dreams can tell the future. It was in my parents' possessions, so they must have known something about demons. Unless they didn't understand what the book truly was. I wish they had told me everything they meant to, and that my dad hadn't left me when I needed him most. There is still a great deal I don't understand concerning my parents and myself."

"Did you read the file Vitas gave you?"

"It basically said we were a typical family; nothing about who my parents were or where they originated."

"That's strange. Everyone's file should reveal everything about them. Every moment we experience gets written in the file. This conversation is being written as we speak."

"That's creepy."

"Very." We returned to unpacking and had nearly finished when we heard tapping on the door. Pyre squinted through the peephole, groaned and opened the door.

"Hey, Big Brother!" Eira exclaimed, wrapping her arms around Pyre's neck.

"Hey, Eira." Pyre muttered, rolling his eyes.

"Hey, Kira!" She ran over and gave me a hug too.

"Hi, Eira."

"Wait a minute! Why is the oaf here?" Pyre yelled as Eros walked up to the door.

"He's helping me." Eira stated adamantly.

"In that case..." He slammed the door in Eros' face.

"Pyre!" Eira yelled at him as she opened the door for Eros. "Why must you be so mean to Eros?"

"I don't have to, I want to."

"For crying out loud, why?" She got closer to him, in his face, and with her hands on her hips said, "Why? Why?! WHY?!"

"I don't know." Pyre walked over to stand slightly behind me. He opened his eyes wide, trying to appear innocent and shrugged. I gaped in disbelief at Pyre and he crossed his arms.

*Why didn't you tell me the oaf was coming?* Pyre demanded telepathically.

*I wasn't aware either of them were coming.*

He thought for a second and turned to Eira and Eros. "Why are both of you here?"

"We brought something for the Christmas party."

"The party isn't for another week and a half." Pyre rubbed his forehead.

"I realize that, but I wanted to bring it over early."

"What's in the box, Eira?" I watched curiously as Eira opened the box and produced a smaller wrapped box.

"It's for you, Kira, but you're not allowed to open it until the party."

"Why bring it now?" Pyre grew more irritated by the minute.

"I don't want it to get broken. Apparently nothing is safe at my house when boys decide they want to train. Or just fight with each other for the fun of it." She glared at Eros disapprovingly, who stared at the ceiling with a sheepish expression.

"I'll find a safe place for it." Pyre took the box from her and disappeared.

"We'll see you later." Eira sang and pushed Eros out the door.

"But you —" I didn't even get to finish.

"We still have more to do." She waved as she closed the door behind them.

*I will never understand her.* I shook my head, baffled.

*Now you know how I feel.* I turned to see Pyre standing in the doorway of his bedroom. *My sister is so unconventional.*

"She is utterly eccentric, but lovable."

"I do love my sister but she is the quirkiest fire demon I've ever met."

"You're not exactly a normal fire demon." I smiled impishly.

"How would you know? To my knowledge, you've only met two fire demons. Are you a fire demon groupie?"

"Well, you haven't known me that long. It'll take time to tell you about all the demons I met before you."

"You're not exactly normal for a human now that I consider it." He walked closer and wrapped his arms around me.

"I would hate being normal. I would prefer to be completely abnormal."

"I wonder what you'd be like if you were a demon." He played with my hair while he studied me. "You'd either be fire or ice I'd bet, possibly an animal type."

"What kind of animal?" He thought about it for a moment.

"If you were fire, I'd guess you'd be a fox. You're remarkably clever and you can sometimes be aggressive like a fire type. If you were ice, you'd probably be a snow leopard. You're independent and highly observant. I'm hoping for the fire type of course."

"Of course."

"I'm going to bed." He gave me a good night kiss and went to his room.

*It has been a long day.* I laid down on my bed and fell asleep within minutes.

The next morning, I pulled a small wood box off my shelf that my mom used to store her old recipes. I went through them and found my favorites, while missing baking with my mom. The door creaked open behind me. Pyre appeared to have just woken up as he rubbed his eyes, yawned, and scratched his belly.

"Good morning." I giggled and shook my head.

"No such thing. What are those papers?"

"They're my mom's old recipes."

"Recipes?" He walked over and picked up one of the cards.

"My mom loved to bake. She wrote all the recipes down so she wouldn't forget and I could learn to make them too."

"What kinds of food did she make?"

"She made so many things that if you named it, she made it. My favorite was her chocolate chip cookies." I held out the recipe to him.

"We should make some of these for the party."

"That'd be fun. We need to pick out which ones we want to make and check whether we have the ingredients."

"We're definitely making the chocolate chip cookies." He wrapped his arms around me. "Can we choose them all now?"

"I don't see why not." We went to the living room and sat on the couch together. "I can't believe it's nearly Christmas. Where did November go?"

"You needed to study for exams and finish the semester. I needed to move my belongings from out of town. On top of which, Vitas has kept me extra busy fighting demons and training. I haven't even had time to unpack until now."

"We both realize why he's keeping you busy." Pyre gazed at the floor with a puzzled expression on his face. "You do, don't you?" He bit his lip and shook his head. "Vitas is trying to make sure we spend as little time together as possible. He believes you're too dangerous for me."

"Vitas might be right." He sounded serious, but when he caught me watching him, he brightened. "Maybe I am too dangerous for you." He ogled me ominously.

"Down, teddy bear." I returned my attention to the recipes.

"Teddy bear?" He exclaimed as he faked being offended. "Teddy bear?"

"Teddy bear; and you're a grumble bear when you're angry."

"In what way am I like a teddy bear?"

"You're sweet, cuddly, lovable, and you would never hurt me no matter what happened." He thought it over for a minute before nodding.

"My baby understands me so well." He wrapped an arm around me. "Not in front of the guys though."

"Never." I crossed my heart as a promise.

"What can I call you?"

"You call me baby and sometimes angel. What else would you want to call me?"

"How about... Firefly?"

"Firefly?" I couldn't grasp it. "How am I like a firefly?"

"You're beautiful to observe, possess the best communication skills I've ever seen, and you light up my world."

"Aw, who says you're not romantic?" He picked up some of the recipes.

"Only when I want to be." A knock at the door interrupted our conversation. "What do you want?!"

"I came to give you something." Lowell answered.

"We don't want it!" Pyre threw a pillow at the door.

"It's for the party!"

"What is with you people? You can wait to bring it on the day of the party!" I stood up and walked over to the door.

"You'll want it before the party." Lowell asserted as he walked into the apartment.

"I still don't want it." Pyre crossed his arms and huffed.

"I'm the youngest, but you're the one behaving like a five year old." I said.

"It's because you're a girl." Lowell stated with conviction. "Girls mature considerably faster."

"Even faster than demons who are hundreds of years old?" I asked.

The guys looked at each other and said in unison, "Yep."

"Why do I even bother?" I threw up my hands and walked back to the couch.

"What did you bring us, Wolf?"

"It's more for you, Pyre." Lowell held out a small box and displayed it to Pyre. I stared suspiciously at the box, and then at the boys.

"Is that it?" Pyre was much too excited for my

comfort. Lowell nodded with a conspiratorial smile. "I won't say this ever again, but, Wolf, you're awesome." Pyre ran over to Lowell and snatched the little box. I grew extremely confused and uneasy about what it might be.

"Pyre, you're alarming your girlfriend." Lowell said.

"A little bit." I admitted.

"Firefly, you're going to love this." Pyre pulled me up for a hug and ran off, letting me go so fast I plopped back down on the couch. I was still bewildered and regarded Lowell quizzically.

"It's something he asked me to search for as a favor." Lowell said as if that explained everything. I continued to stare at him questioningly. "You'll see what it is at the party." I tapped my fingers on my knee and stared at him obstinately without blinking. "I promise... Firefly." He chuckled, with emphasis on my new nickname.

"Do you wish to live?" I queried softly, and in my creepiest voice.

"I've got to get going. Tell Pyre I said bye." He practically ran through the door.

"The human is still confused." I looked to Pyre for answers when he came back into the room.

"You won't be after the party. It's something I know you'll love." Pyre embraced me in his arms and kissed my cheek. "Let's get back to the recipes now." He sat down next to me and picked up more recipes. "This day keeps getting better and better."

"The day just began not too long ago."

"True, but the day has been perfect so far." He examined the recipe cards in his hands. "Ooh, pecan pie."

A thought instantly occurred to me. "You cook frequently and you're exceptional at it. Don't you use some recipes of your own?"

"Nah, I mostly cook by instinct. Any recipes I use are all in my head, and that's where they'll stay."

"You won't even share them with me?"

"Nope!"

"Well, why not?"

"If I share the secret of my cooking, you'll learn to do it for yourself and won't need me to cook for you anymore."

"I doubt there's any real concern there. Even with a recipe, my cooking is usually a disaster."

"That bad, huh?"

"Let's simply say you don't want to mix up baking soda and baking powder. And if there's a smoke alarm anywhere near the stove, such as in the next room, it will go off."

"Note to self. I alone will feed the family." He laughed but noticed me gaping at him, obviously disconcerted. "Back to tiny little pieces of paper."

As we continued going through the recipes, I told him stories about my mom, and memories of baking with her. Pyre took a small break to get dinner started. After a few hours, we finally decided on some choices.

"We chose chocolate chip cookies, sugar cookies, peanut butter cookies, pecan pie, pumpkin pie, chocolate pudding cake, and cherry whip." I said.

"Will that be enough?" Pyre asked.

"Seven desserts for ten people."

"You're right; we need more."

"Pyre, it'll be more than enough as long as we make plenty of each."

"How much is enough?"

"Let's see, with how Caedmon and Eros eat, we should make triple just for them. Let's say three to five times what the recipes require? There should even be enough left for everyone to take some home."

"You're not counting Eira or me in the ten people, are you?"

"Yes, why wouldn't I?"

"You don't want to know." I faced him with my hands on my hips. "Trust me, you don't want to know. If you'll make a list of the supplies we need, I'll go shopping tomorrow after I'm done doing chores for Vitas."

"Nice change of subject. It won't take me long to make a list."

"While you do that, I'll finish cooking dinner."

"Why shouldn't I include you in how many people will be here?" I pulled out a pen and paper to make a list of everything we would need.

He made a big show of searching through the cabinet. "Where did I put... Oh, there it is." He pulled out a pan from the cabinet. I went through the fridge to figure out what we needed. "How's the list coming?"

"Nice change of subject... again! It's almost done. I'm checking to see what we have."

"Dinner will be ready soon too."

"What're we having?"

"I'm making lasagna."

"I love your lasagna. I don't understand how you can make such delicious lasagna."

"That's my secret." He flashed me a toothy smile. I walked over to him and leaned my head against his shoulder. "What's wrong?"

"I want you to tell me why I shouldn't include you in the count of people. You and Eira aren't planning to leave before the party, are you?"

"No, of course not. Where did you get that idea?"

"Why else shouldn't I count you both?"

"It's not a big deal. We merely can't consume sugar."

"What?"

"Fire demons can't ingest anything that contains sugar. If we do, we experience a serious sugar rush."

"Sugar rush? You made me nervous over a sugar rush?"

"It's much worse than a human sugar rush. I didn't mean to worry you, but why would you think I would leave?"

"I thought there was some reason you wouldn't be there, or couldn't be there, which made me anxious you might disappear again, like you did before my birthday."

"I promise I'll never do that again."

"Good." I yawned.

"Are you all right?"

"I'm a bit tired."

"It has been a busy day. Go sit down and I'll bring you a plate when it's ready." I agreed but didn't move. "Kira, go sit down before you doze off where you stand."

"I'm not dozing. It's virtually impossible to sleep while standing, isn't it?" He wrapped his arms around me, picked me up and headed for my bedroom.

"Either way, I'm putting you to bed."

"But the lasagna..."

"Will be there in the morning." He kissed my forehead as he headed to my room. He set me down on my bed, and I laid down right away. "Where is the shopping list?"

"Right here." I held up the list. He took the list from my hand and scrutinized it. "I'm sorry I couldn't stay awake."

"No problem." He kissed my lips before leaving the room.

*Why am I this fatigued? I realize I had a lot to do the last few days but I shouldn't be this tired.* I pondered for a few more minutes before falling asleep.

# Chapter 2
# Christmas Party

    The next day Pyre went to the store and bought what we needed for baking and for Christmas dinner. When he got home, we worked on finishing his unpacking. He had several boxes since he moved all of his worldly goods from his hometown. We wondered if we'd ever be done, so it felt satisfying to see his floor. He wasn't much of a packrat, thankfully, but still, he had lived one hundred and eighty years and had accumulated a huge assortment of possessions. Helping him unpack reminded me of my own belongings I left behind in Nashville.

    "Pyre, you never told me how you moved all of your boxes here." I picked up a marble off his shelf.

    "It wasn't hard. I left my belongings with my parents when I came here, so everything was mostly packed. My parents and some friends packed the rest and hired movers to drive them here."

    "That's it?" I waited for him to say more.

    "How else would we have done it?"

    "I don't know, but that's so mundane, and human; and after all, you are a demon."

    "I see." He chuckled. "You thought because we're demons, we would move things in special or supernatural ways."

    "It's not that. Not exactly that anyway. I wondered since you seemed to move your boxes so fast. Where is your hometown?" I sat down on his bed twirling the marble between my fingers.

"I lived outside Scofield, Utah. It's a terrific little town, supposed to be the smallest town in Utah. You would love it there. Perhaps I'll take you there sometime."

"I'd like that. What's it like there?"

"It's a beautiful area. There's a green valley where wildflowers grow, surrounded by hills, mountains and forests. Uinta-Wasatch-Cache National Forest is to the north and Manti-La Sal National Forest is to the south. The reservoir and Scofield State Park are nearby and offer camping, fishing, and lots of nature activities. You can go bird or animal watching or hunting for dinosaur fossils. They also offer skiing and snowboarding during the winter. There's a neat convenience store in Scofield called the Snack & Pack. They sell all kinds of things including fast food, sporting goods and camping supplies. They're only open about May through October though because of the hard winters."

"It sounds so beautiful. I love being outdoors and going animal watching."

"Not only that but the area is full of history. People came there originally for ranching but then coal was discovered and the railroad came to the area. A few outlaws are even rumored to have followed the railroad, including some of the Wild Bunch."

"The Wild Bunch? As in Butch Cassidy?"

"Yep. If I remember correctly, he was born about 1866 in Beaver, Utah, located south of Scofield."

"That's fascinating! Did you ever meet him?"

"Butch Cassidy? No, I never met him, but I met Matt Warner once. He rode with the Wild Bunch for a time, but later became a lawman in Price, a town near Scofield."

"How did you meet him?"

"Um, I'll tell you about it sometime. Let's just say I met him after he became a lawman and leave it at that for now."

"Sure. You said Scofield is a small town. With all of its history and sights to see, why isn't the town bigger."

"Not all the history is good. In May 1900 one of the worst coal mine disasters in history occurred there at the Winter Quarters Coal Mine. There was an explosion when a random spark ignited the coal dust. About two hundred men and even some teenage boys died, either in the explosion itself, or later from carbon monoxide poisoning. Many people left the area at that time, others moved somewhat later. The town had a population of nearly seven hundred and fifty people in 1910, but now it's down to roughly twenty people. The school closed up in the 1960's so families with school age children eventually moved rather than send their children on buses to schools in other towns."

"How horrific; those poor men! It sounds like a ghost town now."

"It practically is. Only a few buildings remain from the time of the disaster. It's still an active town, but very few people stay all year long. The area is also said to be haunted. Some say there's a headless man who wanders around, presumably a victim of the mine disaster, and there are reports of mysterious lights seen in the cemetery."

"Ghosts fascinate me, I must admit. I was convinced I saw my mother and brother in our living room after they died. I've been interested ever since that experience, so you've got me sold on going." He walked over to his bed and sat beside me. He stared at the floor for several minutes with his pensive expression. "Pyre, did I say something wrong?" He merely shook his head. I sat beside him, held his hand and waited quietly until he could vocalize what was troubling him.

"The disaster left over one hundred grieving wives and girlfriends and well over two hundred and fifty fatherless children. Two huge funeral trains carried the bodies to the cemetery for burial. So many lives were devastated that day." He took a few deep breaths before speaking again. "The disaster has tormented me for years because I've felt responsible."

"Why, Pyre? How would you be responsible?"

"I lived in a cave in the area in those days. The day of the explosion, I was extremely angry, but back then I was always angry. I changed into demon form and threw fire at the wall of the cave where I lived. What if... I always wondered if... it was my fault."

"What? No, that's not possible. How could it have been?"

"What if my cave was connected somehow to the mine, and a spark got through to one of the shafts? Or perhaps I heated the air so much it caused a spark within the mine."

"Did you ever research into it?"

"Somewhat. The news stories I read only mentioned a stray spark."

"Sit still, I'll be right back." I went to my bedroom, grabbed my laptop and hurried back to Pyre's room. "I can find anything on the web." We searched for the cause of the Scofield Mine Disaster and found several sites which said the same thing he had. I finally found one that mentioned something else. "Look, Pyre. Here it says basically a large batch of powder caused the ignition of the coal dust. It created a sort of chain of events throughout the entire mine which couldn't be avoided in that moment. If your cave had been connected, it would've burned too. The information came from the state mine inspector's review of the accident, so it's well researched and believable. There's no possible way it could've been your fault, honey"

He read through what I found and exhaled heavily through his hands. "That's a relief. I've agonized for so many years and been consumed with guilt. Still, Kira, I've done horrible things in my life. Should my guilt be assuaged because this one event ended up not being my fault?" His eyes held mine and vividly displayed the tortured self-condemnation he held in his heart and soul.

"I don't know what you've done in your past, but it doesn't matter to me, because that's not you anymore. I believe you aren't supposed to bear guilt for things which aren't your fault, and everyone does things in their lives they aren't proud of, or that they regret. It's hard not to harbor guilt for those things. It's easier to forgive others than to forgive yourself, but you must find a way. The guilt will eat you up inside until there's nothing left. It's as poisonous as carbon monoxide. You need to let the past go and hold on tight to the present. You learned from your mistakes and changed your life."

"Thanks to you, my angel."

33

"No, honey, you feel remorse for your mistakes because you have a conscience. That's always been there and is part of what makes you the man I love."

He grabbed me unexpectedly and held on tight, burying his face in my neck. I detected wetness on my shoulder as I held onto him and stroked his back. I didn't want to say anything, but finally was forced to, for self-preservation.

"Pyre? I forgot to say that when you hold on tight to the present, don't forget to let it breathe."

"Oh, I'm sorry. Are you okay?" He loosened his grip some but still held me, and I inhaled deeply.

"I'm always okay when I'm in your arms." I gazed into his eyes and kissed him gently. He stared back thoughtfully for a moment, appeared to remember something and moved to crouch in front of me, taking my hands in his.

"I can tell whenever there is something on your mind. Why did you get so curious about how I moved?"

I peeked up at him to find his knowing expression staring back at me.

"I want to get my stuff from Nashville. My life is here now, with you. I won't be going back there again except to visit. I also need to let go of the past and move forward."

"When do you want to leave?" He smiled at me and brushed the hair from my face.

"I thought possibly the Monday after Christmas."

"That works."

"What do you mean?"

"I'm going with you. I don't want you going by

yourself in case a demon attacks. Not to mention, you probably have a lot to pack and move, and I want to come help."

"I appreciate that. I'll inform Juniper that we're coming."

"Juniper?"

"Juniper is the woman who took care of me after my dad left. All of my stuff is at her house."

"Will she object to me coming with you?"

"She's eager to meet you. This woman has known me since I was five years old and she wants to meet my first boyfriend."

"Should I be nervous?"

"Certainly not."

"What all have you told her about me?"

"Everything. Minus the demon part of course."

"Will she approve of me?"

"Only one way to find out for certain."

"Monday?"

"Monday. Thank you, Pyre." I threw my arms around him, kissed him and went to the living room to call Juniper. She was ecstatic I was coming and curious to meet Pyre. I felt moderately nervous about them meeting, but excited about moving my things to Russellville.

We spent the next several days cleaning and decorating for the Christmas party. Vitas sent Pyre on a few jobs, and Lowell came by often, both of which annoyed Pyre tremendously. While Pyre went out on his jobs, I went shopping for a present for him and for Lowell, without luck or success.

I woke up the morning before Christmas Eve, got

dressed and called Eira.

"Hi, Kira. You're up early. What's up?"

"I need your help with finding gifts for Pyre and Lowell for Christmas and wondered if you'd—"

"I'd love to. I'll be there in a few minutes." She hung up before I could say anything else. I grabbed my purse and snuck out of my room. I was nearly out the door when a hand landed on my shoulder.

"Where do you think you're going?" Pyre interrogated suspiciously.

"Out."

"Out where?"

"I'm going out with Eira."

"Why?"

"I need to go shopping."

"Because?"

"Because I do." Eira knocked on the door insistently. She made it in record time. I thought she might be even faster than Pyre when she wanted to be.

"Are you ready?" She bounced up and down with excitement.

"Yep."

"Wait a minute—" Pyre raised a finger in the air, about to say more.

"Great! Let's go." Eira seized my arm and started running.

"Get back here!" Pyre yelled at us.

*Can I keep my arm, please?* I glanced back and waved bye to Pyre. I was relieved, but also surprised he didn't follow us.

Eira and I went to several stores. I found a necklace

with a tree pendant for Lowell, but I still hadn't found a gift for Pyre. We sat on a bench in front of a store with drinks and tried to come up with ideas.

"That was a fun day of shopping. I'm sorry we didn't find anything for Pyre, but you'll think of something. He'll like anything you get him." Eira stood up and gathered up her many bags. She had a successful shopping day, but she never seemed to be at a loss for something to buy when she shopped. "I've got to get home. Eros, Laya, and Caedmon are coming over for a double date."

"Have fun." I watched as she bounced away. *What am I going to do? Christmas is two days away and I'm still clueless as to what to get Pyre.* I vaguely sensed someone had walked up to me, but I was lost in my thoughts.

"Kira?"

I looked up toward the source of the voice. "Hi, Vitas."

"What're you doing here?"

"Shopping for a gift for Pyre for Christmas, and failing."

"Wow, last minute. What's the problem?"

"I don't know what he would want." I gazed down at my hands.

"You'll find something."

"But what if I can't? I'm running out of time and I'm all out of ideas."

"Why are you this agitated about it?"

"Pyre does so much for me. I want to show him how much I appreciate him."

"You don't need to get him a gift to show your appreciation."

"I realize that, but it's also our first Christmas together. I want to give him something special. Plus what if he got me a present? I'll feel even worse."

"What are his hobbies?"

"He collects swords." I leaned back against the bench.

"What about any activities he enjoys?" I bit my lip and thought.

"Training with Lowell, cooking, picking on Eros."

"Does he have any other interests?"

"If he does, I'm not aware of them yet."

"I might have an idea. Come with me." I got up and followed him down the road.

"What's your idea?"

"Not too long ago I came across this sword. I found it buried deep in a cave near Pyre's hometown. The sword was rumored to belong to the greatest fire demon who ever lived."

"Never mind." I spun around to return to the mall.

"What?"

"He was the greatest fire demon who ever lived. No one could stop him until one day he died a mysterious death, and the sword was lost forever." I over stated. "The story's been done. Every ancient civilization had a fabled sword legend."

"That fire demon happened to be Pyre's grandfather." He peered at me with a smug expression on his face.

"His grandfather? You don't say." I walked back over to him.

"His name was Kai, and he was an amazing fire

demon. He and I were long-time friends. We used to talk all the time. Kai was tremendously proud and happy when Pyre was born. He had this sword made especially for Pyre. Pyre's father didn't approve of it and wouldn't allow Kai to give it to him. Kai told Pyrrhos he wouldn't give it to Pyre until he turned seventeen in human years, but Pyrrhos wouldn't listen. Pyrrhos took the sword and buried it in the cave to hide it. When I discovered it, I recognized it, realized it belonged to Kai and returned it to him. Pyrrhos cut all ties with Kai, so Pyre never knew about the sword or his grandfather."

"What happened to his grandfather?"

"He's still living near the town, still waiting for Pyre to come for the sword." He put a hand on my shoulder. "And we're here." He pointed to a door. I surveyed our surroundings and discovered we were in the middle of nowhere.

"Where are we, Vitas?"

"We're at Kai's house."

"How did we get here?"

"It's part of my power." An exceptionally old man opened the door when Vitas knocked.

"Hey there, Vitas!" He hugged Vitas like an old friend. "Still as young as ever."

"And you're still as old as ever."

"Eh, old is just a word. As far as I'm concerned, I've still got a few kicks left in me." He threw a few fake punches at Vitas, who pretended to shield himself. "Who's the girl?"

"My name's Kira."

"Pleased to meet ya, Kira. You smell like a

human."

"I-I am." His scrutiny made me uneasy, but that was true about the whole situation.

"You've got a hint of demon mixed into your scent."

"I'm dating a demon."

"Ooh, girl lives on the edge. What type of demon? Better yet, tell me his name. I might be familiar with him." He sounded curious and excited.

"His name is..." I glanced at Vitas and he nodded to me. "Pyre."

"Pyre?" He turned his gaze to Vitas. "My grandson Pyre?"

"Yep." Vitas said.

"You're dating my grandson?" He shook my shoulders.

"Y-yes, sir." I stammered.

"Ah-ha!" He picked me up and spun me around the room. "My grandson is dating a human! That's my grandson!" He put me down and examined me appreciatively while I waited for my head to stop whirling. "My, my, what a beaut you are."

"Thank you." My face grew warm as I blushed.

"You must be here for the sword." He ran into another room.

"That's Pyre's grandfather?"

"Yep." Vitas beamed at me. He obviously held great regard for Kai.

"How'd he know we came for the sword?"

"That's part of his power."

"Here ya go, little lady." Kai came back with the

sword. "I wanted to give it to him myself, but you go ahead. Give this to my grandson and tell him his grandpa hopes he's doing well. Tell him to come for a visit sometime." He handed me the sword in its sheath.

"I'll tell him. Thank you for this." I said.

"Vitas, you old goat, you need to come over more often."

"I've been insanely busy." Vitas said.

"You're an old stick in the mud." I lowered my eyes to hide my grin and pretended to inspect the sword and sheath.

"It's time to go, Kira." Vitas said, putting a hand on my shoulder.

"Come back anytime." Kai said.

When I looked up to say goodbye, Vitas and I were standing in my bedroom.

"I must get going, Kira. You'll now be able to give Pyre an extraordinarily special gift."

"Thank you for your help, Vitas." I turned to face him but he was gone. *Gone again. I wonder if I'll ever get used to that.* I had only partially wrapped the sword when a knock on the door startled me. "Who is it?"

"You know very well who it is." Pyre sounded angry, but I couldn't imagine any reason he would be.

"One second." I quickly hid the sword under my bed before opening the door. "Yes?"

"I thought you were out with Eira." He appeared as angry as he sounded, with his crossed arms and his rigid posture.

"I was but now I'm home."

"How did you get home?"

"I walked."

"By yourself?" He raised an eyebrow.

"No." *Cue ominous music here.* I could see where the conversation was headed, and Pyre would not be happy about it.

"Who walked with you?"

"Vitas."

"What did he want? And why didn't Eira walk home with you?" He rubbed his forehead.

"Eira needed to hurry home because she had plans. Vitas appeared as she left and offered to help me with something."

"What did he help you with, Kira?"

"Something important."

"If it was that important, why couldn't I help you?"

"It was..." I was embarrassed and closed my eyes. I realized it was time to face the ominous music. "I went out to find you a Christmas present."

"That's not necessary." He rubbed my arms.

"I know, but I want to give you something." I looked at him.

"Why didn't you tell me?"

"I wanted it to be a surprise."

"Please tell me next time. I was somewhat panicky at one point when I couldn't sense you in town."

"Sorry." I tried to sound contrite, although I thought he was being overly protective.

"No need to apologize." He kissed my forehead. "Come on, dinner is almost ready."

While we enjoyed Pyre's savory parmesan chicken, we talked about the plans for Christmas and what all needed to be done. Pyre was tremendously excited about it, just like a little kid. I was relieved I finally found a present for him and now eagerly awaited Christmas so I could give it to him.

The sun woke me up Christmas Eve morning. I sat up and rubbed my eyes.

*Why did I agree to host the party here again? That's right, because I love getting up early to bake. How could I forget? At least Pyre will be here to help.* I went to Pyre's room and knocked on the door. "Pyre, it's time to get up." I waited a minute but didn't hear anything. "Pyre!" I knocked louder, but still no response. I opened the door to find him still sleeping. "Pyre, get up." He didn't budge at all, so I walked over to him. "Pyre, wake up." I touched his arm and immediately regretted it. He swung his arm and nearly punched me in the face. I barely dodged his fist.

"Don't touch me you feathered freak!" I stared at him and tried to catch my breath.

"Never mind." I walked out of his room and into the kitchen. "I'll get the ball rolling and hope you wake up soon." I sorted the recipe cards we pulled out last week. "The chocolate pudding cake will be more time consuming than anything so I'll make it first." I put on some Christmas music to set the mood. While I pulled out mixing bowls, utensils, and ingredients, I filled the sink with water for washing dishes as I used them. "First, I need to combine all ingredients in a large mixing bowl and beat at medium speed. That doesn't sound too hard." I added ingredients one by one to the bowl. When I reached for the eggs, I accidentally dropped one. "Oops. Clumsy me."

43

When I cracked the eggs into the bowl, pieces of eggshell fell into the mix. After fishing out the shells, I added the remaining ingredients.

"Now I blend it at medium speed for four minutes." I pulled out the electric mixer and plugged it in the outlet. I lowered the beaters into the mix and set it at medium speed, but nothing happened. I turned it off and pulled it out of the bowl. "What's wrong with this thing? Is it broken?" I put it back in the bowl and tried again. Still nothing. I inspected the beaters and discovered one wasn't locked in place. "You should work now." I inadvertently turned it on without putting it in the bowl and immediately regretted it. The mix on the beaters splattered all over the place. I quickly turned it off and cleaned up the mess. "Terrific. I hope that's the worst thing that will happen today."

After I finished beating the mix, I poured it into a greased and floured pan and put it in the oven for forty minutes. As it baked, I got to work on the next item on the list. More things went wrong, including slipping on the mess on the floor. After a few hours, and one disaster after another, I had a conglomeration of all the mixes and ingredients in my hair, on my clothes, and covering my face. I finally leaned against the counter.

"This is hopeless." I slid gradually to the floor. "I can't cook. Why did I even try?" As I rubbed my forehead, a hand landed on my shoulder.

"Having trouble?" Pyre surveyed the catastrophe in the kitchen.

"Yes." I stared at him with slight accusation.

"I take it I was sleeping hard." I nodded and pouted while he rubbed my face. "Why don't you go take a hot shower and I'll finish and clean up the kitchen?"

"You don't mind?"

"Not at all. I've got this. Besides you need to get the cookie dough out of your hair." I gaped at him in confusion before touching my hair and pulling out a squishy wad of dough.

"How did I... on second thought, never mind." I tried to stand and slipped. I sat there and kicked my feet. Pyre chuckled and helped me to stand.

"Go take a shower." He pushed me out of the kitchen. "Let me finish baking the sweets and cleaning." He pointed toward the bathroom.

"Okay, I'm going."

I went to my room for some clean clothes. *I should help Pyre with the rest of the work; although, he is a better cook. I guess I need to let him take care of it.*

After I showered and dressed, I went to the kitchen to see if he needed any help. I was amazed that everything was finished. The kitchen was even cleaned and decorated.

"Wow, Pyre!" I exclaimed in surprise.

"I told you I've got this."

"You did." *I still should've helped more.*

"Since everything's done, why don't you go take a nap?"

"I'm fine."

"Let's at least go sit on the couch."

We sat together, and I leaned against his chest. "Thank you for finishing the baking."

"It was my pleasure." He held me close, rubbing my arm. "Can I open my present now?"

"No." I eyed him with my best chastising

expression.

"Please!"

"No!" I got up and ran for my room.

"Please?" He caught me and wrapped his arms around my waist, lifting me up in the air.

"No, you are required to wait until tomorrow."

"What if I don't want to wait?"

"You won't get it. It's the rule."

"Fine." He lowered me back to the floor. "Then what do you want to do?"

"It's Christmas Eve night. We can go out to see Christmas lights, or we can stay in and drink hot chocolate and watch Christmas movies."

"I like the sound of movies but no hot chocolate for me. I'll make your hot chocolate if you pick out the movie you want to watch."

While we were doing all of that, we heard singing coming up the street. A group of kids had decided to go caroling. We went outside to listen, gave them candy canes and hot chocolate and thanked them for coming. After that we snuggled together on the couch with drinks and some of the cookies we baked while we watched "White Christmas." We both dozed off before the movie ended.

I woke up Christmas morning to the aroma of food cooking. I got up and went to the kitchen, finding Pyre standing at the oven.

"Good morning, Kira. How do you feel this morning?" He made a sweet picture, standing there in an apron with a Christmas tree on it. I wondered where he got the apron, but didn't ask so he wouldn't become self-conscious.

"Joyful, and in the Christmas spirit." I walked over to him. "How about you?"

"I'm fantastic!" He wrapped his arms around me and held me close. "Merry Christmas."

"Merry Christmas, Pyre."

"You're not wearing your pajamas in front of the others, are you?"

"Why not? That's what you made me do for my birthday."

"You need to go change."

"Our friends won't approve of blue fleece and penguins?" He gave me his best disapproving face, shook his head and pointed. "Fine, Mr. Bossy Pants." I started to leave the kitchen, but he stopped me.

"I want my morning kiss first." He gave me a long, sweet kiss, put his forehead against mine and caressed my face.

"Is something bothering you?" I asked.

"I'm good. No need to brood about me." He hugged me tight and went back to the oven. "Now go change."

*I hope he's all right. I wish he'd talk to me about his nightmares.* After I changed clothes, I went back to the living room and sat on the couch. Shortly after I sat down, insistent pounding on the door reverberated off the walls.

"Pyre, they're here." I got up and headed for the door.

"Can we send them away?" He came out of the kitchen, making a face.

"Not after we invited them and everything! Would you stop that?"

47

"Why? I don't want them here. Ever since we moved into the apartment, they haven't left us alone."

"And you don't understand why, do you?"

"I realize why and I wish they'd stop." I rolled my eyes as I opened the door.

"What's his problem now?" Caedmon asked, bringing in a bag full of presents.

"You." Pyre mumbled and expelled his breath when I smacked his stomach.

"We love you too, Pyre." Lowell joked, handing me a present with 'To my Kit' written on it. "I hope you like it." He also handed one to Pyre.

"Really, Wolf?" Pyre sounded annoyed, but Lowell just laughed.

"What?" The expression on Pyre's face instantly made me curious.

"Read what it says." Pyre held it out to me. I read the label and had to laugh too.

"To Mr. Hot Head."

"I should've killed you a long time ago." Pyre walked away from Lowell.

"But then you wouldn't be with Kira." Lowell stated. Pyre stopped and spun around to face Lowell.

"I hate it when you're right." Pyre walked back to me and grasped my hand.

"Lowell, would you help me with the trays of food, please?" I asked.

"Certainly." We were about to leave the room when he nudged my arm and winked at me. "Anything for my favorite girl."

"Wolf, if you don't shut up!" Pyre yelled.

"I'm kidding. Can't you take a joke?"

"Not when it involves Kira." Eros said.

"The oaf dies first." Pyre said.

"Bring it, Shrimp." Eros rolled up his sleeves and Pyre stalked toward him.

"Pyre!" I stomped my foot, getting his attention. "You promised." Pyre put his hands in his pockets.

"Ooh, who's listening to his girlfriend." Eros mocked. "Looks like someone would rather please his girlfriend than get his butt kicked and get his hands dirty."

"Eros!" Eira exclaimed, crossing her arms. Her facial expression showed a distinct lack of amusement. "Get the presents out of the bag."

"Yes, ma'am." Eros walked over to dig into the bag.

"Boys." I whispered and walked into the kitchen. Lowell followed behind me.

"I didn't mean to create a fuss, Kira. I was only joking."

"I realize that. Pyre'll get over it."

"Or not." Pyre said as he entered the kitchen.

I walked over to him with a tray in my hands.

"He will or he'll wait until next year for his present."

"I'll behave, but only for you." Pyre eyed Lowell obstinately. He took the tray, and I gave him a kiss on the cheek.

"Thank you." He walked back to the living room. I turned to see Lowell with a pensive expression on his face. "What?"

"Nothing." Lowell regarded me with watery eyes.

"Lowell, talk to me."

"You and Pyre make an amazing couple." I walked over to him as Pyre walked back into the kitchen.

"You're not allowed to be depressed tonight." I took his hand and held it in both of mine.

"How can I be with a friend like you?" He pulled me into a hug.

"What about me?" Pyre punched Lowell's arm.

"You too, Pyre." Lowell punched him back.

"Thank you. Now let go of my girl and help me carry out the food. I'm hungry."

"Sure." Lowell chuckled, letting me go. "Thank you, Kira." We carried the last of the trays to the living room and everyone started eating. More precisely, Caedmon and Eros devoured their food, the rest of us ate.

"Can we open presents now?" Caedmon swallowed his last bite, caught his breath and emitted a small burp. I thought I noticed the walls shake. We all looked at him in surprise or disgust.

"Can you grow up now?" Laya asked. "The rest of us are still eating."

"Do I have to?" Everyone laughed.

"Caedmon, why don't you and Eros sort the presents while we finish eating?" I suggested it as a distraction since Caedmon and Eros started to scuffle, and Pyre's annoyance began to escalate.

"Okay!" Caedmon and Eros yelled.

"Kira, how do you do it?" Iris asked.

"Do what?" I asked her in between taking bites of a cookie.

"Figure out a way to make those two and all of us

happy, at the same time." Gabby said.

"I'm just good with kids I guess." Everyone laughed again.

"We're done!" The boys yelled.

"Sit down because we're not." Pyre yelled back.

"But..." The boys pouted.

"He's kidding. We are done." Lowell said.

We each picked out our spots to unwrap presents. Lowell gave me a beautiful bracelet that resembled ivy vines intertwining. Eira made Eros a scarf with blue flames at each end. Caedmon bought Laya some beautiful green earrings in the shape of stars. After we opened all the presents, we all sat on the floor with drinks and desserts and talked about past Christmas experiences. Caedmon told us about the time he put a frog in Laya's present when they were kids.

"I learned not to do that to Laya again." Caedmon said.

"What about you, Kira?" Iris asked.

"Yes, please tell us a story about your Christmas experiences." Vitas beseeched.

"Nobody wants to listen to my embarrassing stories." Everyone yelled at me about how mistaken I was. "Okay! Don't kill me." I put my hands up in defense. *Which story should I tell?* "My favorite Christmas memory happened when I was about four years old. We visited Santa Land pretty much every year, but this was the first one I can remember. My mother made me a beautiful Christmas dress. It was blue with a silver snowflake print and silver trim. When I tried it on, she told me I was her sweet angel, and I felt like one. I insisted on wearing my new dress to visit Santa Claus.

"We got to Santa Land and it was so much fun. The ground was covered in a thick layer of fresh fallen snow. They had reindeer you could feed and even pet and a huge bonfire for getting warm. A vendor made hot chocolate and fresh-baked sugar cookies, still warm from the oven. Elves took children for rides on a kiddy train. Parents could ride with their children in Santa's sleigh pulled by reindeer, which carried you around the area to see all the Christmas lights. People sang Christmas carols; if the singers took a break, music played through speakers hung high on poles. They had other things to see and do, but those were my favorite, next to seeing Santa Claus. The whole place was extraordinarily magical.

"We got in line to talk to Santa and Mrs. Claus. A boy and his parents stood in line directly in front of us. The boy was about thirteen years old and didn't understand why he had to wait in line. He started to misbehave, acting impatient and rude to his parents, so they asked the people in front of them if he could go before them. They said no; they'd waited in line too and their child was little and very excited. Finally it was his turn. This big kid walked up and sat on Santa's knee and told him all the things he wanted for Christmas. He asked for big expensive items — a new TV and video player, stereo, video game system, dirt bike, and the list went on, while Santa looked at him in disbelief. Santa said he'd do his best, but you can't get everything you want. The kid said he would get all of those things, because he always got everything he wanted. His parents simply grinned through it all. My mother later told me she overheard people muttering about what a spoiled child he was.

"At last it was my turn. My mother taught me not to accept gifts from strangers. Before we left home, she said Santa loved kids and wanted to bring them something special; so it was okay to request one or two things, as long as she was with me. I walked up to him and he picked me up to sit on his knee. He quizzed me about things like what I liked and if I had a pet. Finally he asked me if I'd like him to bring me a present. I smiled and responded, 'No, thank you, you don't have to.' He replied that he wanted to, that he liked bringing gifts to kids. My mother reminded me that it was all right, so I said, 'Yes, please.' He asked me what I wanted and I answered that anything he picked out would be fine with me. Finally he said he especially wanted me to tell him what kind of present I had in mind. I thought about it for a minute, and finally said, 'a pink one', since pink was my favorite color. He looked to my mother in a plea for help. She told me later that she mouthed, 'doll house' to Santa. Santa asked me if I'd like a doll house for Christmas, and I said I would and thanked him. I was incredibly excited about it. I gave Santa a hug and went to see Mrs. Claus. I talked all the way home about Santa Land, Santa and Mrs. Claus, and the doll house Santa promised to bring me for Christmas. My mother told me people around us said I was cute and sweet, and it seemed especially delightful next to the greedy kid. Santa stopped her to say that had never happened before so she was proud of me for being such a good girl. She also said she had hoped I'd tell Santa what I wanted since I wouldn't tell her. She'd give me a toy catalog to search through, ask me to make a list, but I wouldn't make one. I'd just say I didn't know what I wanted. I miss my mom all the time, but I miss her at Christmas most of all, and all the things we did together to make it special."

"You're still like that. I've been trying since your birthday to get you to tell me what you want, but you keep telling me you don't know." Pyre said.

"That's because I don't know what I want. I never do."

"What a wonderful story, Kira. You should've seen how your eyes twinkled while telling it. I could easily imagine you as a little girl at Santa Land, and I could tell how much you miss your mom." Gabby said, with tears in her eyes.

"We need to get going." Laya said.

"Laya and I made plans to spend the rest of Christmas alone." Caedmon explained, wrapping an arm around Laya.

"We should leave too. Thanks for having the party. It was so much fun." Eira gave Pyre a hug and then walked over to hug me too. She whispered in my ear, "Thank you for giving me the best Christmas present of all; you gave me back my brother." After I returned the hug, she gathered up her gifts and belongings.

"And dinner was great." Eros added as he rubbed his belly and picked up some of the leftovers to take home.

"How could you tell? You inhaled it so fast, I doubt you tasted any of it." I poked him in his belly and he laughed. "Bye guys." Our friends hugged me as they departed. By the time everyone left, Lowell and Pyre had finished cleaning. "Did y'all leave me anything to do?"

"No." They both said at once.

"I should head home." Lowell said with a yawn.

"Be careful on your way home." Pyre said.

"I will, Pyre." Lowell wrapped his arms around me. "Good night, Kira."

"Good night." I squeezed him tight and patted his back. He kissed my forehead and left. "Do you suppose he's all right?"

"He's just lonely." Pyre wrapped an arm around my shoulders.

"Maybe he shouldn't be alone tonight. Should we have invited him to stay?"

"No, I imagine seeing us together sometimes makes it worse. He'll work it out. You still need to open my present." He pulled a small box from behind his back.

"Why couldn't I open it while the others were here?"

"I don't like being romantic in front of other people."

"After I open it, you can open the one I got for you." We sat down and I opened the small box while he watched me expectantly for my reaction. The box held a gorgeous ring with a small red stone. As I examined it closer, something appeared to move inside the stone. "Pyre?"

"It's a special stone." He took the ring out of the box and put it on my finger. "The stone can hold fire inside of it, which will continue to burn until the stone breaks." The fire comfortably warmed my hand. "It's only a promise ring but now I'll be with you wherever you go." I wrapped my arms around his neck.

"Pyre, it's so beautiful; I love it." I kissed him and

hugged him close. "Now open mine." I pulled the present out from under the couch and handed it to him.

"It was hidden there this whole time?" I nodded. He had, 'Why didn't I look there' written all over his face. He slowly unwrapped the box. When he opened the box to reveal the sword, the expression on his face was priceless. "Where did you get this sword?"

"Funny you should mention it." I scratched the back of my head. "You see I learned about a sword that was created for fire demons, and could only be wielded by the best. But it had been lost over time. I thought it would be the perfect gift for you, and developed an urgent need to go in search of it. Rumors claimed it was buried deep inside an ancient temple in the middle of the forest. I travelled there and met an old villager who agreed to be my guide. He took me to the edge of the woods but refused to go any further. He warned me that unspeakable dangers and horrors existed in the woods, but I had to try. The guide agreed to wait for me until sunset; after that, he would presume I was a goner. He didn't want to be there after dark and would return to his home, and I'd be on my own. As I entered the woods, I sensed eyes watching me. Suddenly I heard a yell, like a battle cry, and had to dodge spears flying toward me from every direction, thrown by members of an aboriginal cannibalistic tribe. Once I got past them, I had to be careful not to step in—"

"Quicksand and burning pits of death?"

"Yes! As I approached the temple, a huge skull crushing hammer came flying at me from way up high. I ducked and rolled and it barely missed me. Once inside the temple, it was completely dark, and I nearly fell. I instinctively put my hand on the wall to steady myself, accidentally pressing a trigger button which—"

"Opened a wall, releasing hundreds of huge deadly spiders?"

"And part of the ceiling, releasing venomous vipers. I pulled out my flashlight and kept going. I continuously inspected the wall, watchful for more triggers or traps. That's when I observed that the walls—"

"Weren't merely stone?"

"They were covered in bones, and different kinds of skulls, possibly human, demon, or animal. I examined them closer and could faintly distinguish carvings on the bones, and realized the carvings were—"

"Warnings to turn back?"

"But I didn't turn back. I was determined to overcome all obstacles in the journey to obtain this sword for you. I kept going until I entered a huge chamber with five walls. In the center of the room, the sword rested on a pillar, suspended in air, surrounded by a circle of branches with thorns a foot long and more snakes. Around all of that was—"

"A circle of fire?"

"The next circle was filled with water that bubbled and smelled odious."

"And around that?"

"Around that was a circle of nothing; no floor at all. Coming up through the vent in the floor—"

"Was a huge blast of wind that would push you upward?"

"Into long spikes that covered the ceiling of the room. I needed to figure out how to get to the center. I investigated the area and found lines on the floor and a tablet with a—"

"Riddle in symbols, instructions for getting to the sword?"

"I had to decipher the riddle and step in the right path so a retractable layer would close the circle of wind and raise the layer of water up to a slant—"

"For the water to spill onto the fire layer to put out the flames?"

"With that accomplished, the dying flames released a noxious steam that killed the snakes. I cut away the thorns and branches and carefully—"

"Seized the hilt of the sword?"

"While also checking for a pressure switch. When I picked it up, nothing happened. I exhaled a huge sigh of relief, which unfortunately—"

"Was a trigger itself?"

"The walls began to shake, and the floor started to rumble. The wind circle started to open again, lowering the level of the water circle—"

"Which allowed the water to refill?"

"And the flames to rebuild. I had no choice but to—"

"Make a flying leap?"

"Over all the circles at once or I'd have been trapped there. The hard part was over—"

"Or so you thought."

"I heard screeching of critters running and looked behind me to see hundreds of man-eating birds flying through the opening of the wind circle, straight for me. I spun around quickly to run, but must've stepped on a trigger, because—"

"The floor opened?"

"And I slid down a ramp into a lake. As I waded out of the lake, a huge—"

"Crocodile lunged out of the water?"

"And clamped his jaws on the sword. I fought him for the sword. I kicked him and punched him in the snout until he let go of the sword—"

"And crawled back into the water?"

"Only after chasing me on land for several feet. But I ran in a serpentine path to wear him down. When he stopped chasing me, I glanced down and was shocked to find I was covered—"

"In giant leeches?"

"From head to toe. As I worked on removing the leeches, I heard scurrying sounds. I searched all around my position and saw a mischief of—"

"Rats?"

"They appeared to be hungry. In desperation, I tossed the leeches to them. The rats launched themselves on the bloody leeches as they hit the ground. Once I tossed the last leech, I started running and didn't look back. Scorpions landed on my arms, spiders slid down in front of my face, giant paws with razor sharp claws reached for my legs. I brushed them away and ran for my life. Finally, I reached the edge of the woods, emerged from the trees, and found my guide. He said he didn't expect to see me alive ever again. I told him it was too important and failure wasn't an option. He took me back to the village, where I caught my ride home."

"That's unbelievable. You would do all that to get

a present for me?"

"Yes! Yes, I would."

He squinted his eyes. "Now, how did you actually get it?"

"Vitas helped me."

"Was this sword the reason I couldn't sense you in town the other day?"

"Yes, Vitas took me to a house in the middle of nowhere, somewhere close to the town where you lived as a child. An old fire demon lived there and possessed the sword. The sword was made for his grandson but he never got to give it to him."

"Why did he give it to you?"

"Because you're his grandson." He became intensely quiet. "Pyre?" He didn't answer. "Was this a terrible idea?" He put the sword down, grabbed me, and kissed me.

"I love it. Thank you so much." He wrapped his arms around me.

"You're welcome." I hugged him back. "Um, Pyre? The human can't breathe." He relaxed his grip partially, but didn't let go. "If you want, we can visit your grandfather sometime."

"I'd like that. Can you tell me about him?"

"He's a little crazy. He's the kind of guy I would want for a grandfather though."

"Do you think he'll like me?"

"Pyre, he'll love you. He relished the fact that you're dating a human."

"Anyone would love you though."

"I am very lovable."

"Come here." He pulled me to sit with him. We sat on the couch the remainder of the night talking about his grandfather.

# Chapter 3
# New Year's

I woke up the next morning to the phone ringing. "Hello?"

"Hey, Kira, it's Eira. Everyone got to talking, and we all voted to go to $E^5$ for New Year's. They apparently throw a fantastic party and stay open until midnight for New Year's. What do you think?"

"That sounds like a great idea." I rubbed my eyes.

"I'll tell the others it's settled."

*You do that.* I went back to my room and laid down again.

"Kira, is something wrong?" I looked up to see Pyre standing in the door way.

"I ate too many sweets last night, so my stomach is queasy." He walked over and put his hand on my forehead.

"You should take it easy today." He left the room and came back with a cold washcloth and some antacid. "Who was on the phone?"

"It was Eira. She wanted to tell us that the New Year's party will be at $E^5$."

"That sounds great." He leaned over and kissed my forehead. "I'll be in my room if you need anything." I watched him leave the room and went back to sleep.

I woke up at around two in the afternoon and packed what I would need for our trip to Nashville.

The next morning we went to the airport in Little Rock and waited to board the plane to Nashville. While we waited, I tried to read a book but the kids in the area were making too much noise. Pyre tapped his foot with irritation and gripped the armrest until it cracked.

"Is it time to board the plane yet?" His posture was now rigid and his fists were clinched.

"It will be soon. They're probably bored, so try to ignore them." I tried rubbing his arm to soothe him, but it didn't help.

"It's kind of hard to ignore something that loud. If I acted like that, my dad would've popped my butt." He said it louder than appropriate.

"Be nice, Pyre." I leaned into him.

"No, they need to accept that if their child acts up, it's their responsibility to discipline the kid."

"I can do whatever I want!" One of the kids ran up to us.

"Beat it, brat." Pyre growled. I grasped Pyre's hand.

"And why should I?"

"Because I don't like bratty kids." Pyre held his other hand up and made it change to his demon skin.

"Mom!" The kid screamed and ran away.

"Now you've done it."

"It was worth it. That kid was getting on my last nerve." The kid came back with his mother and a security guard.

"Sir, can you show me your hand please." The security guard requested.

"Yes, sir." Pyre held out his hands, both of which appeared ordinary.

"He's lying officer. His hand was red and covered

with scales." The kid yelled.

"I don't know what he's talking about officer." Pyre said.

"Ma'am, get your kid under control." The security guard tipped his hat to us and left.

"Mom, I'm telling the truth."

"I don't want to hear another word." The woman admonished as she dragged him away. I turned to glare at Pyre.

"Kids and their imagination these days." He shrugged, and I hit his arm.

After another ten minutes, it was time to board the plane. Pyre shifted back and forth anxiously while we waited in line.

"Will you please calm down?"

"I'm not positive this is a good idea."

"Just don't set fire to anything and try to ignore the people."

"Easy for you to say." We handed the person our tickets and walked down the ramp to the plane. The flight attendant greeted us and we walked to our seats.

"Do you want to sit next to the window?" I asked him as I tried to push my bag into the compartment above our seats.

"It might be better if I didn't." He pushed my bag into the compartment.

"Pyre, is there something you want to tell me?"

"Nothing comes to mind."

"Nothing? You're more edgy about this flight than I am."

"Fire demons aren't exactly made for flying."

"Don't worry. You can hold my hand the whole time." Which he did, tightly; luckily the flight wasn't too long. We left the airport and took a taxi to Juniper's house.

"Wow, it hasn't changed." I surveyed the whole neighborhood during the ride. We walked up to the door. "Are you ready?"

"No." He stared at the door.

"Marvelous." I rang the doorbell. We stood there for a minute.

"She's not home. Let's go." Pyre tried to walk away but Juniper opened the door.

"Kira!" She wrapped her arms around me. "My goodness, it's wonderful to see you."

"It's great to see you too."

"And this young man must be..." Her voice faded as she contemplated him. "Pyre?" She viewed him up and down, making him hugely uncomfortable. "It's a pleasure to meet you, Pyre." She held out a hand to him.

"I'm pleased to meet you too, ma'am." He shook her hand.

"You two must be worn out from your flight. Why don't you come inside and make yourselves comfortable?"

"She hates me." Pyre put his hands in his pockets and followed her.

"I made fresh tea. Would y'all like some?"

"That would be lovely." I said.

"I'll be right back."

"Kira, there's someone else in the house." Pyre whispered.

"I'm aware of that." I replied as I gazed up to the top of the stairs where Crystal stood watching us.

"I see you've returned." Her voice still sent shivers up my spine. I watched her walk down the stairs. "Why?"

"To pick up my things."

"Who's he?"

"My name's Pyre." He stepped in front of me.

"You're not human."

"Could say the same for you."

"Your first boyfriend, Kira. How... disgusting."

"What do you want, Crystal?"

"World peace. For the earth, that is. Not so much for the people."

"What's that supposed to mean?" Pyre's stance was defensive and ready for anything.

"That would be telling. Can't go giving away the fruit before it's ripe." She walked back up the stairs.

"Is she the girl you mentioned?" Pyre leaned into me.

As I nodded, I sensed Juniper standing in the doorway. "I see she's improved."

"I wish she had." Juniper said, with tears in her eyes. "She attacked some people recently and killed a man. She was tried, convicted and committed to the psych ward for the dangerous and criminally insane. I don't know how, but she got away from them. She got here a few minutes before you did. The police will be here anytime now to take her back to the hospital."

"I realized she was dangerous, but I had no idea she would go so far. Juniper, she might even kill again."

"More than likely."

"Juniper, I'm so sorry."

"I've expected something like this to happen for

66

quite some time." She tried to put on a brave face. "Come on, now. Let's don't let it spoil your visit. Who's hungry? I haven't cooked dinner yet but—"

"I'll do it." Pyre walked up to her.

"You don't need to do that. You're my guest."

"I would like to cook for you since you're allowing me to stay in your home." He walked past her and into the kitchen. She gaped at me in astonishment and gestured toward him.

"Just let him. It'll give us a chance to catch up on things." We sat in the living room and talked about everything that had happened since I moved to Russellville.

The police came and took Crystal into custody. As they dragged her out the door, she glued her gaze on me and smirked wickedly. "Slumber well, Kira. I'll see you soon."

"Not if I see you first." Pyre asserted from the kitchen doorway. Crystal blew a kiss toward him as the police dragged her from the house.

Juniper left the room, unable to watch her daughter being escorted away. When she returned to the living room, she had photo albums in hand. We reminisced and laughed as we looked at the pictures. Pyre enjoyed seeing pictures of me when I was younger, so Juniper gave some to us to take home.

When dinner was ready, Pyre brought us each a plate and we all ate. Juniper praised Pyre's cooking skills, sounding surprised and amazed. The police called to inform us that Crystal was safely detained so we wouldn't be uneasy.

After dinner, we all sat and talked. When I got

sleepy, I went to my old room and went to bed. Pyre offered to sleep on the couch. If he slept at all, it was undoubtedly with one eye open all night, in case anything happened.

The next day we packed up my belongings. As I carried a box toward the front door, I noticed Juniper standing near the window, deep in thought.

"I'm glad you found an apartment in Russellville. I'm surprised how much you've changed."

"I've changed?"

"When you left, you wanted nothing to do with boys and only wanted to focus on your school work." She gazed out the window at Pyre as he loaded boxes into the truck we rented. "Now you have a boyfriend. I must admit, I question your choice of boyfriend."

"What do you mean?"

"Don't you think he's somewhat strange? I can't put my finger on it but something isn't quite right about him."

*She's not wrong.* I peeked outside in Pyre's direction.

*I heard that.* Pyre looked toward the window and winked.

"I'm concerned he's the inappropriate type for you."

"He's actually the perfect type. Pyre might appear to be the bad boy type but he's wholeheartedly sweet and caring. He takes excellent care of me and I take care of him too. You just need to get used to him and get to know him better."

"And you're living together. Are you being... you

68

know... careful?"

"Juniper!"

"Hey, I have to ask." She tried to sound open and comfortable, but I sensed it embarrassed her to ask.

"We're roommates, but we're not living together in that way. Neither of us are ready for that yet. It's all still new for both of us, so we don't want to rush things."

"That's wise, and your decision after all. If you're happy, I'll ignore my intuition." She turned back to the window. "On one condition."

*And here it comes.*

"You must convince him to give me his recipes. Pyre's a fabulous cook. The dish last night was so mouth watering, I want to know how he made it."

I laughed, relieved. "He doesn't give out his recipes. Trust me, I've tried to pry them out of him."

"He'll give 'em to me. I'm certain of it." She went outside and left me standing there dumbfounded.

*How did I live with this eccentric woman?* I picked up the box again and walked out to see her already talking to Pyre. She leaned against the truck while he loaded the boxes. *I wonder if she can get him to spill the beans on some of his recipes.* I went up to my old room for the last of the boxes. When I went back downstairs, Pyre and Juniper were laughing. *She's probably telling him embarrassing stories from my childhood, but at least she appears to be warming up to him.* I put the box down and went back upstairs to the empty room. The room felt unfamiliar without all my possessions in it. I looked around it, paging through memories. I walked down the hall and stopped at Crystal's room. I started to open the door, my fingertips inches away from the doorknob. My intuition screamed at me not to, and I pulled my hand away. I instinctively knew no good would come from opening the door. I stared at it for a moment and hoped it was locked up as the room's former occupant now was.

I went back outside and hugged Juniper goodbye. She promised to call if she needed anything or if any more issues arose with Crystal. She also told us to take care of each other, but she clearly intended the message more for Pyre than for me. Even with the incident with Crystal, I enjoyed seeing her and was glad we came. I climbed into the truck and settled into my seat. I gazed back at the little two story house with white windows and felt sad for Juniper. With me gone, and her daughter locked away, I was concerned she would be lonely. I hoped she would get out and enjoy herself and not stay homebound. My eyes found Crystal's window, and I all but expected to see her standing there, watching me like when I left for college. She wasn't there, of course, but it still felt creepy and brought to mind the moment outside her bedroom door. The curtains abruptly fluttered and went instantly still again. I felt silly that it had startled me and thought it must've been a breeze or something. I looked back at the window. It was closed.

I turned my attention to Pyre as he asked, "Ready?"

"All set. Let's go home." We both waved at Juniper as we drove away.

It was fun being on the road together, even like this. We talked, listened to music, and played road games. I imagined what it would be like to travel for fun somewhere together.

When we got home, we unloaded the truck and returned it. The next couple of days, I unpacked my boxes, with Pyre's help. He asked me about this stuffed animal and that figurine, where I got them, and the story behind them that made them special.

The afternoon of New Year's Eve, Pyre and I started to get ready for the party.

"Kira, what are you wearing to the party?"

"I thought I'd wear the dress you gave me for my birthday."

"Should I wear dress up clothes too?" He said, sounding reluctant.

"It would be an excellent idea."

"I'll go see what I have in my closet." He left the room.

I turned around and viewed my reflection in the mirror, wearing the blue and white dress Pyre bought for my birthday. The snowflake necklace with the blue gem in the middle that Eira picked out for me hung delicately around my neck. In my hair I wore the blue and white rose hairpin Lowell gave me. I was amazed at how beautiful I looked. I felt transformed as I gazed down at my dress and smoothed out my skirt. When I looked back up, frost covered the mirror with ice framing the border. My image in the mirror evanesced as a hallway materialized. I reached up to touch the mirror but as I did, the ice from the mirror climbed up my arm. I examined my arm and returned my attention to the mirror to find I now stood in the hallway. I saw people ambling awkwardly and acting strange. One came toward me and tried to attack me, but a man stopped him and led him down the hallway.

"What're you doing out of your room?" Another man dressed like a guard walked toward me. "You aren't supposed to be walking alone." I had the impression he wasn't talking to me, but to someone behind me.

"There's somewhere I am required to be and I mustn't be late." A familiar chill crawled up my spine when I heard her voice. I spun around and saw Crystal standing a few feet away.

"The only place you're going is back to your room."

"That would make me late for her rebirth." She wouldn't look at him. She just stared at me with a deranged expression.

"Rebirth?"

"She will be reborn soon and I can't miss it. The elements chose us for a reason."

"Crystal, you're not going anywhere."

"Like you could stop me." She looked him up and down with a smug smirk. A mysterious ball formed in her hand and the room became uncomfortably cold. "Bow down before the elements."

"Crystal, stop!" I yelled as the ball expanded and the entire hallway was layered with ice. Even the people were frozen in place. Crystal and I were the only ones unaffected.

"I tried to warn him, Kira. You heard me." I was at a loss for words and simply gaped at her. "The rebirth will be beautiful, Kira. I can't wait for the transformation." She slid around the hall on the ice like she was figure skating. "Ice represents water and is the first of the four sacrifices. Next I'll make sacrifices to earth, wind, and fire. The elements, not the band, in case you were wondering.

The rebirth will follow, and will be done with earth." She cackled a loud cacophony which echoed off the walls and the ice and sounded sinister. She rotated to face me as she glided backwards down the hall. "The sacrifice to water is complete. I'll be seeing you, Kira." She snapped her fingers.

I woke up to pounding on my door. The room was as cold as the hallway in my dream. I tried to move my arms to warm myself but they wouldn't budge. I inspected my arms and discovered ice flakes melting. I took a deep breath and screamed as loud as I could. "Pyre!" Pyre and Lowell ran into the room. "My arms." Pyre ran over and worked on defrosting my arms.

"How did your arms get covered in ice?" Lowell asked.

"All I know is I instantly felt enormously tired and wanted to rest for a few minutes. I guess I nodded off and dreamt about Crystal. She was in a hospital and she froze everyone. She claimed it's only the beginning, that the sacrifice to water was made with three more sacrifices to come, followed by a rebirth."

"Rebirth?" Lowell looked quizzically at me and then at Pyre.

"Sacrifice?" Pyre puzzled and wrapped an arm around me. "Definitely sounds like a witch."

"What are we going to do?" I worried as I leaned into Pyre.

"Everything we can to get ready for whatever she has planned. We need to do some research about witches." Lowell asserted and looked to Pyre for ideas.

"My parents might know something or be familiar

with someone who does."

"I hope so." I shivered and Pyre rubbed my arms to warm them more.

"How are your arms?" Lowell asked.

"Cold."

"Make sure you wear something warm tonight." Pyre said.

"I will." I stood up and wiped my face.

"Kira, everyone will understand if you would prefer to stay home tonight." Lowell suggested.

"No, it'll be better if I get out of the apartment. We've all been looking forward to being together to celebrate the new year, and I'm not letting anyone spoil it."

"We'll let you get dressed." Pyre pushed Lowell out as they left the room.

I got dressed, added my accessories and finishing touches, and walked out to the living room. All our friends had arrived, and we would all be going out together. I marveled at how fabulous everyone looked. Lowell, Eros, and Caedmon pulled out all the stops and were extremely handsome. Vitas even showed up wearing his best suit.

*What a transformation!* I looked down and frowned slightly with concern. *Transformation... No, I will not think about Crystal or anything else tonight.* I watched the girls, twirling around, beautiful in their dresses. Their eyes sparkled with excitement. They were clearly thrilled at the chance to dress up and go out for the night. My eyes found Pyre, and I couldn't help but stare. The sight of him took my breath away. For a moment it seemed as if time had frozen, and everyone else had melted away. Pyre held his hand out to me, as I stepped closer to him, sliding my own hand into his. Our eyes remained locked on each other. I barely heard him speak through the heartbeat pounding in my ears.

"Kira, you're breathtaking, so very beautiful." His hand held mine gently to his heart.

"I could say the same about you." I murmured, still breathless. The laughter behind me broke the spell that bound us.

"Pyre, you're so very breathtaking and beautiful." Eros moaned.

"I can't stand to look at you, you're so beautiful." Caedmon groaned.

"What a lovely girl you are!" Eros batted his eyelashes and pretended to swoon.

"That's it! You're all dead." Pyre yelled.

I grabbed his arm. "Pyre, not tonight. You can kill them in the new year."

"Uh oh." Eros muttered, turning white. Caedmon gulped and backed up a step.

Everyone was ready to leave the apartment, anticipating a fun night. When we arrived at the restaurant, we were all amazed. Blue and white lights decorated the outside of the building. Globes with small twinkling white lights hung in the trees, swaying in the breeze and resembling fireflies.

We went inside where the hostess greeted us right away. She offered us party hats and tiaras and escorted us to our table. I tried to give the tiara back to her, but she wouldn't take it. The inside decorations matched the outside, sparkling with blue and white lights. Silver snowflakes and more globes hung in various lengths from the ceiling, their lights seeming to dance above our heads. Music played softly in the background. The tables and chairs were moved to make space for a dance floor. Several kinds of party favors adorned the table, including plastic bottles of bubbles, noise makers, and tiny boxes filled with confetti. Silver draped windows provided a setting for mirrors framed in string lights.

The server came over and took our drink order and brought fresh warm biscuits and the restaurant's special apple butter. She told us to help ourselves to the food being served buffet style for the occasion. Once we all had our plates, we sat down to eat, talking and laughing about all kinds of things. After we finished eating, we decided to dance.

"Don't forget your tiara, Pyre." Eros said as we arose from the table. "Or are you afraid to mess up your hair?"

"Eros, keep it up, and you won't need to worry about Pyre killing you in the new year, because I'll kill you tonight." He laughed and started to make another wisecrack until he saw my facial expression.

"I'm sorry, I'll behave." Eros pulled Eira out to the dance floor, casting furtive glances my way. I turned back to Pyre and beamed.

"That's my girl." He proclaimed proudly and led me out to the floor. The others followed us and we all formed a circle to dance.

The music was fun and upbeat. We were all having a splendid time just being together. Periodically some would sit to catch their breath and have a drink. After several fast songs, they played a slow song.

"One slow dance?" Pyre bowed slightly and held out a hand.

"I'm terrible at slow dances."

"I'll teach you." I slipped my hand into his and he led me out to the floor. He twirled me and waltzed me around the room. I marveled at what an accomplished dancer he was.

"How do you know how to dance?" I asked.

"If you live as long as I have, you will likely have to dance sometime. Since I didn't want to make a fool of myself, I learned."

"I think I stepped on your foot."

"You can step on my foot anytime, just promise me you won't step on my heart."

"I would never do that. I love you, with all my heart."

"And I love you. Always." He put his forehead against mine.

We continued dancing, mostly in silence. We gazed into each other's eyes, kissing lightly now and then. I laid my head on Pyre's shoulder, breathing in his scent — a soothing woodsy scent with a hint of rosemary that always made me feel calm and safe.

"Ladies and gentlemen! It's nearly midnight; let the countdown commence." The manager announced through a microphone.

Everyone counted down and yelled, "Happy New Year." Some blew noisemakers or bubbles, and others threw confetti in the air. Couples kissed, and we all sang when the DJ played "Auld Lang Syne." Everyone stayed awhile snacking on a variety of "good luck" foods. Our group finally decided to head home. We walked outside the restaurant, and Pyre stopped to contemplate the building.

"There's something unusual about this building. Did it appear bigger than usual inside to you?"

"Not that I noticed. Maybe it seemed that way because they moved the tables to make room for the dancing, or the mirrors simply made it appear larger."

"That's probably it."

By the time we got home, we realized how tired we were and decided it was time for sleep.

"Did you have fun tonight, Kira?" Pyre held my hand and kissed it.

"I had so much fun, and I think everyone else did too. How about you?"

"Yes, I did. I enjoyed dancing with you the most." He gripped my hand and twirled me around the living room.

"Whoa, down boy." I made him stop and leaned against him. "I loved dancing with you too. This time last year, I wasn't even aware you existed. Now I can't imagine my life without you. I'm happy we're beginning a new year together."

"The first new year of our future together. I love you."

"I love you, too. Good night."

I gave him a quick kiss and was about to walk away when he pulled me back into his arms. He gazed deeply into my eyes as his hand glided up my arm to touch my hair. My heart beat faster as his fingertips trailed lightly across my cheek to cradle my chin in his palm and he slowly touched his lips to mine, our eyes locked on each other. He kissed me softly at first and then more deeply. All of his emotions and his love burned for me in that one kiss.

"Good night, my Kira. Sleep well."

He turned and walked to his room. He looked back at me and smiled before disappearing through his door. *Sleep well? After a kiss like that?*

# Chapter 4
# Back to School

I woke up extremely groggy late the next morning. *Good thing today is Saturday.* I abruptly started having a coughing fit. Pyre came into the room to check on me when he overheard the coughing.

"I must've caught a cold." I rubbed my forehead.

"I'll be right back." He came back seconds later with a glass of water. "Lowell is on his way. He has a killer cure for colds."

"Thank you." He kissed my forehead.

"How sweet." Lowell remarked from the door.

"Shut up, Wolf." They continued to argue but I quit listening. I almost dozed off, but I went into another coughing fit. Pyre helped me stand with my back to his chest and wrapped his arms around me. "Lowell, did you bring —"

"I've got it right here. Drink up, Kira." He held out a cup full of a mysterious liquid. It smelled horrible and looked even worse.

"What's in it?" I pinched my nose to block the odor.

"It's better you don't know." Pyre hedged and Lowell pushed the cup closer. I stared doubtfully at the cup and shook my head.

"It'll help, I promise." Lowell asserted as he shoved the cup into my hands. Pyre's grip tightened around my waist. "Drink up, Kira." I took a small sip but I couldn't swallow.  It tasted like cough syrup mixed with molasses, ketchup and sour milk.  I wanted to spit it back into the cup but Pyre covered my mouth.

"You've got to swallow, Kira." Pyre said.  I shook my head.

*It tastes awful.*

"Yes, but it'll help and it works fast.  Come on you need to swallow it."  I inhaled deeply and quickly swallowed.  Pyre removed his hand.

*That was hugely disgusting.*

"I know." Pyre said sympathetically.  I noticed Lowell biting his lip.

*What?*

"Lowell, Kira is wondering why you're biting your lip."

"Why don't you tell her?"  Lowell asked.

"Why should I tell her?"

"Because she'll still love you tomorrow."

"I need to finish it, don't I?"  They both nodded.  I raised my eyes up to the ceiling.  *I'll never understand boys.*  I rapidly chugged the mixture.

"That's my girl." Pyre kissed my cheek.

*Shut up.*  I rubbed my stomach.

"I'll be in the living room."  Lowell rubbed my shoulder and left the room.

*Tell him I said thank you.*

"Why don't you tell him?"  Pyre asked.

*I can't.  If I open my mouth, I'll barf.*

"Kira, says thank you."

"Anything for my Kit."  Lowell yelled from the living room.

"You need to lay down and rest." Pyre said.

*I'm wide awake now.*

"You're not required to sleep, only to rest. You're not allowed out of this bed except to use the bathroom."

*Am I quarantined?*

"No," He chuckled. "You've had so much stress to deal with lately that you've made yourself sick. I just want you to relax today."

*Okay. I'm sorry I'm being rude.*

"You're not. After all, we forced you to drink that disgusting potion." He rubbed my face. "Do you want your laptop?"

*No, but I do want my diary.* He pulled my diary out of the drawer and handed it to me.

"Anything else?"

*No, thank you.*

"I'll be in the living room if you need me." After he left the room, I opened my diary to the next empty page.

*Dear Diary,*

*I've gotten a cold. Pyre says I stressed myself too much and made myself sick. I must agree; I've done that in the past. There has been a lot going on between moving, holidays, school, and Crystal. I'll admit I have been stressing too much about Crystal. I realize Pyre won't let anything happen to me. I'm still frightened, especially not knowing what she's planning. It's sweet that Pyre and Lowell are taking care of me, although they seem to enjoy it way too much. Boys just need to be heroes. I don't want to drink Lowell's disgusting concoction ever again. I don't even want to guess about what was in it. I'm probably grateful they didn't tell me. I don't care what they say, the next time I get sick, I'm not drinking it.*

I put my pen down and rubbed my forehead.

"Kira, do you need anything?" I looked up to see Pyre standing by the door. I smiled and shook my head. "Give me a telepathic shout if you do." He went back to the living room. I finally became drowsy and fell asleep.

I woke up the next morning feeling like I hadn't been sick at all. In fact I felt so vigorous, I thought I could take on the world and threw some fake punches at imaginary foes. Pyre knocked on my door at that moment, and I was immediately embarrassed, until I realized he hadn't witnessed my act.

"Come in."

"Someone sounds much better." Pyre said as he walked into the room.

"I feel marvelous. The mystery brew Lowell makes is amazing, even if it is disgusting."

"I'm glad you're better." He wrapped his arms around me. I spotted my calendar on the wall behind him.

"I was until I saw the calendar. School begins again in barely a week." I whined.

He patted my head while trying hard not to laugh.

The week flew by like lightning. I bought my books and everything I would need for my classes. I had other things to do too, but I still wondered where the week had gone.

When my alarm woke me for the first day back to school, I buried my head in my pillow.

*Not this again.* The alarm kept blaring, so I threw my pillow at the clock. *I'm up!* I subsequently yelled at the person knocking on my door. "Come in!"

"Are you still going to school?" Pyre queried as he poked his head in the door.

"I'll decide once I'm awake." I sat up and rubbed my head. He made a face and closed the door behind him.

*Why did it come back this fast?* I got out of bed. *I'm not ready for school to begin.*

*It will be okay.* Pyre tried to be encouraging, but I was irritable and didn't appreciate his eavesdropping.

*How would you know? Are you attending school too?*

*No.*

*Then how would you know?*

*Lowell told me to say that.* I walked into the living room and came face to face with Lowell.

"It will be okay." Lowell said.

"Bite me, Wolf." Lowell stared at me in surprise at first, and then faked being insulted. I walked into the kitchen and made myself a cup of coffee to go.

"Kira, why so grumpy?" Pyre wrapped his arms around my waist.

"I slept very little last night and kept waking up for no reason."

"Why didn't you come get me?" I rotated in his arms and raised an eyebrow. "What?"

"One, I didn't want you to suffer also and two, you sleep like a rock." He eyed me doubtfully. "You also throw punches in your sleep."

"I definitely don't do that."

"I beg to differ. When I tried to get you up to help me prepare for the Christmas party, you threw your fist at my face screaming, 'Don't touch me you feathered freak.'

You barely missed me."

"Feathered freak?" Lowell leaned against the door frame and frowned with concern.

"It's a nightmare I've been having." Pyre confessed.

"A nightmare you won't talk about to anyone. If you don't want to talk to me about it, you can talk to Lowell." I crossed my arms, Lowell nodded, and we both stared at Pyre, waiting for his response.

"It's not that, and I'm aware I can talk to either of you about anything. I just don't think we need to worry about my nightmares, especially when we have other concerns on our minds."

"But they are a source of concern, Pyre. Kira has had dreams which foretold the future or came true in some way. What if yours are foretelling something? Besides, you nearly hit Kira during this nightmare. Even though you were asleep, and it was an accident, I'd say that's something to worry about, wouldn't you?"

"Pyre, please talk to me."

"How about we talk after school?" He rubbed my face.

"Fine, but we are talking." I went back to my room with the coffee and changed my clothes.

The semester was already off to an interesting start, even though it was only the first day back to class. Pyre walked with Lowell and me to campus and caused people to stare.

"Pyre, you're scaring everyone." I said.

"I want to scare everyone. I don't like the looks of many of these people."

"Pyre, you don't like the looks of most people, especially around Kira." Lowell left quickly to find his first class before Pyre could retaliate.

"Why aren't you and Lowell taking the same classes anymore?"

"We signed up for two of the same classes but he wants to study biology or geology. So he's taking more classes involving those areas."

"Why didn't you go into the same courses he chose?"

"Lowell and I have our own individual interests."

"Like what?"

"He's more into science, but I'm more into art."

"So?"

"Pyre." I stopped and faced him.

"I don't like the idea of you being without someone to protect you. I would prefer to be in there with you, but you said the professors might not agree. You're only in two of the same courses as Lowell and he can't sneak into your other courses without getting caught."

"This morning you said it would be okay. And it will be."

"But what if a demon—"

"If a demon attacks, I will run and yell for you."

"What if I don't hear you?" I raised my eyebrows in disbelief. "What?"

"You probably won't leave the campus so you'll most likely hear me." He was at a loss for words. "Yes, you're that predictable. I love you and I'll see you when classes are done." I walked away, but when I got to the door of the building, I thought of something I had seen in the movies. I decided to try it and turned to look over my shoulder. Pyre still stood there, watching me walk away. I smiled at him, and he waved and left.

My first class was an art class. There weren't many people in the classroom yet. A girl who wore a tie-dye t-shirt, feathers in her hair and flowers sewn onto her jeans sat at one of the desks and waved at me.

"Hi there." She greeted.

"Hi, my name is Kira."

"I'm Lur." She yawned. "Excuse me. I was way too excited to sleep last night, so don't mind me if I snooze during class."

"Okay. I may even join you."

The professor walked into the room. "Good morning, class. As you should be aware, this is an art class; specifically, Intro to Drawing. You'll enjoy this class, so let's get started."

The class was fascinating. She instructed us to practice drawing simple pictures first. She caught Lur dozing a few times. Luckily she wasn't too hard on Lur since it was the first day, but I suspected next time she wouldn't be as lenient.

When class ended, I met Lowell in the library.

"How was your first class?" He asked.

"It was a lot of fun. And yours?"

"Not bad, but I suspect psychology isn't for me." We talked more about our first classes on the way to our second.

"Will this class require us to dissect anything?" I took a seat at one of the desks.

"Did you read the book?" He set his books next to

mine. I bit my lip and looked up and around the room. "That's a no. No, we won't."

"You know me so well." Two girls joined us at our desk. I recognized one of them as Lur. The other girl had long brown hair worn in a single braid with blue ribbon weaving in and out of each link. She wore a dark blue shirt with stars all over it and plain blue jeans. "Hello again, Lur."

"Hey, it's my sleepy time buddy."

"Sleepy time buddy?" Lowell crossed his arms and scrutinized me.

"Well, I slept and Kira sat in the next seat." Lur explained with a smile. "This is Luna."

"H-hi." The girl stammered shyly.

"Hi, I'm Kira and this is Lowell."

"It's nice to meet you." Lowell said.

"N-nice to meet you."

The professor walked in, putting an end to our pleasantries. "Everyone take a seat. Quiet please. Welcome to Biology 101. We have a copious amount of information to cover this semester and not much time, therefore I expect your undivided attention at all times. You are partnered up based on where you sat. The desks are put into a box so four of you will work together. Every group project I assign will be with the groups you're in now. Let's waste no more time."

"I certainly won't be snoozing in this class." Lur proclaimed. We all laughed, but quietly.

The four of us had fun trying to figure out how to work the microscopes. We kept losing the sea monkeys we managed to catch. When class ended, Lowell walked with me to the building for my next class, which was mythology.

"First demonology, now mythology. Is there something you want to be when you grow up?"

"Yea, I want to be able to understand my boyfriend when he goes crazy."

"I'm on my way to chem class."

"Don't blow up the building!"

He turned and lifted his hands. "But that takes all the fun out of it!" I watched him walk off before going into the building. When I entered the classroom, I recognized Luna sitting with another girl. Luna looked up at me and waved. Once I got closer, I could see the other girl better. She wore black headphones that covered her ears, a punk style shirt, and jeans with quotations written all over them. "This makes two classes with you and Lur."

"I guess so." Luna mumbled.

"Don't worry. She'll open up after she gets better acquainted with you!" The other girl yelled. "Name's Stella!"

"I'm Kira."

"What? Hold on one sec." She couldn't hear me due to the headphones and pulled them off her ears. "What'd you say?"

"My name's Kira."

"Nice to meet you, Kira." She shook my hand until my whole arm vibrated. "How do you know Luna?"

"We had biology together." I rubbed my arm.

"I have another friend in biology too."

"Let me guess; her name is Lur."

"How'd you guess?"

"Bio and art with Lur."

"Small world. All three of us will have the same speech and geology classes tomorrow."

"Seriously? Did y'all know each other before or did you just meet?"

"We met last semester. We all had a few of the same classes together. Why?"

"I wondered if you took the same classes on purpose, or it just worked out that way."

"Nope, it just worked out that way. A cosmic co-inky-dink." She laughed at herself. She put her headphones back on and began singing out loud. I gaped open-mouthed at her like she was a little nuts.

"Luna, can I see your course schedule?" She handed it to me and I compared it to my own schedule. "We are all in the same speech class tomorrow. I'm taking a different geology class than the three of you though."

"Totally awesome!" Stella yelled.

The other students stared at her like she was crazy too. *What an interesting coincidence.* Stella resumed rocking out to the music on her phone and Luna began to draw peculiar circles all over her notebook. *But after last semester, I don't believe in coincidences. I wonder what Pyre and Lowell will think of this.* I watched as Stella nearly fell on top of Luna. *On second thought, I won't tell them yet. I want to try to figure this one out on my own.*

"Hey, Kira!" Stella yelled.

"Yea?" I tried to stop the ringing in my ears.

"The four of us, counting Lur, should totally hang out soon."

"That would be fun." Luna said.

"Terrific idea. Since we're in some of the same

classes we should study together occasionally. We could meet at the library or at my apartment where we'd be more comfortable."

"Forget studying! We'll have a party!" Stella exclaimed so loudly she startled the other students, and they stared at her in admonishment.

*It might be a coincidence this time.* Luna and Stella continued arguing about what we would do until the professor walked into the room.

"Welcome to Classical Mythology. This class will focus mainly on Greek and Roman mythology. I expect you to work hard, but enjoy yourselves too."

The class was engaging and went by fairly fast. Stella and Luna walked outside with me. We spotted Lur and Lowell standing together near the fountain. *This day just gets more fascinating.*

"How was class?" Lowell asked when he saw me.

"Great. And yours? Anything... new?" He squinted at me and made a face.

"It was AWESOME!" Stella yelled.

"Stella, calm yourself. It's like you're trying to throw your aura at everyone." Lur rebuked. I glanced quizzically at Lowell, who simply shrugged.

"Lur, there is nothing wrong with my aura!" Stella yelled. Luna and I looked at each other and shook our heads.

"We'll see you later." I said to Luna and walked away with Lowell walking slightly behind me. Another set of footsteps approached us.

"What's going on?" Pyre asked Lowell.

"I don't know." Lowell replied.

"Kira, is everything all right?" Pyre caught up to me and wrapped an arm around me.

"Yep." I wrapped an arm around his waist and leaned my head on his shoulder.

"Are you sure?" Lowell came up on my other side.

"Yep, but stay out of my head until we get home."

"Okay." I detected the uncertainty in Pyre's voice.

"It's nothing you did." I kissed his cheek and patted his chest.

It didn't take long for us to reach the apartment.

"How was the first day back?" Pyre asked.

"It was... satisfactory." I replied reticently.

"What happened?" Lowell asked.

"Last semester we had all the same classes, and you turned out to be a demon." Lowell nodded.

"Where are you going with this?" Pyre inquired, confused.

"Luna, Lur, and Stella are in most of the same classes as me this semester."

"That's a coincidence, Kira." Pyre said.

"Yea, they're not demons." Lowell said.

"Are you positive? We weren't aware Melissa was a demon until she tried to kill me." They glanced at each other.

"It wouldn't hurt to keep an eye on them." Lowell suggested.

"It'd probably be an excellent idea." Pyre agreed, sounding distressed. I sat down on the couch. "What's wrong, Kira?"

"Is this how my life will be from now on? Everyone I meet might be a demon and they all want me dead." Pyre sat down and wrapped an arm around me. "I don't want to be suspicious of everyone I meet."

"You don't have to be." Pyre sounded like his heart was breaking. I looked from Pyre to Lowell and noticed he appeared miserable too.

"What do you mean? And why are you both suddenly unhappy?"

"It is kind of our fault. If I had just erased your memories like I was supposed to..." Lowell muttered as if it pained him to say the words.

"He still can if it would make it easier for you." Pyre leaned forward, hung his head with his eyes closed and clasped his hands in front of him.

"How can you even consider that?" I stood up and confronted Lowell. "If you'd erased my memories, we might not be friends, and I undoubtedly wouldn't be with Pyre. I'm glad you didn't erase my memories." I turned to Pyre. "And you! How can you condone such a thing, much less suggest it to me! Don't you have any idea how I feel about you? I can't imagine my life without you now. I don't care if everyone I meet for the rest of my life turns out to be a demon. I'll face every stinking demon on this planet if necessary if that means I can be with you."

Pyre continued to stare at the floor and inconspicuously wiped his eyes. "I only want what's best for you, even if it's not me."

I sat back down and reached for his hand. He held onto my hand and squeezed it like he never wanted to let go. "Pyre, you are what's best for me. More importantly, you are the man I love and want to be with, not some Joe College. We're better together. We don't do well apart.

So, both of you, don't even think of erasing or changing my memories ever again. Understood?" They both nodded, and I relaxed partially. "I just wish I could tell who's a demon and who's not."

"That's what we're here for, Kit." Lowell tried to be comforting. He and Pyre exchanged glances. I sensed they were talking through telepathy. That made me feel ignored, so I sat back quietly and stared at a spot on the wall. Finally, my eyes closed, despite my efforts to keep them open.

When Pyre accompanied me to school the next day, he escorted me straight into my speech classroom.

"Are the girls here?" His eyes scanned the room and everyone in it.

"Not yet." The girls walked up to us as I finished pulling my books out of my backpack.

"Hey, Kira!" Stella yelled.

"Why is she yelling?" Pyre leaned over and whispered.

"I don't think she realizes she's doing it." I pulled off her headphones.

"Why are you messing with my jams?"

"You were yelling."

"Oops. Who's the stud?" Stella, Luna, and Lur all appraised Pyre appreciatively.

"This is Pyre, my boyfriend." I squeezed his hand.

"Boyfriend?" Lur and Stella asked in unison. Luna tried to hide her face.

"No wonder she's not with Lowell." Lur whispered to Stella.

"This boy would give him a run for his money."

Stella ogled Pyre too suggestively for my comfort.

Pyre got my attention through telepathy. *If they're demons, our whole world is in danger.*

*You might be right.* I observed Luna trying hard to be invisible. "Luna, are you still with us?"

She barely nodded without raising her eyes and tried to shrink down smaller into her seat.

"Hello, class." The professor walked into the room. "Please take your seats and we'll begin."

"I'd better go." Pyre said, making a face at the professor. "Be careful."

"How much fuss can I cause in speech class?" I gave him a sly grin.

"Knowing you, you'll answer that question all on your own." He squinted his eyes at me and turned to leave.

"Bye, Pyre." Stella and Lur said together.

Pyre whirled back and raised an eyebrow at them. They waved at him with goofy expressions. He seemed intimidated as he spun around and practically ran through the door.

"Kira, he's a cutie." Stella exclaimed.

"How did you meet him?" Lur asked. She sounded relieved that I had a boyfriend.

"He's kind of scary." Luna observed quietly.

"Lowell introduced us. They're close friends." They all gaped at me with mouths wide open. Even Luna.

After speech class ended, I headed over to geology. I was relieved the girls weren't in the same geology class with me. With them, a little goes a long way. Lowell waited for me outside the classroom, leaning against the door and twirling a flower in his hand.

"Hi Lowell." He didn't seem to hear me or even realize I was there. "Lowell?" His eyes focused on some distant place. I poked his nose.

"Kira, what're you doing?" He frowned at me while swatting at my hand.

"I thought I saw a bug fly up your nose." I walked into the classroom.

"How thoughtful." He sat down next to me.

"Why were you so distracted?"

"I was... wondering if we'll face a new threat any time soon."

"Let's don't beg for trouble. I'm getting used to it being quiet, so hopefully Crystal will stay locked away and won't cause any more problems." I suspected he had been contemplating more than impending danger.

"With your dreams and those three girls, there's no telling what might happen."

"At the moment, I don't care what will happen. I just want to get through geology."

# Chapter 5
# Meeting the Parents

I was doing my homework when Pyre poked his head through my bedroom door.

"Kira, do you mind if I don't walk you home from school tomorrow? Vitas wants Lowell and me to do something." Pyre seemed irritated about helping Vitas.

"Of course not."

"Are you sure?"

"Pyre, are you sure?"

"No." He scratched the back of his head. "Since Melissa's attack last semester, I don't like for you to walk home alone, especially since you don't live on campus."

"I'll be safe. The campus isn't far away, and it's a direct path."

"Don't take your time and come straight home."

"I will."

"Anyone you run across is a potential demon, so be careful."

"I'll be careful." I kissed Pyre's cheek, and he wrapped his arms around me.

"I don't want to lose you."

"You won't. Not anytime soon at least."

"I'd better not lose you ever. Don't stay up too late doing your homework."

"I won't."

"I'm going to bed." He hugged me tight and left the room.

*I love having a worry wart for a boyfriend. From the sound of it, Melissa's attack affected him worse than I originally thought.* I glanced over at the picture of us at the park. *I wonder if that's why he's been having nightmares. We never got to talk about it.* I quickly finished my homework and went to bed.

I woke up to my alarm the next morning. After hitting the snooze button a couple of times, I got up and got dressed. Pyre knocked on my bedroom door while I gathered my things for class.

"Come in!"

"Good morning." Pyre greeted me as he walked into the room. "How are you this morning?"

"I'm all right, how 'bout you?"

"I'm okay. Are you certain you don't mind walking home from school without me?" I walked over to him.

"How many times are you going to ask me before you're convinced?"

"A few hundred. I still don't like the idea of you walking home by yourself. I'm apprehensive, maybe even paranoid, that a demon might attack you when I'm not with you."

"I'm aware of that, and you're definitely paranoid, but with good reason. I promise I'll be careful and I'll come straight home."

"If we get done early enough, we'll meet you at the school. Otherwise, we'll see you here." He didn't give me a chance to respond before asking, "Are you ready to go?"

"I just need my bag."

"Well, grab it so we can leave."

"Are you in a hurry?"

"No." Even though he said he wasn't, he obviously was, so I got my bag and he pulled me into his arms. We arrived outside the building for my first class in a flash. I held his hand and looked into his eyes.

"Pyre, be careful. I don't want to lose you either." He took me in his arms, and kissed me deeply. A few people whistled around us. I blinked to clear my head when the kiss ended. *How will I concentrate on class now?*

"I'll be thinking about you too. See you later."

I watched him go and walked to my first class. Lur was already there when I walked into the classroom.

"Hey, Kira!" Lur waved at me as I walked over to her. "What's up?"

"Not much. How about you?" I took my seat in the chair next to her.

"Can't complain. I have a question."

"Fire away." I grinned faintly at my own "inside" joke.

"Would you be interested in posing for a painting?" She had the most peculiar expression on her face I've ever seen.

"I don't know, but that smile is creeping me out."

"No, it's not creepy. When I walked by this particular tree, the sun was shining behind it and it was so beautiful, the picture remained in my head. I want to paint it but the thing is, I want someone in the picture. You would be the best person for it."

"Why me?"

"I'm not sure how to explain it but there is something about you that feels... What's the word I'm looking for?" I waited and watched as she tapped her chin.

"I sense you're genuinely in tuned with nature, meaning you possess a strong connection with nature." I continued to stare at her with a dubious expression. "You seem in balance with everything. Not to mention, you're highly artistic. People who maintain a strong bond with nature are generally artistic."

"What would I do in the picture?"

"Just pose, nothing disturbing. I haven't seen you in a skirt or dress yet. Would you be willing to wear one?"

"I don't particularly like them but as long as it's not too short, I'll wear one."

"What are you doing on Friday?"

"I'm free."

"Awesome. We'll go shopping on Friday."

"Goody." *What have I gotten myself into?* I opened my bag to get my books and supplies.

"You don't like shopping?"

"How'd you guess?"

"All we need is a dress and a few accessories and we'll be good to go. Stella and Luna can come too. When you shop with us, you always have fun."

"Guess we'll see on Friday."

"Guess so." We talked for a few more minutes before class started.

When class was over, we walked to the library and met up with Stella and Luna. Our biology class was canceled since our professor needed to go to a wedding, so we used the time to study.

"Kira and I are going shopping on Friday. Y'all should come too." Lur said.

"You are?" Luna asked me, and I nodded. "It'll be

so much fun."

"Apparently Kira doesn't like shopping." Lur announced.

"You'll love it with us. What'll be the mission for this trip?" Stella said.

"We'll be searching for a dress for Kira to wear when she poses for my painting." Lur explained.

"You always have a new painting you want to do." Stella said.

Lur and Stella were busy talking to each other, so Luna asked, "Do you know any other friends who like to shop?"

"Yes, but they're the kind who shop because they want to shop, not because they need to shop."

"Why would anyone simply want to shop?" Luna made a funny face.

"I have no idea."

"Would they want to go shopping with us?"

"I can ask them."

"More people are going shopping with us? Awesomeness!" Stella said.

"The more the merrier." Lur said.

"I'll see if they can come." *These girls are something else. I hope everyone gets along.*

We got busy studying and having more fun. After a while, I spotted Lowell standing in the doorway. He appeared to be gazing at Lur. I waved at him and he walked over to us.

"What are you ladies doing?" He asked.

"Planning a shopping trip." Stella responded.

"Shopping trip?" He turned his attention to me.

"Lur wants me to be in a painting so we are planning to go shopping."

"Sounds like fun."

"Wanna come?" I asked.

"Yes, Lowell, come with us and spend the day surrounded by beautiful women." Stella winked at him and nudged Lur, who turned almost as red as Luna. Luna hid behind one of her books.

"Spending the day holding our bags, waiting outside of dressing rooms. Who wouldn't want that?" Lur tried to inconspicuously give me the stink eye.

"As intriguing as that sounds, I think I'll pass. The girls might want to go though. They were planning a girls' day out anyway."

"Perfect! We're going to have so much fun." Stella exclaimed loudly.

"Kira, can I talk to you?" Lowell motioned with his head for me to follow him.

"Sure." I stood and walked with him over to a bookshelf. He stopped and cautiously observed the girls.

"I want you to be careful around those girls. Go nowhere alone with them."

"Are they demons?"

"We aren't certain yet."

"I might be spending the day with a bunch of demons. Wait a minute, I do that all the time." Lowell laughed, but was still concerned.

"Eira and the others will probably want to go too."

"I hope so. Knowing Eira, I can count on them going."

"Kira, could we talk sometime this week?"

"Of course. What about?"

"I'll tell you later." He ruffled my hair. "I've gotta go. Pyre is bound to be wondering why I'm taking so long. He told me to tell you to—"

"Be careful on my way home. And go straight home. Tell him I will." He squeezed my hand and left. I walked back to the girls.

"Where'd Lowell go?" Lur sounded disappointed.

"He had something to do."

"Does your boyfriend go to school here too?" Stella asked.

"No, he doesn't go to school."

"Did he graduate?" Luna asked.

"That's a long story."

"How did they meet?" Lur asked.

"They work together. They've been friends a long time." *That's an understatement.*

"Does Lowell have a girlfriend?" Stella nudged Lur again.

"Stella, will you stop that?" Lur demanded quietly through gritted teeth.

"Not that I'm aware of." I responded to Stella as all of us peered impishly at Lur.

"What?" She asked.

"Nothing." We all snickered and got back to studying.

We studied until time for the last class. When it ended, I said goodbye to the girls and headed for home. On my way back to the apartment, I saw a man trying to carry a bunch of bags in his hands but one had a hole in it. A stone fell out and rolled near my foot. I picked it up and ran over to him.

"Do you need help?" I held out the rock for him.

"What I need is for my wife to stop shopping in every store we pass and help me find our son." He glanced at the rock in my hand. "Keep it. I obviously have plenty of them."

"Thank you. It's beautiful." I examined the stone and saw a flaming heart carved into it. Numerous stones remained in the bag, so I slipped my backpack off my shoulders and pulled out my pencil bag. I dumped the pencils into my backpack and held the bag open so he could pour the stones from the ripped bag into the pencil bag. "I hope this helps."

"Thanks."

"If you don't mind my asking..."

"Why do I have a bunch of stones?" I nodded. "They're for my son. We've been told he finally has a girlfriend. He's had girlfriends, but not like this one. He has apparently changed his attitude all together. My wife wants to give these stones to the girl who has thoroughly transformed him."

"Why are there hearts carved into them?"

"Our son carved them. Every time a girl broke his heart he would carve a heart into a stone."

My eyes grew wide as I scrutinized the bag. "That's a bunch of girls."

"He also carved them for other reasons. For example, he carved the one you're holding when he was a kid. He used to say, 'When I find the right girl, I'm going to give her this stone and tell her that I give her my heart.' My wife loved it."

"That's so sweet. Perhaps I shouldn't keep it."

"No, you go ahead. My son has lots of them. He carved one almost every year until he was thirteen years old. That year he decided he was too old to carve them anymore. When he was fourteen, he fell in love with a girl who was older than him. She crushed him when she told him she was getting married. That's when he began carving again. Every time he got his heart broken, he would carve a heart into a stone."

"Poor guy." I stared down at the stone.

"Unfortunately, as he grew up, his outlook on the world changed. He came to Russellville, caused some trouble, and now he is forced to live here. His sister moved here to watch over him. In the meantime she found a boyfriend and decided to stay. My son was given more freedom but he wasn't allowed to leave the town." He looked thoughtfully down at the ground. "I guess it was for the best if he met a girl who changed his attitude." I twirled the stone in my hand.

*This sounds familiar.* "What's your son's name?"

"It's—"

"Firefly, I'm ready to go." A woman came out of the store. "Who's this?" I stared at the couple in stunned silence.

"Firefly?" I uttered. *This is very familiar; this can't be a coincidence.* I realized they were both staring at me, and they both appeared confused. "I'm sorry, my name is Kira." I said, shaking the woman's hand.

"I dropped one of the stones and Kira helped me. She even gave me a bag. Wish you had given me one before we left the house." The man said.

"You shouldn't have rushed me, and if I recall correctly, you were the one who dropped the box that contained the stones. At any rate, we must leave now to visit our son. It was a pleasure meeting you, Kira." They left without another word.

*What a quirky couple! Their son reminds me of Pyre. I wonder if... No, it couldn't be. Could it? And Firefly?* I walked the rest of the way home, my mind preoccupied by the extraordinary encounter. Pyre and Lowell got to the apartment the same time I did.

"We made it just in time. How was class?" Pyre asked. I peered at him speculatively, noticed the resemblance between him and the couple, and silently walked into the kitchen. "Kira?"

"Class was fine." I said with a slight smile.

"Did something happen? Did those girls do something?" Lowell said, sounding excessively anxious.

"No, not the girls. I met a peculiar couple on my way home." I made myself a drink and offered one to the guys. "They're in town to pay a surprise visit to their son." I walked back to the living room.

"What's so unusual about that?" Pyre asked. Someone rapped lightly on the door at that moment.

"That's not the unusual part. This is." I said as I opened the door, and gestured with my hand to the couple standing there with shocked expressions.

"Mom? Dad? What are you doing here?"

"We came to see how you're doing." His mother said as she hugged him.

"And to meet your girlfriend, but it seems we already have." His father held out a hand to me. "My name is Pyrrhos. My wife didn't let me introduce myself earlier."

"Oh, please, like I could stop you. Besides, I wanted to see my son and you were busy flirting with yet another cute, young girl." She walked up to me. "My name is Celosia. You can call me Cel, and perhaps someday Mom?"

"Um... thank you." My eyes landed on Pyre, seeking help.

"Mom, it's bad enough Eira is planning our wedding. I don't need you helping her."

"Pyre, relax. You know I want another daughter." She pushed some hair out of my face.

"She would be a cute daughter-in-law." Pyrrhos joked, nudging Pyre's arm. Pyre looked like he wanted to find a place to hide. Lowell gazed at the floor to hide his smile.

Pyrrhos handed me the bag of rocks. "I guess you should put these with the other one." He winked and squeezed my hand.

*What does 'the other one' mean?*

*I'll fill you in later.*

"Pyre, does Kira—" Cel began.

"Yes, Mom, she's aware." Pyre finished for her. Cel walked over to Pyre and his father. They stood there, looking quietly from one to the other, gesturing now and then.

Lowell walked over to me and whispered, "The dreaded meeting of the parents. Always fun."

"I guess they don't like that I know they're demons."

"That's not what I'm hearing." He beamed at me, like he just learned a secret. Pyre and his parents glanced over at him.

"We should get going, but we'll see you later. Kira, don't you go disappearing on Pyre now." Cel said as she hugged her son.

"I'll do my best."

"If you do, he'll find you." Pyrrhos said. Pyre made a mortified face at his father.

"I should hope so."

"You take care of her, Pyre." Cel said.

"I will, Mom." Pyre replied.

"Bye for now, kids." Pyrrhos waved as he stepped through the door. Lowell locked the door behind them.

"That was interesting." Lowell said.

"Yep. Even demon parents can embarrass their kids." Pyre stated emphatically.

"They didn't stay long." I said.

"They wanted to visit some friends while they're here. They'll be in town awhile, though, which means, they'll be back."

"Oh." I said hesitantly, biting my lip.

"They love you." Pyre wrapped his arm around me.

"Really?"

"Trust me, they do."

"They're not upset that I know they're demons?"

"Nah, they're more concerned about you not being a demon."

"We'll make certain she lives well into her hundreds." Lowell immediately realized he'd said the worst possible thing since a human wouldn't live as long as a demon. We both looked up at him.

"Why are you still here?" Pyre demanded.

"You haven't kicked me out yet."

"And why haven't I kicked you out yet?"

"Because you realize I wouldn't go even if you did." Pyre seemed to contemplate his next response.

"Do you want to go to the park?" He asked, focusing his attention on me.

"Yes, I do. Let's see if everyone will go with us." I grabbed my jacket. Lowell opened the door and we headed to Caedmon's apartment.

Everyone loved the idea of going to the park. Caedmon's apartment was so small, and crowded with everyone there, that Pyre and I waited outside.

"What is taking them so long?" Pyre growled impatiently. "Did Eros need to put on his makeup?"

"Pyre, be nice." I reprimanded him, but laughed nevertheless. "Not everyone can move as fast as you."

"They can move faster than this."

"What's wrong?" I grasped his hand.

"Nothing, why?"

"You've been extra grumpy lately." He wrapped his arm around me and pulled me closer.

"I haven't been sleeping well lately."

"Are you still having the nightmares?"

"Not as much."

"Maybe you train too much."

"I only train while you're in class."

"Which is at least three hours a day five days a week."

"So?"

"So I think you need to slow down periodically."

"I'm a demon. I can't slow down." He put his fists on his hips like a superhero.

"You're a living being. Even demons need to slow down sometimes." He stared obstinately in my direction, but I crossed my arms and returned his stare.

"You two are so cute." I glanced over and saw Eira and Lowell standing by the door to Caedmon's apartment.

"Where's the camera?" Lowell asked. Pyre growled again, and Lowell actually growled in response.

"Where are the others?" I asked, trying to change the subject, as I grasped Pyre's hand and rubbed his arm with my other hand.

"Caedmon and Laya got into another fight. Eros tried to step up for Laya which ended up in a fist fight between the two boys." Lowell said.

"This is ridiculous. Why do they fight so much?"

"They grew up together. So they have a brotherly bond." Eira explained.

"To keep the bond they fight?" Eira shrugged her shoulders. I shook my head in disbelief. At that moment, I observed a girl staring at us from across the street.

"Pyre, you and Kira should head to the park and we'll meet you there." Eira stared back at the girl and plainly didn't appreciate her presence.

"You were the one who said we should wait for y'all."

"I changed my mind." Eira sounded harsh and rude. The girl approached us with lithe and deliberate movement. "Now would be good, Pyre."

"Why do you want us to leave?"

"Hello, Pyre." She spoke in a flirty voice and leered at Pyre. "How have you been?" Pyre's arm tensed up beneath my fingers. He glared at the girl with utter disdain.

"Aella." He sounded disgruntled to see her.

"Well, yes, I've been well, but I've missed you." She appraised me up and down and chose the polite approach. "I'm Aella." She held her hand out to me, but Pyre pulled me away from her.

"Her name is Kira." He sounded impatient and defensive.

"What kind of demon are you, Kira?"

"She's human." Eira stepped in between us.

"Eira, I didn't even see you there." Aella claimed, obviously lying and not remotely caring about what Eira said. "How is little Eira?" Eira crossed her arms. "Hmm, I see you're still mad. So, back to you, Kira. What kind of demon are you?"

"I'm not a demon."

"Stop lying. You must be a demon because Pyre would never date a human."

"She is a human and I am dating her." Aella looked back and forth between Pyre and me.

"This is a joke, right? You? Dating a human? Weren't you the one who said humans are disgusting creatures who should be eradicated?" Aella looked directly at me when she said the last part.

"That was a long time ago, Aella. I've changed." He reached for my hand.

"What makes this human so special?"

"She loves me for me; for who I am. She took the

time to get to know me. We're still learning all about each other. We don't keep secrets from each other, the way you did from me."

"Some secrets are necessary for relationships to work." She spread her hands in front of her in a placating gesture.

"While I'll agree to that, the ones you kept weren't."

"I only kept them to protect you."

"You cheated on me, Aella, and when Eira caught you, you threatened her. Which, by the way, was your worst mistake."

"The past is the past, Pyre. I've changed too." She tried to snatch his hand but Pyre yanked it away before she could touch him. "Pyre, I want you back."

"I don't want you back. In case I didn't make myself clear, I'm with Kira now, and I love her." He looked to Lowell with a silent message and turned to face me. "Let's go on ahead." I nodded.

"We'll meet you there." Lowell stated as he and Eira stood between Aella and Pyre to prevent her from following us. Pyre picked me up and took off for the park. When we got there, he set me on a bench and paced in front of me.

"Sorry about that." He rubbed his forehead. "I thought she wasn't even still in America to be honest." I stood up, wrapped my arms around him and rested my head on his chest. "Mmm, you're so warm."

"I'm warm. To a fire demon?"

"Very." As he pulled me in closer and tighter, a question occurred to me.

"You told Aella that you've changed, and you've mentioned it previously. Your parents said the same thing, that you have been fully transformed."

"Yes, thanks to you."

"How did you change?" I asked.

"I'll tell you later. I'd rather not tell you with ears listening." He pivoted to expose Vitas's presence behind him. "What do you want?"

"I need to talk to you." Vitas said.

"This is not a good time."

"I understand, but it's important." Vitas sounded somewhat apologetic, but Pyre still growled.

"I'll be right back. Stay where I can see you." They walked a short way up the path.

*What am I, five?* I sat on the bench and thought about our encounter with Aella. *I wonder why she came here now. Is there more to it than what she said?* A hand unexpectedly landed on my shoulder which caused me to jump. I stood and whirled around to face the new presence.

"Didn't mean to startle you." Lowell held up his hands and took a step back.

"It's okay." I tried to catch my breath and calm the pounding of my heart. *A heads up would've been appreciated.* I glanced over at Pyre.

*By the way, Lowell's behind you.*

*My boyfriend, ladies and gentlemen.*

"Bringing you out of your conversation, what is Vitas talking to Pyre about?" Lowell asked me as the others walked up behind him.

"Stuff." I sat back down on the bench.

"What stuff?" He leaned over to peer closely at me.

"Important stuff." I tried desperately to keep a straight face. Lowell pursed his lips at me.

"What kind of important stuff?" I quietly contemplated Pyre and Vitas. "Well, Kira?"

"What?"

"What are they talking about?"

"Stuff." He threw his arms up in the air. Pyre and Vitas both glanced in our direction with strange expressions on their faces. I shrugged my shoulders and pointed at Lowell.

"Kira, you're something else. I swear I cannot figure you out."

"That's the plan." Caedmon and Eros walked up to us.

"What're Vitas and Pyre talking about?" Caedmon asked.

"Pyre probably did something." Eros said.

"Ask Kira. She won't tell me." Lowell gestured to me.

"Kira, what're they talking about?" Caedmon asked.

"Stuff."

"What stuff?" Eros asked.

"Important stuff."

"Same answers." Lowell gripped the back of the bench in exasperation.

Eira sat down next to me and asked, "Kira, what's Vitas talking to Pyre about?"

"I'm uncertain. All I know is it's important."

"Seriously?" Lowell yelled, shaking my shoulders. "You couldn't simply say that?"

"I did but you wouldn't listen." I tried to appear innocent, but he only shook his head. Pyre walked over to us as Vitas disappeared into the trees.

"Pyre, you have the most bizarre girlfriend ever. You have my sympathy." Lowell stared at me as I gave him a cherubic smile. Pyre took a minute to register what Lowell said and then my facial expression.

"What did you do?" Pyre raised an eyebrow, obviously not buying my innocent act.

"Nothing. I am completely unaware what he might be referring to." I peeked over at Eira and we both giggled.

"Why don't I believe you?"

"My goodness, Pyre, why wouldn't you believe me?"

"What did Vitas want to talk to you about?" Lowell interrupted and inquired yet again.

"Stuff." Pyre smiled down at me.

"I'm not afraid to hit you." Lowell leaned against the bench.

"We had something important to discuss. I'll tell you later." He stared at Lowell with a serious expression and sat down next to me, wrapping an arm around my shoulders.

"What's going on Pyre?" Eira asked. Laya, Iris, and Gabby walked up with some drinks.

"I'll explain later. Is Aella gone? Please say yes."

"She's gone for now. My intuition tells me she'll be back though."

"Not soon, I hope. Let's enjoy ourselves for now."

"We actually wanted to ask Kira a question." Laya said.

"What's the question?" I asked, reluctantly.

"It concerns why you moved here." Caedmon said.

"We realize you moved here for school. But we wondered if there might be more to it." Gabby said.

"We were curious why you chose to move from Nashville to Russellville." Eros said.

"Why do you ask?" Their unanticipated inquisitiveness confused me.

"Aella showing up reminded us of why Pyre moved here. We realized you haven't ever said why you moved here." Eira explained.

"I wanted a fresh beginning in a new place. Nashville holds sad memories for me." I said.

"What kind of memories?" Iris prodded.

"Just memories." I stood up and took a few steps away from the bench and stared at the trees to avoid discussing it.

"Like what?" Eira queried. They weren't letting this go easily. I looked up to the sky in frustration.

"Like my family dying or disappearing and my best friend changing for the worse and attacking me." Pyre placed his hands on my shoulders.

"You're not obligated to tell them." Pyre whispered into my ear.

"That's true, but they're my friends and they asked. There's no real reason not to answer them."

*They don't need an answer. Personally I'd tell them to mind their own business. Or at least keep them guessing.*

*I can believe that, but perhaps they do need to know. If Crystal attacks, she might involve them, so they*

116

*should be prepared.*

I detected movement from the corner of my eye and swiveled my head to find Eros had raised his hand. "Would the idiot like to ask a question?" Pyre smirked at him, crossing his arms.

"Shut up, Shrimp!" Eros yelled at Pyre with a scowl. "I was going to say that she doesn't have to answer if it hurts too much."

"It does hurt, but it gets better with time. I can talk about it now. For starters, you've probably noticed I rarely talk about my family." They all nodded. "My mom and brother died in a car accident." I paused and took a deep breath. "After the funeral, my dad thought it would be easier for both of us if he left."

"He left you all alone?" Iris asked.

"Not entirely. I went to live with my childhood friend and her mother. Not that my friend was happy about it."

"What do you mean?" Caedmon asked.

"My friend's name was Crystal. We had been friends since we were five years old and did everything together. We both changed as we got older, but only in small ways. She still loved the color pink but didn't play with her dolls as much. I liked the colors black and red and I grew to hate shopping. Clothes shopping at least, and only because I had to try them on to be sure they fit. Despite the few changes we remained close friends. At sixteen she still wore pink clothes and makeup. She had a new boyfriend almost every week and had to be in the popular crowd. I still loved the color black, but I became moderately more colorful with my clothes, wearing more earthy colors. I was definitely not part of the popular crowd. The day of my sixteenth birthday, her mother called to tell me Crystal was in the hospital."

"What happened to her?" Gabby asked.

"I still don't know the details. She never told anyone exactly what happened. All I know is she was driving her car and had an accident. I don't know who it involved or where it happened. She acted strange after that."

"In what way?" Eros asked.

"Crystal changed completely. She despised everything pink and burned every pink thing she owned. She no longer hung out with her old friends, or had any friends at all for that matter. She behaved terribly rude and hateful to everyone, including her mother. She dyed her hair pitch black, wore all black clothes, and got into witchcraft. She would lock herself in her room all the time. Everyone became scared of her. The day I moved here, she was so angry that I was leaving, she lunged at me with a knife and made a huge cut on my arm." I showed them the scar.

"That's a bad scar. It must've hurt." Caedmon said.

"She gave you that scar?" Iris walked over for a closer inspection.

"Yes, and if I wasn't afraid of her before, I'm terrified now." Pyre stared at my arm with rage in his eyes. I could imagine what was going on in his head. "I left right after her attack. The sooner, the better." The silence was deafening. Hours seemed to pass by instead of mere minutes.

"We're sorry, Kira." Laya said. "If we had known..."

"If we had been there..." Gabby said.

"It's not your fault. You didn't know me then, so you couldn't have been there. You were here fighting your own battles. Besides, she's now locked up in a psych ward in Nashville. She escaped once and could again. We think she's planning something and using witchcraft to do it, but we're unsure what it might be. She came to me in a dream on New Year's Eve. I awoke with my arms frozen. Nothing has happened since, so hopefully it's over now. Regardless of what happens, I'm confident Pyre won't let her near me."

"You got that right!" Pyre wrapped his arms around me.

"None of us will." Lowell asserted and rubbed my shoulder.

"We'll teach her not to hurt you again." Caedmon said.

"We will do everything it takes to protect you." Eros said.

"Thank you. Please be careful if you see her. She's deeply disturbed and extremely dangerous."

"She won't know what hit her." Caedmon said as he punched Eros.

"Ow!" Eros lunged at Caedmon and we all laughed. You had to love Caedmon and Eros — your one-stop place to shop for comic relief, twenty-four hours a day.

"It's been interesting, but I'm ready for some fun now." I said.

"Can we eat first?" Eros asked mid punch.

119

"Where do we want to go?" Laya asked.

"How about $E^5$?" Eira suggested.

"Yea, that place is fantastic." Gabby said.

"Then let's go." Caedmon said as he pushed Eros off of him. Everyone cheered and headed down the road. The boys immediately began comparing their scars.

*What is it with boys and scars anyway?* I never would understand them.

"Chicks dig scars, don't you know?" Pyre had lifted his sleeve to show off one of his own. Even Lowell got into the exhibition, raising his shirt to display a particularly long scar on his lower left side.

"Chicks? Chicks can dig whatever they want. Grown women prefer their men to possess style and maturity." The girls and I all tossed our heads and started walking again. The boys blew it off and continued with their comparisons. The other girls giggled and looked back to ogle the boys. *What is it with chicks and scars anyway?* I caught myself sneaking a peek at Pyre as he showed off his scar trophies. He ogled me playfully and flexed his muscles.

*Caught ya looking.* I felt my face turn flaming red, faced forward and continued walking. *If it pleases you to look, you can stare all you want. Unless of course you're too much of a grown, mature woman for that.*

*Bite me, Pyre!*

*Perhaps we'll try that later.*

I spun around and stared at him in shock, embarrassment, consternation, aggravation, and a wide range of other thoughts and emotions which played themselves out within seconds. All of which left me speechless. I whirled around and started walking again. "Argh!" I yelled and shook my hands.

"Kira, what in the world is wrong with you all of a sudden?" Eira stared at me, confused by my outburst.

"Boys! That's what's wrong with me. Boys, boys, boys!" I heard laughter behind me and turned to glare at them. I couldn't resist a slight grin as I turned back around and resumed walking.

# Chapter 6
# Parents, Painting and
# Other Nightmares

We sat down at the table and ordered. The special of the day was "all you can eat" fish and shrimp with fries, and cobbler for dessert. We all ordered the special, which was probably a mistake. The guys ran the waitress ragged getting them free refills and still tried to snatch shrimp from the girls' plates. The waitress took it all in stride and even joked around with us.

"You seem to enjoy working here." I commented to the waitress.

"It's not bad."

"What's your boss like?"

"He's nice, and funny too, as long as you work hard and try to do your job well. He can be a real bear if you don't."

"I like bears."

"Not like this you don't. Trust me."

"Well, I was wondering, are y'all hiring at all?"

"I think so. I'll go ask."

When the waitress walked away, Pyre leaned over and asked, "What are you doing?"

"I need to get a job and make some money. This seems to be an acceptable place to work, so I thought I'd try it."

"And if you get hired here, we can come and torture

you." Caedmon looked conspiratorially at Eros. They grinned and laughed evilly.

"You're the first ones I ban from the restaurant."

The waitress came back to the table with the application. She told me to fill it out and leave it, and to come back after two o'clock on Wednesday for an interview. I glanced over at Pyre and noticed him surveying the place.

"What's the matter?"

"Nothing." He looked down at my hand. "Are you determined to work here?"

"You don't think I should?"

"No, it's not that. Okay, maybe a little, but you don't need to work. I can give you money."

"Thanks, but I was raised to be independent. Eros, don't you swipe any more of my shrimp. Don't think I don't see what you're doing."

"You've got enough shrimp — sitting there next to you brooding. Ow! Who kicked me?"

"I did. Eat your own shrimp and behave yourself. You act like you were raised in a barn." Eira chastised Eros.

"Maybe I was."

"Were you the chicken or the egg?" Caedmon needled Eros and they scuffled in their seats. Pyre and I both stared disapprovingly for a moment and resumed our conversation.

"I worry when Lowell and I aren't with you. What if something happens?"

"You can't be with me all the time, and I can't live my life that way, being paranoid every minute about some danger lurking around the next corner."

"I understand that, but we're aware the danger is definitely out there, and coming for you."

"If I work here, it's close to school and the apartment, and I'll be surrounded by people all the time. I should be completely safe."

"I guess, and I could walk you to work and be here when you get done."

"Then why are you brooding?"

"I can't shake the notion that there's something strange about this place."

"I'm still going to apply."

"And I still wish you wouldn't."

"At the first sign of trouble, I'll quit."

"I guess that's all I can ask, for now."

"Thank you." As we walked into the parking lot, I spotted a man getting out of his car, and he seemed familiar. I grew uneasy and asked, "Pyre, could we go on ahead?"

"Why? What's wrong?" He wrapped his arm around me and searched my face.

"I just want to leave. Let's go now, please? I'll explain later." The man noticed us and I turned away to prevent him seeing my face. *Please don't let it be him.*

"Kira, what's the matter?" Lowell asked.

"Nothing. I simply want to leave. Right now, please."

"Kira?" The man stood right behind me. I closed my eyes and faced the man.

"Hello, Dad." I mumbled as my friends whispered to each other.

"How have you been?"

"Good." I looked away.

"Are you going in to eat?"

"We're finished, and we're leaving." I seized a tight hold on Pyre's hand.

"Let me take you home."

"Pyre will take me home."

"Who's Pyre?" He sounded considerably displeased.

"I am. I'm her boyfriend." Pyre held out his hand to him.

"Boyfriend?" My dad questioned as he shook Pyre's hand. "I didn't realize my little girl was finally interested in boys."

"People change. Little girls grow up." I said.

"Pyre, you can call me Cal."

"It's nice to meet you, sir." Pyre said.

"These kids must all be your friends." My dad said affably, as if he hadn't been away, acknowledging each of them.

"Yes, they are. You might know my friends if you'd been around the past year."

"We have a great deal to catch up on."

"Maybe another time. Shall we make an appointment for the same time next year?" I pulled on Pyre's hand. *Please get me out of here.* Pyre nodded, wrapped an arm around me, and we walked away.

"How about we talk tomorrow?" My dad asked.

"We'll see." I said, without stopping or looking at him. *Is he gone?*

*He's back in the parking lot.* Pyre checked to be

certain and chuckled. *Eira stopped him and is chattering away about the weather and other nonsense.*

*That's a relief. Remind me to thank Eira. I can't believe he's here.*

"Pyre, why don't you take Kira home. We'll see you tomorrow." Lowell suggested as he caught up to us.

"Sounds good. Kira, come here." He pulled me close to him before picking me up and I wrapped my arms around his neck. When we arrived at the apartment, he took me all the way to my room and set me on my bed. "Can I get you anything?"

"No, I'm all right. I'm sorry."

"About what?"

"About him. I had no idea he was here. Seeing him, out of the blue, no warning at all. I got flustered I guess."

"Which is why you shouldn't be sorry." He lifted my chin. "You're sorry when you shouldn't be or for things that aren't your fault. That's one of the quirky things I love about you." I frowned doubtfully and kissed him good night. "I'll see you in the morning."

*Pyre's right. I shouldn't be apologizing for my dad. It's not my fault my dad did what he did. I shouldn't stress about it, but I have countless questions. How did he know I was here? Where has he been? Why show up after all this time?* I immediately felt drained of energy. I laid down and fell right to sleep.

I stood on the sidewalk at the Nashville airport watching people as they walked. I recognized the cab driver who brought me to the airport the day I moved to Russellville. He leaned casually against his cab.

"Looks like you've been doing well." The cab driver walked toward me. Time seemed to stop around us. "You didn't heed my warning about danger though."

"I tried, but it found me anyway."

"You're old friend is causing disorder in the natural world." He pointed behind me, so I turned and spotted Crystal.

"How can I stop her?"

"Not my problem. I try not to meddle in human affairs."

"I was right — you are a demon. But if you won't help, why are you here?"

"To give you another warning. The rebirth will happen and there's no stopping it." His eyes changed color like the first time I met him. "The rebirth also isn't what you speculate it is."

"What is it?"

"The rebirth won't bring someone back from the dead. It will transform a living person into something different, and not in a good way."

"Who is to be reborn?"

"That should be obvious, especially to a smart cookie like you." He walked back to his cab and time resumed. I watched as Crystal walked into the airport and followed her. Security guards instantly surrounded her and pointed guns at her.

"Miss, put your hands on your head and get on your knees." One of the men commanded. Crystal rotated her head in his direction.

"But I'll ruin my dress." She argued.

"Get on your knees!"

"I only get on my knees to pray and I'm not praying to you." She raised one of her hands and opened it to display a small bit of dirt.

"Miss, get on your knees! Now!"

"I have work to do and no time to spare for you to take me back to that prison." The bit of dirt in her hand floated up and flew around the room, becoming more plentiful and dense. I watched helplessly as the cyclone surrounded the security guards and other people in the area. When the dirt finally fell to the floor, and the air cleared, everyone had disappeared. A tree stood where the main security guard had been standing. Crystal turned to me. "Don't you just hate when people keep repeating themselves? The earth sacrifice has been made, which only leaves wind and fire. Once they are concluded, the rebirth can begin." She walked closer to me. "The world will be a better place soon. You're bound to be filled with anticipation, but for now, it's time for you to wake up."

I jumped awake. My body except my head was covered in dirt and I couldn't move. I raised my head to look around and discovered a plant at the foot of the bed.

*Kira?* Pyre asked me through telepathy. *Kira, what's happening?*

*I'm buried in dirt.* Pyre ran into the room with Lowell right behind him.

"Kira!" Pyre picked me up out of the dirt and held me close to him. I broke down and cried into his shirt. Lowell grabbed the flower and tossed it out the window. "We need to make this stop, Lowell."

"Take her to the living room. I'll clean up in here." Pyre carried me out to the living room and sat with me in his lap.

"What happened?" Vitas asked, somewhere behind me.

"Kira's nightmare came to life again." Pyre said while rubbing my head.

"That explains the dirt." Eros stepped in front of us. Caedmon leaned on the back of the couch and Vitas stood next to him.

"What happened in the dream?" Caedmon asked. I closed my eyes and buried my face again.

"We'll tell you later." Pyre leaned his cheek against my head. They continued to talk, but I quit listening. I didn't look up until another hand caressed my head.

"The dirt's gone, Kit." Lowell wiped my face.

"Thank you." When I looked in his direction, I realized the clock behind him read roughly ten o'clock. "What day is it?"

"Thursday." Pyre replied.

"I'm late." I tried to get up but Pyre wouldn't let me.

"You're not going anywhere."

"Pyre's right," Lowell said. "After last night, you're in no condition to go anywhere."

I thought about it for a moment and finally agreed. "It would give me time to work on my art project that's due tomorrow."

"I'll tell Lur to notify your speech professor and I'll talk to the geology professor."

"You've been stressed and have gotten little sleep since these nightmares began. I'll stay here with you." Pyre offered.

"Thank you." I leaned on Pyre as he pulled me back into his lap.

"We're leaving now, but I'll find out what I can about all of this." Vitas said.

"Call if you need anything." Caedmon said and Pyre nodded gratefully.

"I won't mention this to Eira." Eros said.

"Thank you. All of you."

"I'm going too." Lowell said.

"Wait, Lowell. What kind of flower was at the foot of my bed?" I just remembered seeing it there.

"It was a peace lily. It means rebirth."

"Rebirth?" I processed the symbolic implication. Lowell nodded and seemed uneasy.

"Crystal sent it, didn't she?" Pyre asked. I nodded and laid my head back on his chest.

"She's getting closer." Lowell exchanged looks with Pyre.

"We'll stop her." Pyre continued rubbing my hair and trying to soothe me.

*I hope so.* The apartment walls seemed to close in on me, making it hard to breathe. I had to do something. Crystal would not turn me into a cowering wimp. "I need to get ready for school."

"Kira, why don't you stay home and—"

"No, it'll be better for me to get out of the apartment. Besides I promised the girls I would go shopping with them tomorrow, and we need to finalize our plans. If I don't show up today, they might assume we aren't going after all."

"Why are you going shopping? You hate

shopping."

"I do, and they are already giving me a hard time about that. But Lur wants to find something for me to wear for the painting. Lur, Stella, and Luna, are going and they wanted to meet Eira, Laya, Iris, and Gabby."

"Kira, shopping can wait. Stay here with me. We'll relax together and do whatever you want."

"I need to go, and I couldn't unwind right now anyway." I looked down at my hands. "Please stay close?"

"I will." He rubbed my face.

Once I was ready for school, Pyre walked with me to class. I wasn't able to focus during classes because I kept deliberating about the dreams and Crystal.

"Kira, what's wrong with you today?" Lur inquired, snapping me out of my trance.

"I'm extremely tired and have so much work to do. How can it already be Thursday? It should still be Monday."

"I can't believe it either." Luna said.

"Are you still up for shopping tomorrow?" Stella asked.

"As much as I am ever up for shopping." They looked at me like I was a space alien.

The professor walked in and began talking about the day's assignments. Even though the classes went by fast, I was extremely relieved when they ended. I was even more relieved when the day was done and actually looked forward to Friday. I only set myself up for disappointment.

Friday was such a lousy day! Ink from my drawing pens smeared all over my clothes in art class. I got drenched with water during biology and had to go to the campus bookstore to buy a t-shirt. I tripped ten people on the way out of mythology; although, come to think of it, I only tripped the first person. He fell into the redhead, bumping her into the next person, and so on, like a line of dominoes. So, glass half... nope, that glass was empty.

When class was over, we walked outside to meet up with Eira and the other girls. After I introduced everyone, we all headed to the mall. They all seemed to get along well with each other. I had the impression of being watched but when I searched around, I didn't see anyone or anything out of the ordinary. Eira kept an eye on Lur and the girls, but tried to be nonchalant about it.

"Eira, what are you doing?" We finally got a few minutes away from the group.

"I'm trying to figure out if they're demons or not."

"What's your best guess?"

"I can't be positive, but they don't appear to be demons."

"Do you sense that we're being watched?"

"No, I haven't noticed anything."

"Stay nearby, okay?"

"Oh, Kira, you know I will."

When we arrived at the mall, we decided to all spread out, since we were such a large group. Lur and Eira stayed with me and the other girls went off together to do their own thing. We ran into them a couple of times and agreed to meet at the food area for dinner. We walked through the mall, going into several stores. I still had the nagging notion of being watched or followed, but I couldn't see anything suspicious. My intuition hadn't been wrong before, so I continued to check my surroundings and stayed alert. One time I swore I saw Lowell, but I looked again and he wasn't there. Another time I was sure I saw Pyre. I walked over to where I thought he'd been, but he wasn't there either. Finally I was positive I had seen Lowell again. I ran over to where I'd spotted him, turned the corner and ran right into Luna, Laya and the other girls. I even knocked Luna down in my haste.

"Wow, Kira, where's the fire?" Stella asked as she helped Luna back to her feet.

"Did any of you see Lowell come this way?"

"No, we haven't seen him." Gabby looked at me quizzically.

"I could swear he was just here. What about Pyre? Have y'all seen him?"

"No, him neither." Iris also stared at me like I had lost my mind. Maybe I had. I probably left it behind in one of the stores on the clearance rack — one lost, slightly abnormal brain, now 90% off.

"Never mind. See y'all later."

I went into the store that Eira had just entered.

"Kira, where'd you go?"

"Eira, it's the weirdest thing. I've been convinced I've seen Lowell and Pyre at times today, but when I look again, they aren't there. I wanted Pyre to stay close, but this is kind of freaking me out."

"Kira, it's probably nothing."

"Have you seen or sensed anything?"

"No, Kira, my demon senses aren't tingling." She laughed and wiggled her fingers in the air.

"What about the girls from school? Do you like them?"

"Yes, I do. They seem very nice, and they are a lot of fun. Stella's a little out there."

"That's an understatement."

"I wouldn't worry until we are certain there's a reason for it, but remain careful and watchful."

"Thanks, Eira. So, what're you looking for today?"

"I want a new dress for Valentine's Day, something that will make Eros go weak at the knees. Are you having any luck?"

"No." I leaned on the wall and pouted.

"Uh oh, what's the problem?"

"I've found a few things, but Lur didn't like them. She claimed they just wouldn't be in tune with the nature of the painting. The outfits Lur chose, I wouldn't be caught dead in."

"You don't care much for dresses."

"No, I don't, but it's not that. I told her nothing too short, too low, or see-through, but that's all she has brought me. She doesn't... dear Lord, what has she got now?" We watched as Lur walked toward us with a small scrap of fabric on a hanger in her hands.

"Kira, this is ideal, isn't it?"

"Absolutely not." I crossed my arms and stared at her obstinately.

"Eira, what do you think?"

"I think I should keep looking for a dress for Valentine's Day."

"Come on, help me convince Kira, please?"

"Okay, let me see it."

"This is it."

"Where's the rest of it?" Eira searched around to

check if Lur had dropped something.

"Eira, this is all of it. This is the whole dress."

"I see." Eira sounded skeptical as she took it, looked it over and held it up to me. I placed my hands on my hips and stared at her. Her eyes grew wide, and she made a face. "Hun, that's not a dress, it's a tunic; an incredibly short tunic."

"She'd wear leggings with it. She'd resemble a forest nymph."

"Cover it up however you want, her butt would still stick out."

"Oh, come on, Eira." Lur argued, getting exasperated.

"No, Lur, you come on. I'm still standing right here you know. I told you — nothing too short, too low or too revealing. That's all the above!"

"Fine, I'll keep hunting. But we've been through practically everything in every store here."

I walked off to another store by myself. I was ready to tell her to forget the whole thing when I happened upon a rack with earthy style clothes. They were even on sale. I browsed through them, sliding the hangers one by one. *Too big. Too small. Too ugly. What in the world? Not a chance! How do you even put that on? That's too much cover. Oh well, it was... hang on a minute. What's this?* I pulled it up to inspect it. The dress was beautiful. It had a curling layered silk and chiffon skirt in various shades of brown, bronze and green. The bodice was fitted in a textured brown which sort of reminded me of watercolors due to the way the colors blended and shifted in the light. Vines of leaves and flowers were embroidered from the shoulder angling to the waist which would give the illusion of wrapping around the abdomen and disappearing over the hip. The left sleeve was similar to the skirt in silk and in a flutter style. The right side was a strap that came around the back neckline and over the shoulder in a beautiful forest green with small flowers and cutouts. It resembled a flowering leafy vine that reached across the shoulder and ended at the neckline with a removable bronze locket. The locket was decorated with an interlaced Celtic-style design and a green stone.

Lur found me evaluating each side of the dress. "Kira, that's perfect!"

"I agree, and it's on sale. I'll go try it on, and you can give me your opinion." Eira had joined Lur by the time I came out of the dressing room.

"Kira, you're so beautiful." Lur circled around me to get a view from all angles.

"That's such an attractive color on you, and the fabric is so soft." Eira felt of the sleeve and the skirt.

"I love the way it's cut, and the fabric is gorgeous. We can make an accessory for your hair." Lur said.

"You could even wear it going out or on special occasions or something." Eira said.

"And the best part is, it's on sale." They both shook their heads at me like I was odd for saying that. Once again, I felt the sensation of being watched. I looked out of the store, and this time I absolutely saw Pyre disappear into the crowd.

"You know how you know when you truly love someone? You see their face everywhere you go. That's been happening to me all day."

"Again, Kira?"

"Yes, but this time I'm positive it was him. What's he doing, following us?"

"I doubt it. Kira, you're merely being jittery."

"What are you two talking about?" Lur sounded totally confused.

"All day I've felt like I was being watched or followed. A couple of times I thought I saw Lowell, and other times I thought I saw Pyre. I'm confident I saw him standing outside this store, staring at me in this dress."

"I'm actually glad to hear you say that because I've been feeling the same way today. It was kind of disturbing."

"Lur, why didn't you say something?"

"I figured I was being weird or paranoid."

"Okay, I believe both of you now. I definitely caught Lowell peeking in here, resembling a lovesick puppy. What are those two up to?"

"More importantly, ladies, what do we do about it?" I raised my eyebrow and smiled mischievously.

"This is going to be good." Eira laughed and the three of us put our heads together to hatch a plan.

We picked out some cute tops, a hat and a big bag for me and a scarf and sunglasses for Lur. Eira took them to the counter for us along with the dress she had chosen for herself. We gave her the money, and she paid for our items. We went back in the dressing rooms to change. Lur pushed the lenses out of the sunglasses so they'd appear to be regular glasses. After we changed, we appraised each other's appearance thoroughly.

"I doubt they'll be able to recognize you in that hat

and with your hair pulled up." Lur said.

"There's no way they'll recognize you with the scarf and glasses."

Eira walked into the dressing room area and clapped when she saw us. "This will be fantastic! I can hardly wait to see their faces. You should leave one at a time and go in opposite directions. I'll stay in the store where they can see me. I'll bring something in here after a few minutes and then look some more. With any luck, they'll assume you're still in the dressing rooms, and won't detect when each of you leave. Once you've had enough time to get away, I'll leave and head for the food strip. The other girls will probably get there shortly too. With any luck, the guys will follow me and wonder where you are."

"I like it. I'll go first, okay, Lur? If Pyre recognizes me, he'll follow me, and we'll know they're onto us."

"Perfect! I'll wait a minute or two and be right behind you. You go right, and I'll go left."

I left the store and walked right past both Pyre and Lowell. Neither of them paid me any attention. Lowell was terribly cute as he hid behind a cart of floppy hats and peeked into the store to find Lur. I stepped into another store on the other side, so I could watch when Lur left. She came out and walked the other direction as planned. Pyre and Lowell both continued peering into the store trying to find us and didn't even glance at Lur. I walked out of the store and headed for the food shops, following in Lur's path. After I caught up to her, we staked out spots where we would be inconspicuous and could watch. I sat at a table and pretended to read a magazine I found laying in a chair. Lur stood near the bathroom, pretending to talk on her cell phone. Eira walked in and gave a thumbs up without looking at either of us. She went to a counter to order some food and a drink and picked out a table in the center of the area to sit and wait. It wasn't long before I caught Pyre peeking around a corner. Lowell tried to be invisible as he walked by and hid behind a sign, watching but trying not to be obvious. Pyre came out of hiding first, walking over to a counter and leaning against it while pretending to peruse the menu. He casually glanced around, trying to locate us. Lowell came out from behind the sign and scrutinized everyone in the food area. I was sure he made me out for a second, but then his eyes moved on to another table. He hunted all around, resembling a parent searching for his lost child. He finally shrugged at Pyre and they both walked over to Eira's table.

Eira looked up from her food and smiled. "Hi guys, I didn't realize you were coming here today. How's it going?"

"How's it going? Where's Kira? That's how it's going." Pyre demanded, obviously extremely agitated.

"Kira? Oh yes, Kira. She and Lur went off together on their own."

"On their own? Why'd you let them do that?"

"I saw no harm in it, big brother."

"No harm? No harm?! What if Lur's a demon? And where is everybody else?"

"The other girls wanted to go do their own thing too, so I'm simply sitting here and enjoying the scenery. What are you guys doing here anyway?"

"I'm here to... Kira wanted me to stay close by, in

139

case she needed me."

"I doubt that meant stalking."

Before Pyre could respond, Lowell said, "I suggested we follow them to keep an eye on her. Them. Kira."

"Hmm. That's so believable. Not at all. Besides Pyre, can't you sense where she is?"

Pyre searched all around and began to panic. "No, she must be blocking me. Or worse, she might be unconscious. Where could they be? What if that girl's done something to my Kira? What if Crystal has? If something has happened to Kira, I'll never forgive you, Eira, for letting them out of your sight. I'll never forgive myself."

"Pyre, before you continue your rant, I should tell you something." Eira looked seriously at him.

"What is it?" He asked, distracted and still searching the area for me.

"I think I should warn you that you are not alone."

"Of course I'm not alone. You're here. Lowell's here. There are hundreds of people here. The only person not here is..."

"Kira, who is behind you and about to kick you in the backside!" I stood there with my hands on my hips.

Pyre jumped and spun around in place. "Kira, hey there. Um, look, Lowell, Kira's here. Hi Kira." He paused and took in my facial expression. It was hard to keep a straight face and pretend to be mad. "Um, baby, you know I love you right? And you love me too. Remember?"

"What are you two goofs doing?"

"Pyre wanted to make certain you were safe, and I

thought we should keep an eye on all of you, in case Lur and the girls are demons."

"Did you enjoy the view while mooning over Lur all day?"

"What? I have no idea what you're talking about, Kira." He tried to sound so innocent and clueless. He failed.

"In that case, who were you ogling all day?" Lur crept up behind him, and stood there giving him the stink eye. Lowell jumped at the sound of Lur's voice and circled around the table, presumably to use it as a protective barrier between Lur and himself.

"Ogling? No, I wasn't ogling. I needed some... something and invited Pyre to accompany me to the local shopping mall. We just happened to run into you, and isn't that a coincidence?"

"Lowell, did you leave your brain on the clearance rack too?" I appraised him as if seeking clues.

"What?"

"Never mind. Here come the other girls. Let's put some tables together and get something to eat."

"When did you figure out we were following you?" Pyre asked me.

"On the way here from the campus. You might be losing your touch." I hugged him and gave him a quick kiss on the cheek so he'd be assured that I wasn't truly mad. "And thanks, for watching out for me."

"We watch out for each other."

"Always."

The other girls joined us and we hung out at the food strip until everyone decided they were getting tired.

Stella, Luna, and Lur headed back to the campus with Lowell watching Lur walk away. Lur stopped a short distance away, pivoted and looked at Lowell, holding his gaze for a few seconds. Then she smiled and turned away again. *Oh yea, love is in the air. I hope Lowell takes a big whiff.* Pyre and I said goodbye to Eira and the others. We stood there for a few minutes before deciding Lowell had drooled long enough.

"Pyre, do you suppose he'll still possess a brain by tomorrow?" I asked taking Pyre's hand in mine.

"With the thoughts wandering around in his skull, I'm not entirely satisfied he ever had one at all."

Lowell punched his arm. "Stay out of my head."

"What fun would that be?" Pyre asked with a mischievous grin as he wrapped an arm around me.

"What was he thinking?" I assumed a conspiratorial demeanor.

"Oh, girl, you can't imagine. I couldn't believe what I was hearing. He was thinking—" Pyre did his best imitation of a gossipy girl.

"Don't tell her!" Lowell hit Pyre on the back of the head.

"But she asked me a question and I simply must answer her." Pyre said, still acting his part.

"No, you don't!" Lowell's face turned bright red. "There are some things she doesn't need to know."

They continued to talk and started to ignore me. I walked over to the wall and leaned against it while they argued. I smiled at the scene as I struggled to stay awake. Pyre finally noticed me yawning and rubbing my eyes.

"I'd better get her home before she falls over."

Pyre walked over to me. "I won't give away your warped musings and reflections."

"Thank you for respecting my privacy, Pyre."

"She'll weasel it out of you later anyway." I held my arms out to Lowell.

"Give me a hug." He leaned down and wrapped his arms around me while I wrapped mine around his neck. "I hope you were considering asking Lur out and don't deny it. I've seen the way you look at her. The two of you would be great together and I want you to be happy."

He tightened his grip around me for a moment and then pulled away. "I'll see you later."

I leaned my head pensively on Pyre's shoulder and watched Lowell disappear. "Do you suppose he'll be all right, Pyre?"

"He's got some issues to work out on his own, but he'll be fine." He rubbed my arms. "I've got to get you home before you catch another cold."

"You could warm me up if there's something else you want to do."

"Or we can go home." Once we got home, I kissed him good night and went straight to bed.

The next day turned colder, so Lowell, Eira and the others all came over to our apartment. We played games and listened to music. Vitas popped in during the afternoon with some news.

"What is it, Vitas? What have you discovered?" Pyre demanded.

"Unfortunately, I don't have much information yet, and the news I do have is distressing, to put it mildly. Perhaps I should tell you and Lowell privately."

143

"No, we're all in this. Just tell us."

"Fair enough. I haven't learned anything yet about Kira's nightmares, Crystal's plan or how to stop it. I've sent demons after her, but they can't find her. But we will find her, Kira. I'll keep working on it. Now here's the news. First, a report popped up about a girl who escaped the psychiatric unit in Nashville. The story caught my attention since the staff at the unit were found dead. They were all frozen."

I closed my eyes and reached out for Pyre's hand. "Is there anything else, Vitas?" I hoped there wasn't more, but I knew I hoped in vain.

"I'm afraid so, Kira. Since you had the second nightmare, and your dreams are coming true, I began watching for news stories. The humans don't know exactly what happened. They reported that a freak dust storm or possibly a tornado tore through the Nashville airport, even though there was no damage to the outer walls or roof of the building. They said there was dirt everywhere, and several people were missing. The reporter noted the random appearance of an unusual tree a few feet inside the airport doors. No one offered an explanation for how it got there, or how it was firmly rooted through the floor and into the ground. Both stories were exactly like your nightmares and happened during your nightmares. Kira, we will locate her, and when we do, she'll be... handled."

I couldn't say anything. What could I say? I nodded and rested my chin on my knees.

"Kira, I need to ask you something. Each time she says the sacrifice was made and there are more to come. What's supposed to happen in the next one?" Vitas crouched in front of me to question me.

"In this last nightmare, she said wind would be next, followed by fire. The rebirth will be in earth, whatever that means."

"Anything about how or where?"

"Unfortunately no, that's all she said."

"Try not to worry and keep me informed. We'll keep working on it." Vitas left as abruptly as he had arrived.

"Pyre, my nightmares are real. They aren't simply coming to life in my bedroom. She's actually doing these things."

"Kira, it's—"

"Pyre, please don't tell me it will be okay. People are dying, and it's because of me. No, it's not my fault. But she's doing all of this because of me. What are we supposed to do?"

"We're doing all we can do for now, but hopefully Vitas will learn something soon. I'm familiar with the demons he would send out after her, and they're relentless." Pyre only wanted to reassure me, but it didn't work.

"We can try to figure out what she'll do next in her plan." Eros suggested.

"If you can think like a lunatic, be my guest." Pyre growled at him.

"Pyre, he's trying to help. I think it's a good idea and better than doing nothing. Let's try it." Eira sat down next to me and scrunched up her face in contemplation. Either that or she had a muscle cramp. "Now, let's see here. She's a witch, right, so she's probably doing a spell of some kind. She wants to transform someone or something."

"No, it's undeniably someone. In the ice nightmare, she said, 'she will be reborn' while looking directly at me. The cab driver in my last nightmare said it should be obvious who will be reborn, so I conclude it's meant for me."

"Cab driver?" Pyre asked.

"Some weirdo demon cab driver who took me to the airport when I first came to Russellville appeared in my dream. He said he doesn't meddle in human affairs, but he wanted to warn me."

"Lowell, do you know a demon cab driver?"

"Pyre, all cab drivers are demons. It might be anybody, but we'll check with Vitas anyway."

"Back to our thinking board." Eira began again. "The third part of her spell will be wind. What do we know about wind. Wind blows. You can run like the wind. What kind of damage could she do with wind?"

"Extensive damage if she can make a tornado." Caedmon suggested, sounding unsure of himself.

"That's an outstanding idea, Caedmon. I've heard of witches who can manipulate the weather, at least to some extent. But this is tornado country. That could be anywhere." Eira stated, still searching for a solution.

"Anywhere with lots of people to kill." I laid my forehead on my knees.

# Chapter 7
# Finding Forgiveness

Monday morning dawned much too quickly. I was grateful for the three day weekend, but it passed too fast. At least I still had one more day off from school. The day was supposed to be warm, so I tried to decide what to do to enjoy it. The phone rang and interrupted my musing. Lur called with the answer to my dilemma.

"I had so much fun shopping with you Friday. Can we do the painting this afternoon around 2:00? I realize it's short notice, but the weather's supposed to be unusually pleasant today." Lur suggested.

"Absolutely. I was trying to come up with ideas for what to do with my day when the phone rang".

"Shall I meet you by the fountain on campus?"

"Great. I'll see you then." I replied.

"Who will you see when?" Pyre asked.

"That was Lur on the phone. She wants to work on the painting this afternoon. I knew you and Lowell had to work today anyway, so I agreed."

"By yourself? She might be a demon, possibly a threat, and you're going out with her alone?"

"Pyre, you met her and you didn't sense a threat. We could be worried for nothing. I'll be careful, and you can keep your crisis prevention hotline open, just in case." He thought it over for a moment and finally surrendered.

"We shouldn't be too long. If we get done early enough, we'll come find you."

I kissed him goodbye as he left for work. After doing a few chores in the apartment, I changed into my dress, grabbed my coat and walked to the campus. Lur was there when I arrived.

"Have you been waiting long?" I asked.

"Nope. I just got here too. Come on, the tree's this way." She led me to the tree, not too far away. She was right, the tree was magnificent. I could easily imagine that with the sun shining through it, the tree would look amazing.

"Lur, I have no clue what I'm supposed to do." I grew more self-conscious now that I was here.

"I realize that, but I'm going to tell you. Come stand right here. Now be as clay, and I will mold you."

"Uh, no, I don't think so."

"It's not peculiar. I merely want you to be pliable so I can pose you the way I want."

"Okay, I guess so. How long will this take?"

"Not very long if everything comes together the way I want it. I took pictures of it before, so I got to work on it earlier."

"So what, thirty minutes?"

"Kira, you're so funny."

*Uh oh.*

Lur placed me in several poses, both sitting and standing. She moved me to this side and that and moved my arms in every which way. She shifted my head until she got precisely the right angle for my face. It felt like she would unscrew my head from my neck. Once she finally had me where she wanted me, she proclaimed, "Don't move!" I was sore and tired already from being pulled,

148

prodded and poked.

When Lur finished with me, she sat down on her stool. She moved to the left and back to the right, forward and then backward. She stood up and sat down again. If she had done the hokey pokey and turned herself around, I wouldn't have been at all surprised. She finally found the spot she liked the best, the spot where she began in the first place. *If I survive this, I'm going to smack her a good one.* I watched her from the corner of my eye as she went to work with her brushes and canvas. She stopped now and then to contemplate me and the tree. She tilted her head to the side periodically and would come over to adjust my pose because my arm, chin or something had dropped a hundredth of an inch. During this extreme torture, I detected noises somewhere behind me.

Lur jumped up and yelled. "Go away! Shoo! Stop that!"

I thought it might be an animal of some kind. I tried desperately not to move my face when I asked, "Lur, what is that?"

"It's Pyre, Lowell and a couple of other guys. The guys I don't know are trying to mess with you, to startle you or make you laugh I presume. But it's not funny!" Her voice grew louder as she spoke and ended with yelling the last part.

"It's only us, Kira, with Caedmon and Eros." Pyre said.

*I was right. It was animals.* "Guys, please go away. Don't make this any worse. I don't want to be frozen in place any longer than necessary."

"Sorry, Kira, we'll make them behave." Lowell

approached Lur in an attempt to view the painting.

"No! You can't see it until it's finished. Shoo! Be gone!"

"Artists! If we sit over here, totally quiet, and we don't bother you or Kira, can we stay and watch?" I heard Pyre's voice, but I couldn't see him. I detected the smirk in his voice though.

"Yes, but be as a tree — stoic, still and silent." She enunciated and emphasized each word.

"Lur, you get weird when you paint. And that's saying something, considering you're by nature a bit odd." I made the mistake of talking, so she marched over to adjust my chin again. Since she was exasperated, she wasn't gentle.

"Ow." I grunted, without moving any muscles at all.

"I'm nearly finished, so be still and quiet. Everyone." She eyed all of us menacingly. Caedmon and Eros mocked cringing in fear, but only after she walked past them and had her back to them.

I stood there for what felt like another eternity. I grew hungry and tired and urgently needed to go to the bathroom.

"Kira, I want you to meditate on something that touches your heart. Perhaps something that makes you both sad and happy when you recall it, or something you remember fondly. Visualize it and feel it, allowing it to show in your eyes, mouth, face, hands and so forth; but don't say anything or move whatever you do. You get the idea?"

"I'll try." I tried to speak like a ventriloquist,

without moving my lips.

*Meditate on something that I remember fondly that's both happy and sad.* I thought of my mother and my little brother. I remembered playing with him at the park, chasing him and playing hide and seek or tag. We had such fun. I reminisced about baking cookies with my mother. *How I wish they were still here. There's so many things I'd like to talk over with my mom. Juniper is happy to listen, but it's not the same. I wish they could see me here at college, and that they could meet Pyre. He would like them, and I think they would like him. I miss them immensely, all the time. I'm extraordinarily lucky I found Pyre. Being with him helps ease the pain of missing them. I love him so completely, I feel it in every part of me. He's in the air that I breathe. I kiss him, and my soul melts into his. I never want to lose this feeling. Whatever the future may hold, it's wide open in front of us. We can handle anything that happens as long as we're together.* I imagined the future with Pyre. I envisioned the usual things, what we would do, where we would go. Would we have children, and grandchildren? I pictured us old and gray, and I sucked in my breath. I wondered how old a fire demon would have to be to grow old and gray.

Finally, Lur said, "Finito!"

"Lur, tu parli italiano?" Lowell queried. Lur looked at him like he just asked her an outlandish question.

"What?"

"I said, do you speak Italian?"

"No, I don't. I only learned the one word. I can say 'finished' in several languages. When I finish a painting, I say it in whichever language strikes my mood at the time. I perceived this setting as Celtic, but I don't know how to say it in Celtic. So I went with Italian." Her voice sounded happier by the minute. "Do you speak Italian?"

"A fair amount."

I developed a muscle cramp. "Can I move now? 'Being as clay' has made me rigid."

"Huh? Yes, you can move now. Come on over here and look at the painting. I'm dying to get your opinion."

"Can someone help me move, please? My limbs are numb."

Pyre walked over to me and helped me to stand, stretch my muscles and get moving again. Sitting in one position for so long can certainly make you stiff. I reached my hand up to touch his cheek, and he kissed my palm. We stared into each other's eyes for a moment.

"Come. You should see this."

I went over to the easel. The moment I observed the painting, the stiffness instantly fell away, and it was all worth it.

"Well? Come on, Kira, say something. What do you think?"

"I can't... I mean... Wow! Is that truly me?"

"Of course that's you, silly! Do you like it?"

"It's magnificent, Lur. You are exceptionally talented." I sat down on her stool and gazed at the painting. I took it all in, every nuance, every stroke and blending of color. She perfectly captured every detail of the tree and the surroundings. The sun wasn't shining through the trees, but the picture leaned on the easel next to the canvas for me to compare. The painting was so extraordinarily vivid, I could virtually feel the warmth of the sun shining through the painted tree. I viewed myself in the painting. Did I honestly look like that? I was speechless, and my eyes filled with tears. All my emotions and thoughts were portrayed there in my eyes, on my lips, and in the fluid softness of my hands and fingers.

I stood up abruptly and hugged Lur. "Thank you. Thank you so much for letting me pose for you. I'm sorry if I was irritable or uncooperative. You possess such a wonderful gift." Lur hugged me back and wiped her own eyes.

Eros and Caedmon got bored and left. The rest of us were ready to leave a few minutes later. Lowell watched as Lur walked away, standing there for such a long time that Pyre and I realized he had forgotten we were there.

"So?" I asked, bringing him back to earth. "Parli italiano?"

"Sì, parlo italiano. Parli italiano?"

"No, I just wanted to give it a try."

"Pyre, la tua ragazza è male."

"Lo so."

"Farai parlare con lei."

"Lo farò."

I stared at Pyre. "You speak Italian?"

"Sì mia signorina." He put one hand over his heart and gestured with the other. He leered and wiggled his eyebrows, clearly quite full of himself.

"What did each of you say?"

"Lowell said you were horrible." Pyre instantly ratted out Lowell and nodded for emphasis.

"And Pyre agreed." Lowell said in self-defense.

"Well, Lowell said I should have a talk with you."

"And Pyre agreed again." They started to scuffle.

"I hate you both." I walked away.

"Ma il mio amore." Pyre stepped in front of me. I stared questioningly, and he translated, "But my love."

"Do you speak any other languages?"

"No, but Lowell can speak a few others."

I turned to Lowell. "Ask Lur out in English."

"Yes, ma'am." Lowell blushed.

"Do you speak any other languages, Kira?" Pyre asked.

"I took two years of Spanish in high school, but I don't speak it."

"Huh?" Both Lowell and Pyre said at once, confused.

"I unfortunately haven't had anyone to speak Spanish with since high school, so I've forgotten most of it."

While Pyre and I walked home, he tried speaking to me in Italian. Admittedly, it was both beautiful and romantic. After a while, though, I simply wanted to understand what he said and only shook my head at him. He decided to try what little Spanish he knew. From bad to worse in two seconds flat! He stopped when he caught me glaring.

When classes were done the next day, I put my backpack on my shoulders and left the classroom with Lowell. He offered to walk home with me, so we headed out of the building together. We met Lur and the girls on the way to the door and chatted a moment until they needed to leave. When we got outside, Lowell stopped abruptly and stared at the ground.

"Lowell, is something wrong?"

"Can we talk now?" He sounded like his heart was breaking.

"Of course. What about?"

He hung his head and didn't respond at first. I frowned thoughtfully and reached for his hand. "Can we talk at your apartment? I don't want to do it here."

"No problem. Do you want to travel by demon express?" That didn't get even the slightest twitch of a grin. He pulled me over to an alley and transformed into Ulric. "Has something happened?" I asked as he picked me up into his arms.

"No, I just need to talk to you." He rushed to the apartment. When we got there, he took the keys and opened the door. Pyre stood inside with his arms crossed.

"What's going on here?" Pyre demanded. I shrugged my shoulders.

"I want to talk to Kira." Ulric's voice sounded sorrowful and he hugged me closer. Pyre relaxed somewhat but looked worried about Ulric.

"I'll be out here if you need anything." Ulric carried me to my room and set me on my bed. I would've requested that he put me down sooner, but I had the impression he needed to hold on to something.

"Ulric, what's the matter?" He paced the floor in front of me.

"I don't know."

"Yes, you do. What's wrong?"

"Do you... Do you honestly believe it would be a good idea if I asked Lur to go on a date?" He blushed

155

somewhat, but he looked so despondent too.

"I wouldn't have suggested it otherwise."

"Are you positive?" His body language told me he thought he was being watched.

"What's really bothering you?" He looked away from me. "Does this involve Cadel?" He nodded. "Come sit down and talk to me." He sat down next to me and I held onto his hand.

"I'm not certain I should be allowed to fall in love again."

"Why do you think that?"

"Cadel might be mad if she learned I found someone else." He laid down and stared at the ceiling.

"She would be happy for you and pleased that you moved on with your life."

"Not with what happened to her. It's my fault she was killed." He closed his eyes. Pyre walked into the room.

"What happened that day?" Pyre asked.

"An assassin killed her."

"We're aware of that, but why would she blame you? More to the point, why do you blame yourself?" Pyre walked over to us. Ulric sat up and looked at us with misery in his eyes.

"You need to talk to someone. You've kept this buried inside too long, and we're here to listen." I clasped Ulric's hand again. Pyre took a seat behind me.

"I should start at the beginning. I was running through some fields near Rowe, Massachusetts when I spied a girl around Kira's age being attacked by some demons. At that age I usually didn't care what happened to humans when demons attacked them. I stood there and watched but there was something about the girl. I was drawn to her for some reason and I felt compelled to figure out why. I fought off the demons and took her to the nearest town. I ran off before she had the chance to say anything, but I watched her from a distance. The girl would occasionally go back to those same fields and put a small sack by a tree in the nearby forest. I'd peek into the sack and find food and a drawing. She went to the fields more often, and I began to show myself to her. She tried for months to get me to talk to her. It wasn't until she was attacked again that I finally spoke to her. I said, 'You must be a demon magnet,' and— "

"You told her that?" Pyre interrupted.

"Be quiet!" I admonished, hitting his arm. "Keep going, Ulric."

"She laughed about it. We talked whenever she went to the fields, about anything and everything. She told me she belonged to a coven, what today is known as Wiccan, and she wanted to see the world but her grandmother wouldn't let her. I joked that she should run away with me but as we became better acquainted with each other, I grew to mean it. I fell deeply in love with her. One day I waited for her in the fields but an old woman came instead, and questioned me about my feelings for Cadel. I told her the truth. After I answered all her questions, she left without uttering another word. I hadn't seen Cadel for a few days and I grew worried about her. I finally decided to go to her house. I thought I should take the back way, and stay out of sight. I discovered her sitting in her room crying, so I tapped on the window. She hurriedly opened the window and wrapped her arms around my neck. I asked her where she'd been. I told her I was anxious she had gotten hurt or met someone she liked better. She told me her grandmother made her stay in her room to wait to see what I would do.

"We sat in her room for hours simply talking. Her grandmother brought us some food and gave us her blessing, as well as that of the entire coven. I was allowed to walk around town without a care in the world. They all welcomed me into their lives and homes, and taught me things, including how to change into human form. They told me to hold an image in my head of what I wanted to look like and imagine myself that way. I eventually asked Cadel to marry me, and she agreed. The coven helped us with the planning and preparations. The night before our wedding we snuck out to the fields to be alone. Only we weren't alone." He took a deep, shaky breath. "I didn't detect the assassin until it was too late. When I heard the arrow coming, I spun around in the direction it came from, to face my attacker. I left Cadel wide open to the arrow. I killed the assassin and took Cadel home. She was gone before we got there. I didn't talk to anyone and hardly ate anything. I left after her funeral. I didn't want anyone else in the coven to get hurt. I also couldn't stay there without her, walking where we had walked, every part of me flooded with memories, engulfed with the guilt and pain. I transformed into Lowell Hew and I've never looked back, but I've never forgotten Cadel. Wherever I wandered, Cadel remained with me, carried forever in my heart. I love her as much now as I ever did."

As Ulric recounted the memory to us, he gripped

my hand tighter and closer to his chest. Pyre wrapped his arms around my waist and put his chin on my shoulder. I wiped my face and caressed Pyre's arm with my other hand.

"I'm sincerely sorry, Ulric." I said.

"Now you understand why Pyre is so protective of you. Humans don't tend to survive long around demons. Even the ones they love." Ulric stood up and stared into a distant time and place from his past. I glanced over at my window and spied a mysterious flower growing.

"Ulric, what kind of flower is that?" I pointed at the window.

"That flower wasn't there earlier." Pyre said.

"It's a white tulip. It symbolizes forgiveness." Tears formed in Ulric's eyes as he touched his fingertips to the glass in line with the flower and leaned his forehead against the window.

"Ulric, do you want to be alone for a minute?" Pyre asked. Ulric nodded and Pyre and I walked out of the room. Once the door was closed, Pyre said, "He'd better ask the girl out."

"I agree with you; but still, be nice about it."

"Come here." Pyre wrapped his arms around me. "I love you, Kira."

"I love you too." He kissed me tenderly, embracing me in his arms, obviously contemplating Ulric's story about Cadel's death.

"Where do you think you're going, Wolf?" I looked over my shoulder to see Lowell trying to sneak through the door.

"I was going to..." Lowell pointed at the door.

"We have work to do and you're not leaving it all to me." Pyre walked over to him. "Vitas assigned the job to both of us and I am not doing it by myself."

"Pyre!" He realized I was annoyed but didn't appear to comprehend the reason. "He was probably about to go do what we just got through saying he'd better do, and then you go and do what I told you not to do."

Lowell looked from me to Pyre and back again, obviously confused. Pyre opened his mouth and closed it. He tried again and frowned thoughtfully. "When I figure out what all that meant, I'll form a clever reply."

"It's okay, Kira," Lowell chuckled at us. "Working will be good for me." He walked over to me. "Thank you for listening."

"Anything for my favorite wolf." I winked at him, and he gave me a quick hug before leaving.

# Chapter 8
# First Job

Pyre and I went to E$^5$ for my job interview Wednesday afternoon. Pyre stared at the building like it was a piece of spoiled meat infested with maggots but still encouraged and supported me.

"Good Luck!" Pyre squeezed my hand before I walked into the building.

"Thanks."

"Hello, is it just one today?" The hostess greeted.

"I'm here for an interview."

"Okay, hold on one sec."

I waited in the lobby and browsed in the restaurant's store. They had all kinds of goods for sale, like stuffed animals, shirts, aprons, wooden signs with funny little sayings and pictures, and other little knick knacks.

"Hello, are you Kira?" A man walked around the counter from somewhere in the back.

"Yes, sir."

"Hi, Kira, my name is Dustin. I'm one of the managers here. Come in here and take a seat." I followed him into the smaller dining room. "Do you have any work experience, Kira?"

"No, sir, I don't. This would be my first job."

"Where do you go to school?"

"Arkansas Tech University."

"How old are you?" He sounded shocked.

"Seventeen."

"Wow, seventeen and going to ATU. You must be a smart kid."

"I was eager to get through school."

"Do you have a way to get here when you're scheduled?"

"Yes, sir."

"What position are you seeking?"

"Waitress."

"Are you good with people?"

"Yes, sir."

"When can you start?"

"Anytime."

"How about Saturday at five?"

"That works for me."

"When you come in, you'll need to wear non-slick shoes and jeans. You'll get two free shirts. After that, it's seven dollars a shirt. We'll see you Saturday, Kira."

"Thanks." I shook his hand before leaving. Pyre stood and watched me walk toward him.

"How'd it go?"

"I got the job. I start Saturday at five."

"I'm proud of you." He wrapped an arm around my shoulders. As we walked away, he kept glancing back at the building.

"I'm kind of nervous. I've never waitressed, or even had a job."

"You'll do fine. If you want I can stay and eat at the restaurant Saturday."

"Or you can hang out with Lowell."

"Can I at least stay close by?"

"Like I could stop you." I wrapped my arms around

his waist.

We went home and spent the remainder of the evening alone together.

Pyre walked me to school the next morning. Speech went by fast but I thought geology would never end.

I spotted him as Lowell and I walked out of the building.

"Hello, Kira." My dad said.

"What're you doing here?" I demanded. I was not in the mood for him to appear spontaneously, and I felt more prepared than last time.

"I hoped we might talk." He eyed Lowell. "In private."

"I have a lot of homework."

"Let's sit down over here and talk for a few minutes." He pointed at a bench.

*There are several people here.* "Fine." I looked at Lowell and mouthed, "Stay close."

"I'll be over there." Lowell said, walking over to a nearby tree.

My dad and I sat down on the bench and I put my bag next to my leg.

"How have you been?"

"Splendid, you?"

"I've been doing well, working hard. I've bought a house in the vicinity." I merely stared at the ground, anticipating where this conversation thread would lead. "When school is done, you can stay with me for summer break."

"I have a place."

"Right. Yes, well, good for you. It's fun to have a place of your own. Do you work somewhere?"

"I applied at $E^5$."

"That's great. You'll have to tell me your schedule so I can come see you."

"I'll just have to do that." I responded frostily. The awkward conversation began to bother me.

"Tell me about your boyfriend."

"What about him?"

"Is he good to you?"

"Yes."

"Has he tried anything?"

"No."

"Where does he work?"

"He works for a guy."

"What guy?"

"What does it matter?"

"I want to make sure he's taking care of my little girl."

"Next question."

"Where does he live?"

"In town."

"Where in town?"

"Next question."

"Are you going to answer any of my questions?"

"Why should I?"

"Because I'm your father and I want to assure myself you're being safe." I grabbed my bag and stood to face him.

"You lost that right when you walked out on me." I whirled around and stomped away.

"Kira, come back here." He caught up and stepped in front of me. "Don't you dare walk away from me."

"Why not? It's what you did to me." Pyre walked up to Lowell and assessed the situation.

*Do you want us to come over there?*

*No, I've got this one. I'll be over there in a sec.*

"Kira, I had my reasons for leaving." My dad stated.

"Messed up reasons. What kind of father leaves his daughter after she loses her mother and brother?" He stared at me, momentarily at a loss for words. I walked past him and went to Pyre and Lowell.

"How are you?" Pyre took my hand in his.

"I've been better."

"Let's get you home."

"Don't look now." Lowell said.

"Kira!" I turned to see my dad approaching us. "Kira, I left to protect you."

"You left to protect me, but now it's safe to come back? What exactly was such a danger that you were forced to leave in order to protect me?"

"There are things you are not ready to know."

"You can make inquiries and demand answers, but I can't? You get to show up a year later and immediately need to be apprised of everything about my life, but there are things I can't know? I don't think so." I turned to Pyre and asked, "Can we go now?"

"You're the one who's changed my daughter." My dad tried to step between us. "My little girl never would have talked to me in this manner. You're the reason my daughter hates me."

165

"You leave him out of this. All of this is on you. You have no right to tell him any of this is his doing. It's not his fault and you know it. You can't or won't admit it. You'd rather blame anyone else than be honest with yourself. Or with me. Just... Just leave me alone." I snatched Pyre's hand and stomped away. I pulled him into an alley and wrapped my arms around him. Lowell walked up behind Pyre. "I don't want him to know where we live." I smoldered with anger, but I was also hurt, and on the verge of tears. Pyre nodded and picked me up in his arms. We reached the apartment seconds later. I paced in my bedroom while Pyre and Lowell stood and waited for me to pull myself together. Finally I said, "I'm sorry."

"Don't apologize for him." Pyre said.

"He needed to hear it." Lowell said.

"I'm not apologizing for him, but for how I behave around him. I don't want to lose my temper with anyone, especially not in front of you. But I was so furious when he tried to blame you for no reason. No one does that, not while I'm around."

Lowell beamed and patted Pyre on the back. "That's one feisty girlfriend you've got there, Pyre."

"I'm proud of you for standing up to him, but you didn't need to on my account."

"You'd do it for me."

"Yes, I would. That's what we do." He smiled and embraced me. "When he finally realizes his mistake, he'll come back and apologize. If he genuinely cares about you, he'll try again and he'll make it right." He rubbed my back and shoulders before leaving me alone to do my homework.

*Pyre's right.* I gazed out the window. *My dad is*

*the one who messed up everything. Not me. I shouldn't be apologizing. He has no right to disappear and then show up after all this time presuming he can jump right in as if he never left. No explanations. Blaming everyone else. Tomorrow is bound to be a better day.* I sat down at my desk and started my homework.

Each of my Friday classes got out so early, I wondered why I even bothered going. Pyre and Lowell needed to apprehend a demon, so I had the place to myself. *All this alone time, and I'm spending it studying. I'm being responsible, and not at all boring or pathetic. Yea, right. Keep telling yourself that. If you say it enough times... nope, you still won't believe it.* Someone rapped on the door and saved me from my conversation with myself. I looked through the peephole and opened the door.

"Hi, Cel. Hi, Pyrrhos."

"Hello, Kira, how are you?" Cel gave me a big hug.

"I'm fine, thanks." *Except I can't breathe at all. Wow, she's strong!*

"Is Pyre home?" Pyrrhos asked.

"No, he had a job to do for Vitas today."

"He left you home alone?" Cel sounded concerned. "Why would he leave you alone?"

"He doesn't go far and I have studying to do."

"I don't care. He told me about the girl who used to be your friend. He shouldn't leave you by yourself."

"Now, honey, Kira, isn't a child, and she's a strong young lady. She can take care of herself." Pyrrhos said.

"Against a demon? Kira is merely a human. She can't fight against a demon."

"Pyre isn't far away. I can hear his thoughts."

"She still shouldn't be all alone." She sat down on the couch. "Come here, Kira. We're here now, and we'll stay with you until Pyre gets home." She patted the cushion.

"You might as well get over there." Pyrrhos said as he went to the kitchen.

"Okay." I sat down next to her. "You mentioned that Pyre told you about Crystal. Did you know anything that would help us?"

"Unfortunately we don't. We know a moderate amount of information about witches but this is more involved than anything we've ever seen. We're checking into it though. Don't you fret, dear. We won't let anything happen to you."

"Thanks, Cel."

"Now, tell me how you met my son."

I told Cel and Pyrrhos all about our first meeting and how we came to fall in love with each other. I discovered Cel was a hopeless romantic. Pyrrhos nodded off a couple of times. I asked Cel about what Pyre was like as a child.

"He used to love to build remarkable creations out of odds and ends he'd find around the house. He would take anything — my compact, Pyrrhos's pocket watch, Eira's hair clips. He'd build such incredible contraptions, so interconnected and complex there wouldn't be any way of removing our possessions without destroying the whole structure."

"That's so sweet. What kinds of things did he build?"

"We had no clue what most of his creations were

supposed to be, but in one phase he became obsessed with perpetual motion sculptures. A ball rolls through the whole thing and never stops."

"That sounds like Pyre. He thinks he has to keep going all the time, can't slow down."

"That's very true! He grew out of the building phase as he got older. Oh, I just thought of another story. This one time when he was a little boy, he got jealous of Eira's snowy spirit, which I doubt he even understood what it meant. He wanted to prove he could be snowy or icy too. In the middle of winter, the coldest day of the year, he went outside and filled a tub with water and jumped in while not wearing any clothes. He jumped up and down out there for who knows how long before we caught him. When we found him, he had turned blue from the cold water. See, he didn't realize his fire would go out due to the water. He thought his fire combined with the water would make steam, and when the steam rose it would freeze, making snow that would fall to the ground. We ran outside and he was yelling, 'I'm snowy too' and waving his arms. It took several days and all of us to get his fire going again."

I laughed so hard my sides hurt. "It sounds like he certainly kept you on your toes as a kid."

"Indeed he did. Both Pyre and Eira did as a matter of fact. And if those two put their heads together! What a headache!"

"Cel, you and Pyrrhos mentioned that Pyre changed considerably since meeting me."

"Yes, you've been exceptionally good for him."

"Can you tell me how he's changed?"

"Pyre was such a jovial boy. He was lighthearted

and liked most people until he met a girl who broke his heart. She was only using him and he refused to see it. She was human with demon ancestors, therefore she possessed some special gifts of her own. Pyre grew to despise humans and withdrew from his family and friends. He still dated some after that but he didn't let most of those girls fully into his heart. Eventually he met Aella, who was the last girl he dated before you. She was a demon too. Pyrrhos and I didn't like her from the onset. We could see what she was, but Pyre couldn't and developed feelings for her. She was all trouble and got him involved with an unsuitable kind of crowd. She hated humans and talked him into doing certain things, basic pranks at first, but it became more serious. She consistently managed to convince him it was his own idea, and to get off squeaky clean while he took the heat for their actions. He finally discovered she was cheating on him. We suspected she had been all along. Eira caught Aella making out with another demon. Eira confronted Aella and intended to tell Pyre about it. Pyre overheard Aella threatening Eira from the next room and finally learned about her betrayal and the truth about her character. He tries to act tough and like he doesn't care, but the truth is he cares so deeply it can be hard for him to admit. But that can also make him dangerous. Pyre went into the room and pulled Eira behind him. He wanted to kill Aella for what she did, and would have, but she disappeared. He was enraged and went on a rampage. He... did some awful things, which is how he ended up here. Fortunately, he met you and fell for you. You've helped him change back into the boy he used to be. He's my little boy again, and I'm grateful to you for that."

She reached over and squeezed my hand, but then her mood grew serious. "But I'm apprehensive too. It's hard for demons to date humans. What if something happens to you, or if something goes amiss between you and Pyre? I'm worried about what it would do to him. He has never cared for anyone the way he cares for you. He'd be devastated and would permanently lose himself, so it is imperative for you to be extremely careful. Please?"

"I will, Cel, I promise, and I will do my best to never let anything or anyone hurt him again."

"I believe you will. You both have us and our complete support, and I'm available if you ever need to talk about anything at all."

"Thank you, Cel. That means so much to me." Cel hugged me tight again. "Please tell me more about Pyre when he was younger."

"I just remembered a funny one. One time when Pyre was little, he did something. I don't even remember what, but he realized he would be in trouble. He decided he needed an escape route for when he got caught. He got a marker and drew a picture of the house layout and the yard on the wall. Then he made fire with his fingertip and burned his escape route into the picture and into the wood. When I caught him, he blamed it on Eira. Eira was barely crawling at the time and hadn't gotten her fire yet. That map is still etched into the wall to this day, by the way."

"That's kind of ingenious, coming up with an escape route."

"Except for the part where he left a trail for me to find him if he had escaped." Cel laughed. "Speaking of escaping. There was this one time after Eira was slightly older and was walking, I needed to run some errands. We went into this one store and I was browsing through things we needed for the house. The kids had been giving me fits all day long, and I was at the end of my patience. I gave them a harsh talking to and told them to straighten up and be quiet, or else. They got still and quiet, so I thought I'd finally gotten my point across to them. I returned my attention to my shopping, and I heard Pyre say, 'You go this way, I go that way.' I turned around narrowly in time to see them take off through the door in opposite directions. I caught Eira first, but I had a terrible time finding and catching up to Pyre. Demon children are uncommonly fast! Once I caught him, I took them both home and dumped them in Pyrrhos's lap. I said, 'Tag, you're it.' And I left to go finish my errands. After I was done, I wasn't ready to go home yet, so I went to a restaurant to eat and read a good book. The kids were asleep by the time I got home."

We both laughed so hard that tears ran down our cheeks. Cel shared more stories about Pyre and Eira, so we were still laughing when Pyre got home.

"Mom, Dad? What're you doing here?"

"We were enjoying a pleasant chat with Kira." Cel said.

"I can see that. What all did you tell her?"

"That's not the question, son. You should ask what she didn't tell her." Pyrrhos smiled conspiratorially.

"Mom!" Pyre whined, burying his face in a couch cushion.

"Honey, that's our cue to get going." Pyrrhos put a hand on Cel's shoulder.

"But, Firefly, I haven't told Kira about the time

Pyre was learning how to—"

"Mother!" Pyre's face turned as red as a tomato.

"Shush, Pyre." I got up and wrapped my arms around his waist.

"You've embarrassed him enough for one day." Pyrrhos took Cel's hand and pulled her toward the door. "We'll see you later, kids."

"I love you, baby boy." Cel kissed Pyre's cheek.

"Aw, Mom. Yeesh! Must you call me your baby boy?" Pyre wiped his face.

"I'll see you later, Kira." Cel ignored Pyre and rubbed my arm before leaving with Pyrrhos.

Pyre buried his face in my shoulder.

"There, there." I patted his back. "That's how all parents behave." When he began to relax, I said, "And they always bring pictures."

He groaned and hid his face as deep as possible in my neck. "I want to go fight more demons. Anything but this torture."

"Come on, it's not that bad. You saw my childhood pictures. Come sit with me and tell me more about some of these."

We started going through Pyre's pictures. Some were quite old, and some were more recent. Some were color, and some were black and white. Some were printed on paper, others on thick cards and some were metal. They were old, but he was young in all of them. I grew disconcerted, but I put it aside and listened as Pyre told me about each one. He remembered each moment clearly, some with embarrassment, humor, sadness and even a few tears. I recognized him of course. His parents and Eira were in some as well. He came across a painted portrait miniature encased in an incredibly old frame and simply stared at it.

"Pyre? What is it?"

"I don't recognize this man, but he seems familiar. He looks exactly like me, but I know it's not me. Do you see the resemblance too?"

"Pyre, honey, that's your grandfather."

"My grandfather... who gave you the sword?"

"Yes, and you've never met him at all?"

"No."

"You should. We'll go soon."

"Maybe when the semester ends. He looks exactly like me, doesn't he?" He was distracted and consumed with his thoughts, and didn't realize he was repeating himself.

"Yes, he looks very much like you. But there's something missing."

"There is? What?"

"The way you look at me."

He looked over at me, overwhelmed by his emotions. He pulled me into his lap and held me close, like he feared that if he let me go, I'd be gone. We sat there for a long time, each of us lost in our own thoughts. We stroked each other's arms and backs. He played with my hair and I rubbed his chest. We both realized we were contemplating the same things, even without telepathy, but we didn't speak. His grandfather did resemble him so much that I knew what Pyre would look like as an old man; an old demon man living in a cave waiting to give a sword to his grandson. Alone. Because he would live many more years than I would, possibly even hundreds. He had lived over a hundred years, and had aged slowly, judging by the age of the pictures and his age in them. But I wouldn't. Even if I lived to be quite old, in all likelihood I'd be gone before he even started to age.

What were we going to do? It wasn't like in vampire movies. He couldn't bite me and turn me into a demon. *Wait a minute. Could he? No, of course not. That's just in the movies. This is real life.* We would need to talk about it sometime, but for now, I decided to take things one day at a time, to enjoy this moment and being together. Tomorrow was a brand new day. The sun would come up and I would start a new job, my first job. In the still of the night, shadowy thoughts creep in, distorting your view, but in the light of a brand new day, there is hope and promise.

Resolving to appreciate the present, though still fearing what lay ahead, and loathing myself for having any doubts, I nodded off in Pyre's arms. Which was exactly where I wanted to be.

"Have a wonderful day. Be safe." Pyre dropped me off at work the next day.

"I will." I walked into the building and found Dustin standing up front.

"Right on time, Kira. Are you ready for your first day?"

"Yes, sir, I am."

"Good. Pick out a shirt and we'll find someone to train you." I picked out a turquoise colored shirt and went to the restroom to change. Once I finished, I went back up front to report to Dustin.

"Kira, this is Franq. He's going to train you today."

"It's a pleasure to meet you, Kira. I'll begin by showing you around the restaurant." Franq motioned for me to follow him. He showed me the server hall, expo, walk in cooler, and dry stock.

"Franq, you've got a table." The hostess came to tell us.

"Thanks. Come on, Kira, it's time to teach you how to waitress." We went to the server hall. "First you need to ascertain how many people are at the table. We utilize an advanced method for this — peek around the wall and count how many people are there." He pointed at a booth close to the hostess stand, where two people waited.

"How do you know which tables are yours?"

"Good question. We're set up in sections. I'll show you that after we get their food order." He walked over to the bread warmer. He put two biscuits in a basket, grabbed two plates, and a small cup of apple butter. "Now this cup can be called a ramekin or soufflé cup. It's a small two ounce cup that can generally take care of two people. "We walked out to the table. "Hello, how are y'all today?"

"We're good, and you?" The man at the table responded.

"We're doing well, thanks. My name is Franq, and this is Kira, my trainee. We'll be taking care of you this evening. What can we get you to drink?"

"I want a diet cola." The man motioned to his wife.

"I'll take a sweet tea." She said.

"We'll be right back with your drinks." Franq and I went back to the server hall. "Now about the tea. We serve sweet and unsweet. We arrange the tea urns so we

176

don't get them confused. The one currently on the maker is sweet and so is the one closest to the bread warmer. The one in the middle is unsweet." I watched him make the drinks and followed him back to the table. "Are y'all ready to order?"

"Yes, I'll have the country fried steak, with mashed potatoes and collards."

I noticed Franq wasn't writing down the man's order.

"Would you like gravy on your mashed potatoes?"

"Yes, please."

"Not a problem. For you ma'am?"

"I'll try your famous meat loaf with mashed potatoes and green beans. I would also like the gravy on the potatoes."

"Excellent, we'll bring that right out for you." Franq took the menus and walked to the computer. "This will be the hardest task for you to learn. The computer has a variety of menu bars and a ton of buttons under each one. The man wants country fried steak." He went under the lunch menu and selected the country fried steak button. I watched as he entered the man's drink and side orders and did the same with the woman's order. "Now while we wait for the food to be made, let me show you the sections."

We walked over to the hostess stand and perused the floor chart. I learned that all the tables were assigned numbers and each server had a designated section of tables. He showed me which ones were his and their corresponding numbers. As we finished going over the floor chart, the cook called his name, so we went to the expo to get the food.

"Now most of the plates come with cornbread. The only ones that don't are sandwiches and salads." As we walked back to the dining room, I slipped on some water and fell. "Are you hurt?"

"I'm okay." I stood and rubbed my backside. "I just hurt my pride."

"Are you wearing non-slick shoes?"

"Yes, or at least that's what the box said."

"You'll still slip now and then. Come on."

As the day continued, I slipped, tripped, and fell in practically every corner of the restaurant. I dropped cups in the server hall and the first time I tried to carry a tray, I slipped and it fell. Dustin asked if I was hurt and told me to take a seat in the other dining room.

At the end of the night Dustin let me go home instead of cleaning. I offered to help, but he said it was handled and to come back the next day.

As I was about to go outside to meet Pyre, Dustin called my name. "Kira, a moment please?"

"Yes, Dustin?"

"Not the worst first day on the job I've ever seen. Franq's first day? Way worse! You kept your cool, and didn't lose your head, so don't give it a second thought. Tomorrow's another day."

"Thank you, sir. I'll see you tomorrow." That was kind of him. I almost felt better. Almost. Then I saw Pyre waiting for me, holding a vanilla coffee and a bag of doughnuts.

"Yum! You know what I like!"

"How was your first day of work?"

"It was a disaster."

"What happened?"

"I don't think I'm cut out to be a waitress."

"What do you mean?"

"I dropped several trays of food and slipped and fell. It was extremely embarrassing, but at least I didn't get fired. Yet."

He gave me a hug and the coffee. We went straight home and talked about what happened at work.

Sunday was a better day. I managed to walk in the back without slipping and I only dropped one cup.

"Tonight was a better night for you." Franq said as he walked up to me with Dustin.

"I understand you didn't drop much today." Dustin said.

"Thankfully. I guess I simply need to get used to it."

"That's good, and you will. Plenty servers are scheduled for this week, so I won't need you again until Friday. Is that satisfactory?"

"That'll work."

"And you'll be on the floor without a trainer as well."

"With only one table right?" I was uneasy about being on my own so soon.

"Do you hear her? Isn't she great?" Dustin laughed hysterically as he walked away.

"I was serious." I appealed to Franq.

"Keep your chin up and you'll do fine." Franq walked away.

"Easy for you to say."

After all the cleaning was done, I went outside to

meet Pyre.

"How was work today?"

"Much better. I might get the hang of this."

"Of course you will. You can do anything you put your mind to. But if you want to quit working here, I wouldn't mind."

"Pyre!"

"I know, I know. I worry too much." I nodded vehemently in agreement, he laughed, and we headed for home.

# Chapter 9
# Demon and Wiccan
# Get-Together

My body felt sore all over from my first couple of days at work, but that wouldn't get me out of classes. When I reached the biology classroom, I spied Lowell leaning against the wall trying hard to stay awake.

"Lowell, are you okay?" I asked as I walked up to him.

"I didn't get much sleep last night." He rubbed his face and yawned.

"There's a lot of that going around lately. You should go back to your dorm and take a nap."

"Nah, I'll be fine." Lur walked up as Lowell entered the classroom.

"Is Lowell all right?" She asked.

"He claims he is."

"What's your diagnosis?" We watched as Lowell tried to sit in his chair but almost fell backwards instead.

"Not a chance." I walked over to him and pushed his chair closer to him. "Lowell, you're not okay."

"No, really, I'm okay."

"If you doze off during class, can I punch ya?"

"Yea, of course." He laid his head against his hand. Lur sat down at the desk and watched the scene unfold.

"Can I push a q-tip up your nose?"

"Whatever." He obviously paid no attention to

what I said.

"Can I cut your hair?" I picked up the scissors and snipped them a couple of times. He only nodded.

"Can I paint your face?" Lur giggled and bit her lip as she joined the game.

"That's fine." He mumbled with a yawn.

"He's no fun." I pouted and pointed at him.

The professor walked in and explained the lesson for the day. After a few minutes, I noticed Lowell snoozing away with his head on the desk. During the professor's discussion of chromosomes and cell division, I heard Lowell make a peculiar noise. I leaned over and poked him. His lip twitched, and he started growling.

"Kira?" The professor called. "What's wrong with Lowell?"

"That's an excellent question. Let's ask him." I punched him and he jumped awake and glared at me.

"What?" He asked while rubbing his arm. He became aware of everyone staring at him.

I leaned over to him and whispered quietly. "You were just a cute little puppy dog for the whole class." He looked at me silently for confirmation, and I nodded.

"Sorry. I... watched 'Homeward Bound' last night." His face turned several shades of red.

"No more late nights watching movies about dogs." The professor reprimanded him, trying not to chuckle.

"Yes, ma'am." He hung his head. When the professor resumed the lesson, he leaned over to me and whispered, "Not a word to Pyre."

"Never. But the pictures are going on the refrigerator." I made an air camera with my hands and

182

pretended to take pictures. He picked up his book and hid behind it.

The next day, geology was canceled, so I was eager to get home when speech class ended.

"Hey, Kira, are we still having a study date tonight?" Stella asked as we walked out of the room.

"Absolutely."

"Awesome!"

"I thought I would bring the painting and my paints with me. Do you mind, Kira?" Lur asked.

"Not at all. Sounds fun."

"Perfect! We'll see you at five!" Stella yelled and wrapped an arm around Luna's neck to drag her off, with Lur following behind them.

*Good thing I remembered to tell Pyre.*

*Remembered to tell me what?*

*About the study party at five o'clock.* There was a moment of silence. *You forgot, didn't you?*

*No. Of course not.*

*Pyre.*

*Yes, I forgot; I'm sorry.*

*It's no problem, Pyre.* I walked out of the class room.

*Is it the same three girls who might be demons?*

*Yes.* I met him outside the building.

"And you're letting them in our apartment?" He crossed his arms.

"I thought I would."

"Why?"

"We're in most of the same classes and we need to study. I thought having it at our place would give you an

183

opportunity to figure out whether they're demons or not. If they are demons and they attack, you'll be there to handle it. Would you prefer that I went to their place?"

"No. Good point, but Lowell and I will be in my room, in case you need us."

"But isn't Lowell going to ask Lur out?"

"Don't even get me started on that. He won't stop obsessing about it. He wants to ask her out, but he's afraid she'll say no. He thinks he's in love with her, but what if she's a demon and he has to kill her? Will you please talk to him again?"

"Of course."

"Does this mean we're required to clean?"

"The apartment should already be clean. I cleaned it a couple of days ago, and it was still in good shape when I left for school this morning."

"Yea, about that." He scratched the back of his head.

"What happened?"

"Lowell and I wanted to train before he went to his first class, but Eira got mad at me because I picked on Eros. We left Eira's and decided to train at our place."

"You're getting to the point slowly." I eyed him and crossed my arms.

"We thought the living room would be the best room for training. We moved all the furniture out of the way." He looked ashamed and lowered his eyes to the ground. "While training I accidentally stabbed the couch and the wall." I stared at him and waited for the last shoe to drop. "And the door to the kitchen."

"Is that all?" He nodded. "Let's get home and see

184

what the damage is." He picked me up so we would get there quicker. He slowly opened the door to expose the catastrophe in our living room. The couch cushions were on the floor with stuffing pouring out of them. The door to the kitchen hung off its hinges and the hole in the wall was bigger than my head. My eyes slid over to him in disbelief.

"Eira was supposed to come over to help me clean up the mess." He said sheepishly, biting his lip.

"Pyre, this is hugely worse than how you made it sound. Why didn't you admit how extensive it was?"

"I didn't want to worry you."

"It looks like a tornado came through here!"

"I'll fix it before the girls get here. I promise." He appeared to be moderately scared, walked over to the kitchen door and fiddled with it.

"It's fine, Pyre. If you gather the stuffing, I can fix the cushions while you fix the door and the wall."

"You can sew?"

"My mom taught me." He walked up to me with his hands full of stuffing.

"I'm sorry." He looked shamefaced, but I wasn't ready to let him off the hook yet.

I inhaled in an attempt to calm myself, and said through clenched jaws, "At least you didn't set anything on fire." I took the stuffing and went to my room. He brought the cushions behind me and put them on the bed. At that moment there was a knock on the door.

"It's Lowell. He came to help."

"Good." Pyre ran and opened the door while I tried to figure out how to put the stuffing back in the cushions.

"How did it go?" Lowell asked as he came in the

door. "Did she yell like we thought she would?"

"You do realize I can hear you?" I faced them with my hands on my hips.

"Hey, Kira, didn't see ya there." Lowell laughed nervously.

"Right." I rolled my eyes.

"We're genuinely sorry about all of this. We'll put it back together." Lowell attempted to get back on my good side. It was admittedly difficult to stay mad when they both sounded so remorseful.

"It's fine, just fix it. Fast."

"Kira has a study party at five so we need to hurry." Pyre sounded desperate to please as well.

"With who?" I went back to my room and closed my door so I couldn't hear them anymore. I replaced all the stuffing and patched up the cushions. I sat there for a few minutes, enjoying the peace and quiet, before taking the cushions back to the living room.

"Do you need help?" Pyre took one of the cushions from me. "You're done?"

"Yep, it was only a small bit of patchwork."

"That was fast for a human."

"It wasn't as bad as it appeared at first. Each cushion only had one hole, so that made it quick and easy." I noticed the door was fixed and the hole in the wall was gone. "You two are quite the handymen."

"The wolf is better with tools than I am." Pyre scratched his head.

"Pyre did most of the work. Don't let him tell you otherwise."

"I won't." I wrapped my arms around Pyre.

"When do you plan on talking to him?" Pyre pointed his head at Lowell.

"So, Lowell," I stepped away from Pyre. "You are planning to ask Lur out, right?"

"O-of course. Why wouldn't I?" He seemed embarrassed being under the spotlight.

"Lowell?"

"I-I just don't know how."

"It's easy. You simply say, 'Lur, will you go out with me?' It's that simple." Pyre stated matter-of-factly.

"Says the guy who practically kidnapped his girlfriend to ask her out." Lowell crossed his arms.

"Kidnapping works too."

"Pyre!" I softly hit his arm. There was a knock at the door. "Is it five o'clock already?"

"Ten 'til. We'll be in my room, trying to get a smidgen of courage for a certain wolf." They went to Pyre's room, and I answered the door.

"Come on in."

"We brought snacks!" Stella said.

"And drinks." Luna said.

"And paint." Lur said.

"And books?" I looked from one to the other of them expectantly.

"We brought one book." Luna held up the book.

"We have five classes." I smacked my forehead.

"We thought it would be more fun to party than study." Stella said.

"What would this party involve?" I crossed my arms and stared at them suspiciously.

"We wanted Lur to paint our faces." Luna said.

"I brought some music." Stella said.

"And we wanted to try something if you're open to it." Lur said.

"What?" I asked.

"I'm a Wiccan on my mother's side. That is, sort of."

"What does that mean?"

"I have a varied background and I don't fit neatly into one box."

"If you want me to participate in whatever you're considering, I need a bit more than that."

"It's no big deal. My mother descends from the ancient Celts, through a long line of women who revere the earth and nature. Their practices and beliefs evolved over the years. Modern day Wicca is a recent incarnation. The Wiccans are so open and flexible it was a natural transition for her. My father's line descends from European Christians and Native Americans. So his ancestry was rooted in reverence for the earth too. I've learned a lot from all of my ancestors, and all of it has shaped who I am and what I believe. I'm a unique blend of spiritual paths and beliefs. I prefer not to be labeled, but if I'm forced to choose one, I usually go with Wiccan, because it encompasses the most wide and varied beliefs."

"So what do you believe?" I asked, hoping for insight as to whether she was a demon.

"Personally? I believe in one supreme being with both male and female aspects. I hold great reverence for nature. We could learn so much from nature, but have either failed to do so or have forgotten it over time. There's more in this world than is known or can be seen.

That's why I like to make special herb potions and natural remedies, to find ways of doing things naturally rather than depending on toxic chemicals or processing. This book was my mother's and now I'm learning from it and adding to it. We wondered if you'd like to help or even try some?" Lur explained. I wasn't certain at all about it and hesitated to answer.

"I don't know..."

"It's fine if you don't. We'll understand." Luna said.

"It's totally cool if you're not into that." Stella said.

"Try asking me later." I hedged, ready to change the subject.

"Let's get this party started." Stella yelled. The girls made themselves at home.

*Kira, did Lur say she's a Wiccan on her mother's side of the family?*

*Indeed, she did.*

*Lowell likes the sound of that. He's practically gnawing on my pillow and drooling everywhere.*

*I thought he would.*

*Don't drink or inhale anything they make.*

*I won't.*

"Kira, do you mind going first for the face painting?" Lur asked, sitting near the armrest of the couch with her paints on the coffee table.

"Not at all." I sat down in front of Lur.

"You seem like an icy hot type of girl."

"So I'm muscle ointment?" Everyone laughed.

"No." Lur paused to catch her breath before continuing. "I mean your personality. You're sweet but I bet you wouldn't back out of a fight if you're standing up for what's right."

"You'd be right."

"I know what I'll paint on you."

"Kira, what brings you to little Russellville?" Stella asked.

"Just school." I didn't want to talk about it with people I only recently met.

"Luna says otherwise." I stared at Luna.

"I have a hunch there's a deeper meaning to why you moved here. I sense someone caused you tremendous pain for you to move so far from your home."

"How do you know how far I moved?" I asked.

"That's where I come into it. You don't act like you're from Arkansas. Your personality is in sweet harmony while you're past is in total chaos." Stella declared as I stared at her. "My intuition sees you living in a largely musical area, probably from somewhere in Tennessee."

"I sense either a friend or parent caused you the pain that's dug a hole in your heart. Pyre is doing an amazing job at making the hole disappear." Luna stated with a faraway expression on her face.

"As for letting it control your life, you've done an amazing job of letting go of the past." Lur continued the impromptu evaluation. I stood up and backed away a few steps, shocked and speechless. "Did we go too far?" Lur asked.

"H-how—" I stuttered, unable to form all the words of the question.

"I mentioned I have Wiccan ancestors. Since I'm in

tuned with the earth, I'm able to tell a great deal about people by looking at them. The way a person walks, talks, holds their head up, or their use of arm movements tells plenty about them." Lur tried to explain.

"I can see auras. Your aura is a beautiful turquoise with some brown mixed in, which means there's something unsettling and distracting from your past." Luna continued.

"As for me, I'm just weird." Stella wrapped it up and put her hands behind her head with a huge smile on her face.

"Stella isn't like us, or like Lowell." Lur commented.

"Like Lowell? What do you mean?" I asked.

"I suspect he might be a demon. Pyre might be too since he and Lowell are together so often. I haven't been around him much to determine for sure." Before I could respond, Lowell pulled me away from Lur and stepped in front of me.

"How do you three know all this?" Lowell demanded.

"What do you three want?" Pyre interrogated as he pushed me further back toward the bedrooms.

"We don't want anything." Luna said, hiding behind Stella.

"You must be demons." Stella sounded much too excited about it.

"We came here to spend time with Kira." Lur entreated and looked at Lowell with imploring eyes, but Lowell avoided her gaze. She looked like she might cry.

"How could you tell that he's a demon? How do you even know about demons?" I inquired, looking directly at Lur.

"Because of my lineage, I can tell the difference between humans and demons. Demons radiate a unique energy, so I was aware from the beginning that Lowell was a demon, just not what kind. I only know that it's a cute kind. I mean, nice. Or something." She blushed. Lowell turned quite red in the face himself.

"I thought Wiccans didn't believe in demons."

"Many Wiccans don't. I do because of my varied background. Not necessarily in the traditional religious view, but more like humans with special gifts."

I glanced over at Pyre. *I don't think they're a threat.*

*I agree. I don't sense anything unusual about their intentions.*

*That's a relief. Lowell can relax in that case.*

*I'm fine.* Lowell's face showed his struggle with his emotions; embarrassment, attraction to Lur and concern she might be a demon.

*Obviously, Wolf, but you need to apologize to Lur.*

*Why?* Lowell looked at us, confused.

*Because you made her cry.* I stared pointedly at him and crossed my arms. I perceived the confused expressions on the girls' faces. *And you better do it fast.* I stood up and said, "Lur, Lowell wants to talk to you."

"Why?" Lur asked, nervously.

"Just does." I grabbed Pyre's arm and pulled him closer to me. Lowell gawked at me and shook his head. "Go on." I said.

"Apparently I want to talk to you. Will you come with me for a minute?" Lowell motioned for her to follow him to the kitchen. She hesitated but followed him anyway. He looked back, caught us all watching, and glared at us as he shut the kitchen door.

"Do you suppose he'll finally ask her out?" I whispered to Pyre. Stella and Luna ran to the door and put their ears to it to listen.

"He'd better. I'm bored with him talking about her every day."

"Of course if they start dating, he'll talk about her even more." He growled at the thought of that. Stella and Luna jumped up and down in place.

"He asked her." Pyre and I said at the same time. Pyre wrapped an arm around me.

"About time." He declared.

"Agreed." Stella and Luna ran back to the couch. Lowell and Lur walked in and stared at us for a moment.

"I'm gonna head home." Lowell said.

"You're leaving now?" Lur couldn't hide her disappointment.

"You're welcome to come with me." Lowell looked at her in a way that made her blush a deep red.

"Wrong, Wolf! You're not leaving me with four girls." I raised an eyebrow at him. "Three girls and my girlfriend." I crossed my arms. "Is there no way to say this correctly?" I shook my head. "You're not leaving me." The boys went to Pyre's room.

"Kira, are we okay?" Lur asked. Stella and Luna glanced back and forth between the two of us.

"Yes, we are now." She ran up and hugged me.

"I need to finish your paint." We sat back down, and she started painting my face again.

"What did you and Lowell talk about?" Stella asked.

"Stuff." Lur grinned to herself.

"What kind of stuff?" Luna asked.

"Just stuff." Lur said with such a big smile, she lit up the whole room.

"When's the date?" I asked, smiling back at her.

"Tomorrow." She blushed.

"What are the two of you planning to do?"

"He didn't say. He said he would figure it out and surprise me." She paused for a moment. "Thank you, Kira."

"All I did was introduce you."

"And that's why I'm thanking you."

We had a fun night painting each other's faces and pretending to study. Pyre and Lowell came out and joined us at one point. Lur painted Lowell's face. We all enjoyed watching as they lightly flirted with each other. Pyre even let me paint his face. When it got late, Lowell left with the girls.

"Thank goodness he finally asked her. Maybe now he'll cheer up and shut up about it." Pyre said.

"We can only hope." I picked up the pillows off the floor.

"This paint will wash off, right?"

"Yes. I'm surprised you let me paint your face."

"Why? What did you do to me?"

"Nothing too embarrassing. I'm simply surprised you let me."

"I started not to, but I regretted the mess Lowell and I made of the apartment. I figured I'd make it up to you.

194

Besides he let that girl paint his face. I can't let him show me up." He sat down on the couch. "Come here." I sat down next to him. "How about we clean this mess up later?"

"That sounds good." He held me in his arms. *The end of another amazing day.*

Lowell wouldn't stop chattering about Lur on the way to school the next day. When I finally got away from him, I had to endure Lur. During biology they wouldn't stop flirting and giggling at each other. I finally raised my hand in the middle of biology.

"Yes, Ms. Phoenix." The professor acknowledged me.

"Can I borrow your trash can?"

"Why?"

"These love birds are making me nauseous."

"Kira!" Lowell yelled.

"Well, you are."

Class resumed. I was thankful neither of them were in my last class. Stella laughed when Luna and I told her what happened.

Pyre walked me home so I could change for work. When we were about to leave the apartment, I turned back because I thought I saw someone down the hall. I checked but if someone was there, they had vanished.

"Did you forget something?" Pyre asked.

"No, I thought I saw something."

"Let's get you to work." I walked inside to find Dustin and Franq dealing with a customer. Franq motioned for me to meet him in the kitchen. I quickly clocked in and followed him.

"Kira, would you start making the cocktail and tartar sauces?"

I agreed and watched him walk away. While I worked on the sauces, a woman walked up to me.

"Who're you?"

"My name's Kira."

"You're the new girl everyone has been talking about recently."

"Everyone's talking about me?" *Wonderful! How embarrassing.*

"Only about how you dropped things and fell down your first day."

"That's just... terrific."

"Don't be embarrassed. You'll get the hang of it. My name's Tora by the way." She held out a hand to me. "I'm one of the supervisors."

"Nice to meet you."

"You too, and I promise I don't bite too hard." She walked away laughing loudly.

*I hope that was a joke.* I hurriedly got back to work.

Luckily we weren't excessively busy which enabled me to focus on figuring out how to juggle tables. I managed not to drop anything. The hostess, Clio, didn't sit me tables bigger than four people and made sure I didn't get sat too many times at once. I met a girl named Wynne who might have been a friend of Crystal's before she changed. Wynne was stuck up and bossy. Every time she needed something done, she'd put it off on someone else. Trina was another waitress who was sweet and helped me tremendously. The only other male server was Anntoin.

196

He was a joker. He kept playing tricks on everyone and making us all mad. I started sweeping my section after all of my tables left at the end of the night.

"Kira, come with me please." Tora walked up to me. "I need to show you something."

"Okay." I leaned the broom against the booth and followed her to the other dining room.

"Now when you're cleaning... Make sure you listen carefully to what I'm telling you. When the night is over and you start cleaning... Are you listening?"

"Yes, of course." I didn't understand why she kept repeating herself.

"When you're cleaning, you need to make certain..." She continued repeating herself over and over as we walked to the other dining room. I noticed a box that the disposable cups came in but I didn't pay it any mind. Her voice seemed to get louder as we walked. As she reached the back of the room, Anntoin jumped out of the box and scared me. After I jumped back, I accidentally kicked him in the face.

"She kicked my nose." Anntoin mumbled and held his nose, because I kicked him hard enough to make his nose bleed.

"That was great!" Tora laughed so hard she couldn't breathe.

"What is going on in here?" Dustin walked out when he heard the commotion.

"Anntoin jumped out of a box and scared Kira."

"Now isn't the time for games. There are customers in the restaurant." He glared down at Anntoin. "Don't bleed everywhere." He walked away.

"I guess we learned not to try to scare Kira." Tora walked away still laughing and told the others what happened. They all said they were sorry they missed it.

I met Pyre outside after I finished cleaning my section and rolling silverware. He practically doubled over laughing hysterically when I told him what Tora and Anntoin had done. When he finally stopped, he walked me home. Lowell stood in front of our door, waiting for us.

"What do you want, Wolf?"

"I wanted to ask how work went." He tried to play innocent.

"But you actually want to talk about Lur." I teased.

"Of course not, I'm offended you'd accuse me of such a thing." He pretended to be insulted, but I was aware it was an act.

"I didn't drop anything tonight and I go back tomorrow at five." I walked past him into the apartment with Pyre following right behind me. "Pyre, did you want to discuss anything?"

"I want to talk about butterflies."

"Don't ya just love butterflies?" We both sat and stared at Lowell expectantly.

"Come on, I don't incessantly talk about Lur."

"What do you want to discuss?" I asked.

"I doubt that Lur enjoyed the date tonight." He hung his head and sat down in the chair across from us.

"Why do you say that?" Pyre asked, concerned.

"I took her to a movie and a nice dinner, and it was a catastrophe from the beginning." Lowell rubbed his forehead. "At the movie theater, a tall guy sat in front of us so we moved. A couple sat behind us and started arguing

198

so loudly we could hardly hear. By that time, there were no empty seats available. Then we went to dinner. We had a reservation, but we still had to wait over thirty minutes to be seated. They sat us at a table near the door to the kitchen. It was a swinging door, which bumped her chair every time the staff went in or out of the dining room. She moved her chair as far from the door as possible, but it didn't help. I offered to trade places, but she politely refused. We sat there waiting for the waiter to come over and take our order. He took such a long time, and we didn't even have drinks yet. When the waiter finally came to our table, he dropped the water pitcher on the table, soaking Lur's clothes. I may have growled at the waiter. We left right after that and went straight to her place. I apologized about the waiter, and how the night had gone in general. She said it was fine but I could tell she was upset. I told her I would see her at school and tried to kiss her good night."

"She didn't." Pyre said unexpectedly. Lowell nodded dolefully.

"Didn't what?" I asked, highly confused.

"She gave him the cheek. I am so sorry, man." He patted Lowell's shoulder.

"What does that mean?" They both looked at me in disbelief. "Did you both forget I'm still new to this dating thing? What does 'she gave him the cheek' mean?"

"He tried to give her a good night kiss, but she turned her head and caused him to kiss her cheek instead."

"Right." I nodded like I understood. "And that means?"

"It means I probably won't get the chance to take

her on another date." Lowell finally explained.

"What? No way." I got up and picked up the phone.

"Kira, what're you doing?" Pyre took the phone away from me.

"She should realize none of it was Lowell's fault — not the theater, not the waiting, and certainly not the water. Why would she blame him?"

"It's something for them to work out together. We're only here to listen."

"And yell at her if she's being unreasonable to my best friend. I want to ask her what's going on in her head." I tried to pick up the phone again, but Pyre stood in front of it and crossed his arms, shaking his head. I inhaled deeply to calm down. I walked back over to Lowell and knelt in front of him. "I'm sorry it didn't go well, but it's possible she wasn't angry with you. Maybe she doesn't kiss on the first date." I rubbed his face.

"Maybe I'm not supposed to fall in love again."

"Don't say that." I wrapped my arms around his neck. He buried his face into my neck and squeezed me. Pyre walked behind the chair and rubbed Lowell's shoulders.

"I should get going." Lowell said, pulling away from me.

"Why don't you stay here tonight? While Kira is at work tomorrow, you and I can do something to cheer you up and get your mind off it. We'll get Caedmon and Eros too and have a guys' day." Lowell and I both stared at him. "What? I'm trying to help."

"I'll leave you boys to your bonding time. I'm

going over to Eira's."

"Kira, you don't need to leave." Lowell objected.

"I know but it would be better if I did." I put on my coat and got ready to leave.

"Let me take you. Lowell, I'll be right back."

"I'm not moving, Pyre." Lowell sat and turned on the television. We took off and arrived at Eira's house in no time.

"I'll see you tomorrow before you go to work." He was about to give me a quick kiss, but something stung my arm and I looked down, causing him to kiss my cheek. "Kira, did I upset you?"

"No, I didn't mean to look away; something stung me." I pointed to the big red bump that had already appeared on my arm.

"I see what bit you." He reached through my hair and pulled out a spider. "Eira can heal it for you. Can we try that kiss again?"

"Of course." I kissed his lips with my palm on his cheek. "Go take care of Lowell." I watched as he disappeared. *Tomorrow should be fun.*

I went inside and explained everything to Eira. She healed my arm and let me stay the night in one of the extra rooms.

The next day, she and I hung out until time for Pyre to come by to take me to the restaurant.

"Have a wonderful day." Pyre squeezed my hand.

"I will. Have fun with the guys." He made a face, but he was obviously eager to spend the day with his friends.

I had been getting the hang of the work routine

more each time, so I honestly looked forward to the day as I walked into the building. It was a busy day at the restaurant. Dustin asked if I could stay late, and I agreed. Ike, the other manager, supervised the kitchen. When I'd go to pick up my food orders, he'd yell sporadically, "Keep moving! Keep moving!" I thought I was too slow, but Trina said he constantly said things like that. It was one of his mottoes he liked to say to encourage the staff. I kept up with my tables and didn't fall behind, thus it was a terrific day. By the end of the day, though, I was exhausted. Pyre met me after my shift. Since he saw how fatigued I was, he carried me by demon instead of walking home. When we got there, I had fallen asleep in his arms, so he took me all the way to my bedroom.

Later he told me about the little conversation we had when he set me on my bed.

"Kira, we're home."

"Air Demon, the only way to fly."

"What?" I didn't answer him. "Okay, then, I guess I'm not the only one who talks in their sleep. Good night, Kira."

# Chapter 10
# Love and Hate in the Air

I realized I was sitting in an airplane, unsure of how I came to be there. I looked around and saw Crystal to my left. She appeared to be waiting for something to happen. I disconsolately observed the other passengers. None of them comprehended what was about to happen. The stewardess approached us.

"Is there anything I can get you?" She asked Crystal.

"You can fix your voice." Crystal glared at her.

"Pardon me?" The girl was confused.

"Your voice is too shrill. Fix it." Crystal's voice grew louder and ruder. "Don't bother, I'll fix it for you." A gust of wind blew and built up speed, tearing up the inside of the plane. I closed my eyes and held onto the arms of my seat. When the wind died down, the passengers and the employees had disappeared. "Man her voice was annoying. The wind sacrifice has been made and accepted. The rebirth will be soon." She leaned closer to me. "Just between you and me, I've grown weary from this sacrifice, so if you don't mind..." She snapped her fingers.

I woke up in Pyre's arms.

"I listened telepathically and heard what Crystal said about the sacrifices and the rebirth. She'll be here soon."

"I simply can't wait." I surveyed the damage in the room. "Did a tornado go through my room?" My nightstand leaned upside down next to the door with all the legs broken, some of my knick knacks were thrown into the walls, and my stuffed animals looked like they went through a shredder. "At least I wasn't frozen this time."

"I would rather you'd be frozen."

"P-Pyre?" I was disconcerted for a minute.

"If you're frozen, I have a better chance of saving you. I am a fire demon after all."

"Don't scare me like that again."

"What? You don't want to be my frozen angel?"

"Shut up."

"Why is your face getting red?" He kissed me all over my face.

"Stop it." I looked away from him and down at my bed. That's when I realized he was standing on my bed, holding onto me. "What happened when you came into my room?"

"I heard crashing and bumping noises. I ran in and found a tornado destroying your room and you floating over your bed." He sat down on my bed with me in his lap.

"I take it I was about to fall when my dream ended."

"I was worried you'd hit your head, so I fought against the wind to get to you."

Pyre's mood shifted rapidly from jovial in an attempt to lift my spirits to tense and worried. I decided Crystal had caused enough distress for one day, and to give this moment to Pyre.

"Aw, my sweet fire demon." I wrapped my arms around his neck.

"I do what I can." He wrapped his arms around my waist. Lowell knocked and poked his head in the door.

"What?"

"Everything okay?" Lowell surveyed the room, taking in all the damage.

"Another dream." Pyre said without going into details.

"That explains the room." Lowell walked over to us. "Are you all right?" I nodded as I stood.

"Kira?" Pyre asked.

"I'm sorry." I said ruefully.

"For what?" Pyre stepped in front of me.

"You've got to be fed up with babying me. I feel like such a burden sometimes."

"You're kidding, right?" Lowell chuckled. I looked quizzically at him. "Pyre loves it. He doesn't like seeing you cry, but he loves having you in his arms."

"Shut up, Wolf." Pyre growled.

"He also loves being able to do stuff for you. You're such an independent girl he takes any chance he can get to baby you." Lowell said, ignoring Pyre. "Before he met you, he was just a big, scary demon but now he can play the great big hero." Lowell mimicked something big and scary and then pretended to be a swooning damsel. I struggled not to laugh.

"I said shut up." Pyre was perturbed and spoke through gritted teeth without looking at either of us.

"But do you know what he loves even more?"

"You're dead, Wolf!" Pyre chased him around my room before running outside. I couldn't contain my laugh any longer. I leaned against the wall to stay out of the way of their antics.

*He is my hero, but can he stop Crystal and the*

*rebirth?* I gazed out my window. The branches on the tree blew and reached out as if calling me outside to kill me. *If only I could figure out when the rebirth will happen.*

"Why don't you stay home today?" Pyre leaned against the door frame, watching me get ready for school.

"I need to go to class. Besides, if I'm going to date a big, scary demon, I can't allow a bit of danger to hold me back."

We left the apartment and headed for campus. When we arrived at the building, he raised my hand to his lips to kiss my palm. "I'll see you when you get out of class."

I watched him go and walked into art class.

"Hey, Kira," Lur said when she saw me.

"Lur." I said frostily and took my seat.

"Is Lowell mad at me?"

"Why don't you ask him?"

"I'm scared to, but I want to apologize to him so badly."

"Then apologize."

"Do you expect he'll forgive me?"

"How about you apologize and find out for yourself?" I rubbed my eyes.

"Kira, is something wrong?"

"I'm exhausted. I had a long, hard day at work yesterday."

"Is it only due to work or is it Crystal?" I was astonished she knew about Crystal. "Lowell told me you haven't been able to sleep lately because of a girl named Crystal."

"She's an old friend, and she's hatched some

mentally disturbed plan, but I have no idea what or how to stop her."

"Kira, you should go home and take a nap."

"I'd prefer to be out of the apartment right now." I took out my art supplies. "Besides, I wouldn't want to miss art class. There's no telling what she'll talk about today."

"That's true."

"Lur, there's something I want to talk to you about since we have a few minutes."

"Sure, anything."

"It's about Lowell."

"I knew it, he is mad at me."

"No, that's not it."

"What is it, Kira?"

"Lowell is my best friend, and he isn't like most guys."

"Yea, that's one of the things I like about him."

"Well, here's the thing. Lowell hasn't dated for a long time. His last relationship... it ended badly, and he was deeply hurt."

"That's so sad. Poor guy."

"Let me get this out, okay? Because he was hurt before, it was extremely difficult for him to ask you out. But he genuinely likes you, and he sincerely wanted your date to go well. He's worried you're mad at him. I'm glad you're not because the two of you would make a wonderful couple. I want to make certain... well, that you be fair to him. I don't want to see him get hurt."

"I wouldn't hurt him, I promise."

"That's good. Because I should tell you that if you did, I'd have to kick your butt."

"Fair enough. So, are we okay?"

"Yea, we're good." I smiled and hugged her.

"Good morning, class." The professor arrived and jumped right in to the lesson. "Today's assignment will revolve around spring since spring is around the corner and all." She sat down on her stool. "Who can tell me the purpose of spring?" One girl raised her hand. "Yes?"

"The purpose of spring is to give us all the flowers?" The girl didn't sound confident in her answer.

Her friend sitting next to her said, "Don't be stupid. The purpose of spring is so we can get a head start on our tans before swimsuit season begins." Lur and I looked at each other and shrugged.

"No." The professor covered her face and shook her head. "The purpose of spring is for the earth and everything in nature to be reborn." My head snapped to attention. "Every season has a purpose. Summer is the time when the earth reaches its full potential and beauty. In autumn, the earth cleanses itself by shedding its leaves or dried up flowers. Winter is when the earth slumbers to regenerate, but spring is when the earth reawakens anew. The earth brings in new life and brings hope to everyone. It's a beautiful transformation, and a time when new beginnings are possible. Now I want everyone to draw a picture of what spring means to you."

*Spring is the rebirth. A transformation? Is that what Crystal is waiting for? Spring will initiate the rebirth she has been working so hard for. Since we've concluded it's likely intended for me, the only dilemma now is how, where and what will happen afterwards.*

When class was over, I walked up to the professor.

"What can I do for you, Kira?" She asked.

"I wonder if you would tell me more about spring and how it's a rebirth for the earth."

"Why? Is it important?"

"I've been having dreams that deal with some kind of rebirth."

"I only know a little about spring and even less about dreams, but I know someone who might be able to help you. He's a professor of metaphysics, Professor Dean. I'm about to go meet with him. Would you like to join me?"

"Would you mind?"

"Not at all. Let's go."

We walked over to the next building and up to his office.

"Hello, Cora. Good timing. And who's this?" The man said when we entered his office.

"This is Kira, the girl I mentioned."

"Yes, yes, the girl who has such a vivid imagination when she's drawing. How can I help you?"

"I have some questions and we thought you might be able to help. I've been having disturbing dreams about a girl who is making sacrifices to the elements, and she keeps talking about a rebirth."

"That sounds like a spell for transforming things."

"Transforming? How would it transform something?"

"The spell begins with four sacrifices in ice, earth, wind, and fire. If the sacrifices are made at the correct times, the transformation will happen immediately before the time of the spring equinox."

"What happens exactly?"

"It depends. Can you tell me more about the sacrifices?"

I explained everything to him about each of the dreams and what Crystal said in each one.

"It sounds like she wants to transform a human being into something else. She said the rebirth would be done in earth, thus she might be speaking of a cemetery, or even planting or putting something into the ground. Without more information about how she made the sacrifices, I'm unable to be of much help. All I can tell you is these are merely dreams and dreams can't hurt you."

*You don't know me very well.*

"Here is my number in case you have any more questions. It sounds fascinating. I'd like to hear more about it if you experience any more of these dreams." As he handed me the paper, I caught a glimpse at the clock.

"Yikes, I'm late for bio." I grabbed my bag, thanked him and ran out the door. I barely made it in time.

"Kira, where have you been?" Lowell asked as I walked up to the desk. "Pyre has been screaming at me to find you."

"My art professor took me to talk to a metaphysics professor. I hoped he might tell me something regarding what Crystal is planning. He didn't know much but said to inform him if anything new occurred." I detected Lur out of the corner of my eye. She stood by the door gazing longingly at Lowell. Lowell flipped through the pages of his book, unaware of her presence. When I turned back to face Lur again, she was gone. *I hope they work this out soon.*

Luna walked in and sat in front of me. Lowell wouldn't look up from his book.

"Where's Lur?" I whispered to Luna.

"She was scared to come to bio." She eyed Lowell cautiously. "She wasn't prepared to see him yet."

I glanced over at him and could tell he had stopped reading the book to listen to Luna's words. I became aware of something flying outside the window. A hummingbird flew around a vine slowly growing around the window.

"Everything will work out." Luna tilted her head questioningly at me. "You'll see."

After biology, Luna and I walked to mythology class and told Stella what happened.

"Do you think they'll try again?" She asked.

"Kira says they will." Luna motioned toward me. "It's a hunch."

Mythology class went by fast and I met Lowell at the library. While Lowell and I were studying, Lur walked in and sat down nearby. I caught Lowell casting furtive glances at Lur. He would start to get up but change his mind. I glanced over at Lur and observed her doing the same thing. It was time for an intervention.

"Lowell, Lur spoke to me about your date. She would like to talk to you, but she's nervous that you're mad at her."

"Of course I'm not mad at her. I thought she was mad at me."

"She's not. You should go talk to her, ask her out again."

"What if the second date goes as terrible as the first, or even worse? Maybe it was a sign."

"The only sign was the white tulip of forgiveness. First dates often go bad. Everyone deserves a second chance."

"Even me?" He beheld me with such deep sadness in his eyes, it was heartbreaking.

"Especially you."

"What should I say?"

"Hello? Take it from there and be yourself. Perhaps take her a flower or a plant."

I watched as Lowell did something with his hands under the table and pulled out a potted flowering plant.

"What kind of flowers are those?"

"They're violet hyacinths. They symbolize apology."

"Excellent choice. She'll love them."

He took a deep breath and walked over to Lur. She peered up at him and put down her book. They started to speak at the same time.

"Lowell, I'm so sorry..."

"...so many things went wrong on our date."

"If you're willing..."

"...I'd like to try again."

They laughed and Lowell said, "Okay, let me try this. Lur, would you please accept this token of my apology for our first date, and be my date again on Saturday?" He pulled the flower pot from behind his back and gave it to her.

"Lowell, they're beautiful. Yes, I'd love to go out with you again." He released the breath he had been holding.

"Okay. That's good. I guess I'll see you Saturday."

He was embarrassed and hesitant, and terribly cute.

"Or you could sit down and we could talk. Must you leave now?"

He looked over at me, and I nodded. He sat down and before long they were talking and laughing, inching closer together intermittently, and touching each other's arm or knee.

*I believe he can take it from here.*

*Playing matchmaker?* Pyre jumped into my thoughts as I watched them getting along so well.

*No, just helping some friends. Pyre, are you ready to go home?*

*I'll wait for you outside the library.*

I packed up my books and walked outside. Pyre pulled me into his arms and gave me a deep passionate kiss.

"What was that for?" I smiled as he broke the kiss.

"Just wanted to say I love you."

"Lucky for me, 'cause I love you too." He pulled me in for another kiss. "Mm, Pyre, people are staring." It was my turn to break the kiss.

"Let 'em stare." He gave me a mischievous leer.

"Let's go home." I turned my head and giggled.

Saturday came fast. We heard a familiar knock on the door late that night. Pyre and I looked at each other and we both shook our heads. In unison we said, "Come in, Lowell."

"How did you know it was me?" He closed the door behind him.

"A lucky guess. How was the second date?"

"It was... hmm... amazing." He had a faraway gaze, and couldn't stop smiling or nodding his head. The girl had this boy hooked.

"That's too bad, man. Kira, did you say you had a friend you could fix him up with if this date went sour?"

"Sure do, but you don't mind if she reeks horribly, do you?"

"Guys!"

"We're just having some fun with you. Tell us all about it." I said.

"Since it was such a beautiful day, we decided to spend it outdoors. We went geocaching at Mt. Nebo State Park."

"Geocaching?" Pyre sounded confused.

"It's sort of like a treasure hunt. Someone hides the geocache, and they leave clues on the geocache website. You use the clues and a GPS to hunt for it. It's usually trinkets, but sometimes you find cool stuff. If you take something, you leave something in its place. We had so much fun. I got to teach her about some of the plants, and she got to teach me about some of the rocks. We took a picnic lunch with us. And we talked. We talked about all kinds of things. It was peaceful, relaxing and... it felt like... like coming home."

My eyes filled with tears and I held his hand. Pyre smiled and nodded. Then he realized he was doing it, and said, "Enough of the mushy stuff. What did you find in the geocache?"

"Pyre, you're so romantic." I clasped my hands to my chest and batted my eyes at him.

"Romance? You want romance? I'll give you romance!" He pulled me up on my feet, twirled me and dipped me. He pulled me up and kissed me all over my face. I laughed so hard I couldn't breathe.

"Stop it!" I pushed against him, but then hugged him close. Lowell was still laughing at us as we sat down again.

"Okay, Pyre, I'll tell you about the geocache. It took a while, but we finally located it. Inside were some little toys for kids, like small cars, balls and hair bows. For adults or older kids, they had a deck of cards from Yosemite, a magnet from the Grand Canyon, and other souvenirs like that from various state and national parks. I chose an exceptional guitar pick with a wolf on it. Lur got a small piece of amethyst crystal geode. We put in a tiger's eye stone, a picture of a wolf that I drew, and a picture that Lur painted of the hyacinths I gave her. We also put in a few other odds and ends."

"That sounds like a lot of fun. You had a fantastic day."

"We did. There was also something in the geocache I thought you would like, Pyre."

"Me? What was it?"

"It was another guitar pick, but this one was black with a shimmery red fire-breathing dragon on it."

"Kira, do you want to go geocaching tomorrow?"

Before I could say anything, Lowell said, "You should go sometime, because it is loads of fun. But the guitar pick won't be there anymore. Someone else took it."

"Someone took it? Who?" Pyre slumped in disappointment.

"Me." Lowell pulled it out of his pocket and handed it to Pyre. "I wanted to say thanks for having my back all the time and convincing me to ask Lur out."

"Lowell, I oughta... but I can't. Thanks, man!"

"Pyre, you walked right into that one." As I giggled, a thought occurred to me. "I wasn't aware you two played the guitar."

"Guitar, piano, a few other instruments." Pyre said it like it was no big deal.

I realized Lowell was staring at me with a Cheshire cat smile on his face. "Help me now, what am I about to walk into?"

"Nothing. Lur sensed I'd be coming over here tonight, and that knowing thing takes some getting used to, believe me. Anyway, she got you something to say thanks as well."

He handed me a small drawstring pouch. I opened it and pulled out a silver triquetra charm.

"Lowell, it's beautiful. I can't wait to thank Lur."

Pyre examined it curiously. "I've seen those, but I don't recall what they're called."

"It's a triquetra. It's basically a symbol of unity and spirituality. Christians believe it stands for the Holy Trinity. Some Pagans view it like the ancient Celts, as a representation of the natural elements of earth, air and water. Others believe it symbolizes life, death and rebirth. The circle symbolizes eternity, perhaps God's love, or even the circle of life. Wiccans use them for protection." I scrutinized it thoughtfully.

"What's on your mind, Kira?" Pyre reached over and touched my hand.

"I was musing about what an appropriate gift this is and wondering if Lur sensed that. Maybe she chose this because it's important to her, or maybe she thought it was important for me."

"Can you decode all that for those of us who don't have a clue what you're talking about?" Lowell made a silly face at me.

"Be quiet, you! No, consider what I just said about the triquetra. Natural elements of earth, air and water, like my nightmares. Life, death and rebirth, like Crystal's plan. Wiccans, like Lur, believe it offers protection." The guys looked at each other pensively. "It's probably a coincidence."

"Do you believe in coincidences anymore, Lowell?"

"Not so much, Pyre."

"I think I'll keep it with me, in case it does possess protective powers. It certainly can't hurt anything."

"By the way, Kira, apparently you and Lur had quite the talk about me the other day."

"We chatted awhile. That's how I learned she wasn't mad."

"Hmm. And the part where you told her that if she hurt me unfairly, you'd kick her butt?"

"You said what?" Pyre asked incredulously.

"I told her to be fair to him. And yea, if she didn't, and he got hurt, I'd have to kick her butt."

"Kira? Thanks." Lowell said.

"Anything for my favorite wolf." I stood and gave him a big hug. Pyre was still staring at me, eyes wide with astonishment. "What?"

"You are a constant surprise."

"And you love it."

"I guess I'll head home now." Lowell said.

"Not so fast, mister! Apparently you and Lur talked

some about me too."

"What do you mean?"

"What exactly did you tell her about Crystal?"

"Nothing much. Honest! I only said she was an old friend, and that you were agonizing about her causing trouble. I'm sorry if I said too much."

"No, it's okay. It was somewhat unsettling at first, but I'm more concerned that if she knows too much, she might be in danger too."

"That's all the more reason for her to be advised, at least of some of it. That way she won't be caught off guard. She might even be able to help." Pyre suggested, doing his best to assist.

I held up the triquetra in contemplation. "Perhaps she already has."

# Chapter 11
# Muscles and Sweat

Lowell and I sat in the living room studying. He behaved as if he had something else to do and glanced back and forth between the kitchen door and his books. He finally went to the kitchen to talk to Pyre. Pyre shook his head as they talked, which made me wonder what they were discussing.

"Kira, would you mind if I stole Pyre to go train?"

"Why would I mind?"

"Does that mean it's okay?" I nodded. "She said it's okay!" He yelled triumphantly. I peeked over and saw Pyre slap his forehead. "Thank you, Kira."

"No problem." They left the apartment. *That wasn't strange at all.*

I resumed studying. After a few hours, I got up to go to my room, but the front door opened. Pyre and Lowell came in, sweating and panting.

"Good training?" I asked.

"Very." Pyre said, breathing heavy.

"Are we up for tomorrow?" Lowell asked.

"Totally." They bumped fists. I rolled my eyes.

"If it's okay with you, Kira." Lowell entreated.

"No problem. Maybe next time I can go too."

"You want to come?" Pyre sounded incredulous.

"Eira would enjoy the company." Lowell said.

"In that case, I've changed my mind. If I'm forced to spend time with her, I'll stay home." I tossed my head and stuck my nose up in the air.

"You're not fooling me. You love spending time with Eira. Come on, it'll be fun. You can watch me work out." Pyre said as he flexed his muscles.

"And watch you sweat? Ew, no thank you."

"Do you want to come or not?"

"Oh, okay, I guess so."

"It was your idea in the first place, so why did we end up trying to convince you?" Pyre asked and looked perplexed at Lowell.

"It's the nature of women, Pyre — an unsolvable mystery or puzzle, of baffling intrigue that taunts and challenges us, and which keeps us coming back for more."

"On that note, I bid you both good night." I said in a coy manner and walked to my room. When I looked back they both had perplexed expressions on their faces. I laughed and went to bed.

The next day Eira and I hung out at her place while Pyre and Lowell worked out.

"Do the boys regularly come here when they want to train?" I asked.

"Pretty much. We built a training room in the back of my house that has most everything they need. It's mostly indestructible, thank goodness. If it's pleasant outside they like to go out into the yard."

"Pyre comes here every day for a few hours a day?"

"That's about right."

"How often does Lowell train?"

"He trains with Pyre about three days a week, depending on his schoolwork. But he also trains on his own sometimes." Eira slowly inched closer to the window

220

as she spoke.

"What're you doing?" She motioned for me to come closer. I walked over and stared out the window to where Pyre and Lowell were training.

"Lowell is even hotter when he's training." She spoke like a school girl in love. "Don't you agree?"

"You're kidding, right? He's covered in sweat."

"That's what makes him so much hotter."

"You're disgusting."

"You don't think Pyre is more attractive?"

"I must admit I like watching him train, but the sweat is grossing me out."

"You're the weirdest girl ever." She went back to ogling Lowell. The other girls rapped on the door behind us and rushed in to the room.

"Are we too late?" Iris asked.

"No, come on, ladies." Eira waved. They all ran over to the window.

"Man, oh man." Laya said.

"You said it." Gabby said. I stared at them like they had lost their minds.

*I'll take weird over conventional any day.* "Don't some of you have boyfriends?"

"It doesn't hurt to look." Eira said.

"Do you recall that one of them is my boyfriend?" I crossed my arms.

"We're not looking at him." Gabby said.

"Nah, he's too short for us." Laya said.

"Whatever." I walked away from the window.

"They stopped." Iris said. "Why did they stop?"

*Kira, can you come out here?*

*Of course.*

"What're you doing?" Laya yelled. The girls jumped back from the window to hide.

"Pyre wants to talk to me about something."

I went outside to where the guys were standing. "You called?"

"Haven't they figured out that we realize they're watching?" Pyre asked.

"And that we put on a show for them, just enough to tease them, but inexplicably stop training for the day?" Lowell asked, sitting down on a large stone.

"I doubt it." I openly admired Pyre's bare chest.

"You do realize you're staring?" Pyre leered at me.

"What? I'm not allowed to stare at my boyfriend? I'll stare at someone else in that case. So, Lowell—" I started to turn but Pyre stopped me.

"You're not allowed to stare at anyone but me." He wrapped his arm around my shoulders and I wrinkled my nose. "What?"

"You stink." I pinched my nose. "And you're rubbing your sweat on me." I pushed against him but he pulled me closer, making Lowell laugh at us.

"Kira doesn't think we look good while training." Pyre said to Lowell as I kept pushing on him.

"You don't, Kira? We work hard to look good to give the girls plenty reason to drool."

"I didn't say that, but I don't drool over boys, remember?" I pushed harder against Pyre.

"Then what did you say?" Lowell asked, hovering over me. I peered up at him. "Well?"

"I said your sweat grosses me out."

"Is that right?" Pyre rubbed his hand on my face.

"Pyre!" I yelled. "You're so nasty." As I wiped my face, I spied a snake behind Pyre. I wrapped my arms around Pyre's neck.

"What's that for?" Pyre was shocked by my embrace.

"I thought she was about to smack you, not hug you." Lowell said. I shook my head looking away from the snake.

"What's going on, Kira?" Pyre tried to look me in the face.

"Nothing."

"It's our training buddy." Lowell picked up the snake.

"Hey there, Pal. Kira, this is... Kira?"

"Yes?" I asked.

"Why don't you want to meet our friend?" Lowell asked.

"No reason." Something abruptly touched my neck, and I shut my eyes. *Get it away. Get it away!*

"Take him away, Lowell." Pyre said as I buried my face in his neck. "Kira, are you afraid of snakes?"

*Yes.*

"Why didn't you tell us?" Pyre asked.

"I wouldn't have put him near you if I had known." Lowell said.

"The last time I told someone I was afraid of snakes, they laughed at me." I leaned back in Pyre's arms. "They also played practical jokes."

"We wouldn't do that to you." Lowell asserted, still holding the snake. I stared at the ground.

Pyre pulled up my chin to see my face. "Don't be afraid to tell us something based on how people treated you in the past. We're different."

"Why are you afraid of snakes?" Lowell asked. "If you don't mind me asking."

"I'd rather not say at the moment."

"Of course." Lowell patted my back. "Pyre, we should go take our showers now."

"I'm good. Most of my sweat rubbed off on Kira."

"Ew! Thank you so much!" All the wet spots now on my shirt disgusted me.

"Come on." Lowell laughed. We walked back to the house. When we went inside, the girls all pretended to be busy doing something.

"Hey, guys, how was the training?" Eira asked innocently. I lowered my gaze to hide the incredulous expression on my face.

"You tell us." Lowell teased.

The girls pretended not to comprehend what he meant.

"I'll be right back, Kira, I'm going to take a shower." Pyre flexed his muscles and stretched. "Try not to imagine me washing that nasty old sweat off my bare chest." He laughed as he walked away. I replied with a gagging sound.

"Kira, why did you tell them we were watching?" Eira whispered the accusation.

"I didn't. They figured it out themselves."

"We've always known. We stop as soon as Pyre can sense all of you watching." Lowell admitted.

"That's just mean. You're both mean!" Eira

exclaimed.

"Eira, you've got something on your shirt." Lowell motioned to her. When she looked down to check her shirt, he said, "Looks like you drooled all over yourself."

"It does not!" She yelled at him indignantly. The other girls sat together trying to hide their faces in embarrassment.

"Made you look though." She threw a couch pillow at his head. "Now, what should I say to Eros and Caedmon? Hmm, let me think." He stared up at the ceiling as if searching for the answer.

"You wouldn't!"

"Nah, I just wanted to make you squirm." Eira took a step in Lowell's direction, and he decided he'd picked on her enough, that it was time for him to take his shower.

# Chapter 12
## Phoenix Gets Tough

"Pyre, what all do you and Lowell do on the jobs for Vitas?"

"We mainly apprehend demons who are causing disturbances. Sometimes we search for demon artifacts. Other times we train new recruits."

"Recruits?"

"People like Caedmon and Eros. We teach them how to control their abilities and how to defend themselves against a demon."

"Sounds thrilling."

"Only catching the demons. I could do without training the humans."

"Are they that annoying?"

"It's Caedmon and Eros multiplied. None of them like each other so they get into constant fights."

"My poor fire demon." I leaned in and kissed his cheek.

"It's so hard being me."

"Anything I can do to help?"

"Can you make them all disappear?"

"I wish I could."

"Me too." He hugged me close and brushed my hair off my face. "You should come with us one day."

"I went with you the other day."

"I mean to train."

"Sounds like fun, but I'll pass."

"Come on, you'll like it. You can yell at people."

"And yet, I still pass."

"We actually need you." Vitas appeared out of the blue and startled us when he spoke.

"Why would you need me?"

"Come to the next training, and you'll see." Vitas stated, and promptly disappeared.

"He loves to pop in and out, doesn't he?" I held my hand to my chest and tried to still my thumping heart.

"Yep, and he needs to stop it 'cause one of these days he'll appear and get a sword in the gut."

"He hasn't yet?"

"No, he's been smart, keeping his distance, but one of these days..."

"Make sure you stab him once for me."

"Will do."

"When is the next training day?"

"Tomorrow."

I thought about the dangers we had previously faced, and what lay ahead of us. I thought about Crystal, and the possibility of future dangers.

"Perhaps it's not such a bad idea."

Pyre appraised me suspiciously. "Why the change?"

"You've been fretting yourself that you and Lowell can't be around all the time."

"We'll do everything we can to keep you safe."

"I realize that, but Mr. Hot Head and the Big Bad Wolf can't always be there to save the human damsel in distress. The damsel might need to hold the danger off long enough for them to get to her. Me, that is."

"That's true, I guess."

"And who knows, maybe the damsel might need to save you occasionally."

"You have saved me, by loving me."

"I'm serious, Pyre."

"Is there something from your dreams you haven't mentioned?"

"No, nothing like that."

"Then, why are you so uneasy?"

"I started to consider what happened with Melissa, and now with Crystal. The dangers lurking out there, those who want to hurt me or you — they are aware of how we feel for each other, how important we are to each other, and that they can use it to hurt us."

"Like when Melissa tried to hurt me by hurting you."

"Exactly. And Crystal is capable of that too."

"I'm still concerned that I'm the real danger; that you'd be safer if you'd never met me."

"Pyre! Stop it! Crystal would still be after me. Did you consider that I'm the real danger?"

"But..."

"No! No, buts, and don't be one either!" That got a small smile out of him. "I'm saying we're better, safer, together. Danger would threaten us either way. If we'd never met, Melissa wouldn't have threatened me, and Crystal wouldn't be a threat to you. We'd both still be in danger, and possibly one or both of us would be dead. What they view as our weakness is actually our strength. We're better together, in every way. This time, we know Crystal's coming, and we can be prepared."

Pyre gazed deeply into my eyes. "I know I've said this before, but you are a constant surprise. My life is immensely better with you in it in every way. You are certainly not the normal damsel in distress, human or demon."

"Normal's boring anyway."

"Training it is." He laughed unexpectedly and tried to hide it.

"What's so funny?"

"I had a mental image of me tied up or injured, and you with sword in hand, protecting me."

"That's it, Mr. Hot Head, it is on! Just you wait and see!" Inside though, I was still tormented, about the danger I might pose to him through Crystal, and whether I would be able to protect or save him if necessary. Training wasn't such a bad idea at all. *I'll be ready. We'll both be ready, for Crystal and whoever or whatever else comes our way.*

"Well then, you'll need your sleep. Off to bed so you'll be ready for tomorrow."

"Yes, sir." I saluted.

"That's not funny." He raised an eyebrow.

"I'm not allowed to call you sir?" I pouted.

"No, and you're not allowed to embarrass me in front of my students either."

"Not even a little?"

"No."

"Fine, Mr. Party Pooper." He glared at me. "Don't worry, I'll behave." I kissed him good night and went to bed.

I woke up in the middle of the night to the light in the living room. I got up and walked to the door and found

Pyre sitting on the couch.

"Pyre?" He jumped slightly as if startled.

"I didn't wake you, did I?"

"No, but why aren't you in bed?" I sat down next to him.

"Couldn't sleep."

"Why not?" I held onto his hand. He didn't answer. "Does it pertain to your dreams?" He nodded. "Do you want to talk about it?"

"Not tonight." He laid his head on my shoulder.

"Pyre, I tell you about my nightmares all the time. I trust you. Don't you trust me?"

"Of course I do." He sat up and looked at me.

"Then why won't you tell me about your dream?" He was hesitant to answer, but finally resigned himself to admitting the truth.

"Because it scares me. In the dream, I'm running from something unfamiliar, but it's big and has wings."

"Where are you?"

"It's one of those dreams where you're running down a long, dark hallway that never ends. Someone is laughing and the sound echoes through the hall."

"Laughing how?"

"Cackling to be precise, like a mad man who recently killed his prey." He started twitching and continued. "Whoever is laughing, I realize it means they kidnapped you. I feel completely useless in the dream, the way I did when Melissa attacked." He turned his face away from me. "And it scares me."

I wrapped my arms around him as he buried his face against my neck and wrapped his arms tightly around me. I rubbed his back with one hand and his hair with the other, trying to soothe him. Pyre's previous reluctance to discuss his dreams wasn't caused by a lack of trust or openness. Admitting his fear and vulnerability, and speaking about it to anyone, likely proved to be the hardest thing Pyre would ever do. His willingness to reveal it to me was in fact the most sincere expression of trust he could give. "Do you suppose Melissa's attack is the cause of these dreams, or something else?"

"I'm not certain." He pulled out of the hug and surreptitiously wiped his face. "I only want them to stop. I'm not going to lose you, am I?"

"Never."

"Good." He leaned his forehead to mine for a moment. "You need to get back to bed. I'm not going easy on you tomorrow simply because you're my girlfriend."

"I should hope not." I squeezed his hand and kissed him before going back to my room. "You need to try to get some sleep, too."

"I will."

*I hope you don't have any more nightmares tonight.* I laid down and went back to sleep.

I woke up the next morning and went to the kitchen.

"What're you doing?" Pyre wrapped his arms around me.

"I'm making coffee."

"You're not drinking coffee this morning. You're drinking sports drinks." He handed me a bottle.

"No coffee?"

"No coffee." He pulled me out of the kitchen while I dragged my feet. "You need to go change. Training begins in about an hour, and I want to get you there early to allow enough time to teach you a few techniques."

"How early is 'early'?"

"Within thirty minutes."

"I just got up." I whined.

"I'm aware of that, but the earlier the better."

"You know, I think I changed my mind about training. I don't wanna do it anymore."

He stood his ground, with his arms crossed, and flattened his lips.

"How can you say so much without saying anything at all?" I asked him as I went to my room to change. I put on a tank top and black pants I could move around in easily.

"Are you ready?"

"If necessary." I pulled up my hair.

"Come on, let's go." He picked me up and took me to the training area. There were dodge balls, weights, punching bags, weapons, and other workout gear. "We should begin with a warm up for a few minutes. Watch me and do what I do." He started with stretching his arms and I copied his movements.

"Now, punch me." He held up his hands.

"What?" I thought I had misunderstood.

"Punch me."

"No." I backed away from him.

"Why not?"

"As soon as I throw a punch, you're going to trip me and make me fall to the ground."

"No, I'm not."

"I don't believe you."

"No, I promise. I'll stop the punch but I won't make you fall."

"What are you going to do?"

"I'm going to show you how to block a punch and defend yourself." He got back into position. "Come on, now. Hit me with your best shot."

I steadied myself and threw a punch at him. He caught my fist and pulled me into his arms.

"I forgot to mention I also wanted you in my arms." He kissed my cheek several times.

"Stop it. That's cheating!" I pushed his face away. "Do you do that with all your students?"

"Definitely not. Okay, next, if you aren't as strong or as big as your opponent, there are moves which will use their size or weight against them."

He showed me some of those types of moves until Lowell arrived, followed by Caedmon and Eros, and a few others. I expected jokes from Caedmon and Eros, but they seemed to be impressed I was there, and encouraged me the whole time. I was thankful they didn't laugh or make fun of me when I fell, and I fell a lot. Eros knocked my feet out from under me, Caedmon flipped me onto my back on the ground. Lowell knocked me backward, but caught me before I landed. That was one less bruise I'd endure in the morning. Pyre started to come over and check on me a couple of times, but he stopped himself. Mostly, he seemed to be proud of me. I thought I did fairly well for my first time even though I ended up exhausted. Pyre and I walked home after the training session ended.

"Will I be this sore after every training?"

"That depends on how many times you fall." He

laughed and held my hand. "I'm just kidding. Your muscles will adjust to it the more you train, so you won't be so sore. You honestly did well for your first day. You should've seen Caedmon and Eros their first time."

"That bad?"

"They spent more time on the ground than on their feet."

"But you were most likely harder on them, being guys and demon derivatives."

"Not at all, remember? I promised I wouldn't take it easy on you."

"After that workout, I'm famished. Are you hungry?"

"I'm starving. We'll get some raw meat and raw eggs since you're in training."

"What? No way! If that's the training menu, I quit!"

Pyre laughed at me, and I poked him in the stomach.

We walked along trying to decide where to eat and came across a small store. Pyre stopped to look in one of the windows.

"What are you looking at, Pyre?"

"I was admiring the little dragon figurine." He put an arm around my shoulders and pointed to something that resembled a bird on fire. "It's called a phoenix dragon. Are you familiar with the legend of the phoenix?"

"Of course, I'm familiar with it. I'm a phoenix."

"No, you're last name is Phoenix." He chortled at me.

"That still makes me a phoenix." I wrapped my

arms around his waist. He continued to stare at the phoenix dragon. "Do you want to buy it?"

"Nah, let's get you home, and I'll make us something to eat while you take a shower. You reek of sweat, and it's grossing me out."

"Come here and let me rub my nasty old sweat all over you, then." I raised my hand to swipe his face, but he dodged.

The next day Pyre went to hunt a demon with Lowell. I took the chance to sneak over to the store to buy the phoenix dragon. Luckily it was still there. I was on my way home with the statue when I spotted a black rose on the sidewalk.

*You don't scare me, Crystal.* When I got home, I quickly hid the statuette before Pyre returned.

"Sorry I was gone so long." Pyre said when he walked into the room.

"No problem. I understand that catching demons takes considerable time and effort."

"It's not that, but there was one... on second thought, I'd rather not say." He sat down next to me. "What did you do today?"

"Studied." I gestured to my book.

"Studied, huh?" I looked at him and nodded. "What else did you do?"

"I just sat here and studied. Honest."

"Are you sure about that?" He trapped me in his arms. He interrogated me with an examining expression.

"Of course I am."

"I still don't believe you." He switched tactics and kissed my ear, but I managed to retain a clear head, with difficulty.

"I can't imagine why."

"I sensed you when you left the apartment, and where you went. The general area anyway." He looked me directly in the eyes.

"I remember now. I did go out for a quick errand. I needed something for art class."

"What did you need?"

"Inspiration."

He merely stared at me, waiting for me to give him the answer he wanted. I stared back, trying to appear innocent.

"I guess that's all I'm going to get out of you." He sucked in his lips a moment before giving me his famous toothy grin. "I'll go poke around; check to see whether you bought me anything." He looked under the couch. "I see you didn't use the couch again. I'll investigate in your room." He disappeared. I heard him moving things around in my room, hunting for the dragon. After a few minutes, he came back with a defeated expression. "I didn't find anything so I guess you didn't buy something." He put his hands in his pockets. "What did you do though?"

"I didn't worry you, did I?"

"You went walking around town without protection, aware that Crystal is after you and demons are roaming around town." He leaned on the couch. "You didn't worry me at all."

I raised up on my knees and wrapped my arms around his neck. "I didn't mean to worry you." I kissed him passionately. "But I need to have a life. I'm not a child, and you aren't my excessively over-protective parent."

"Kira, you know it's not like that. But you must be careful right now. Very, extremely, excessively careful. I didn't know where you went or even that you planned on going anywhere. We talked about this at Christmas, and that was before Crystal initiated her plans. For all I knew, Crystal or some demon kidnapped you and took you away somewhere. I tell you when I'm going somewhere, where I'll be, and when I expect to be home. If something happens, someone should know how to find me. I don't do it because I'm obligated to, but as a courtesy so you won't worry. I would do it even if there was no known or present danger at all. Don't you understand? I'm terrified of something happening to you."

As he spoke, he grew more agitated. It was evident how frightened he was, which reminded me of Cel's concern for how Pyre would be affected if something happened to me. "Yes, I understand, and I'm sincerely sorry I worried you. It was only a short errand, and it was in town. I thought it would be safe, but you're right. We aren't certain what Crystal is planning, so we both need to be very, extremely, even excessively careful. I'll tell you the next time I plan to go somewhere." We held each other in a tight embrace until I reluctantly said, "I should get back to studying."

"Tests coming up?"

"Much too soon, and I'm not looking forward to them."

"You'll do great." He kissed me once more and walked to his room.

*At least he didn't find it.* I was on my way to the

237

kitchen for a drink when he came back to the living room.

"Find what?" He wrapped his arms around my waist.

"I forgot to block again." I grimaced and smacked my forehead.

"What didn't I find and where is it?"

"You're keeping me from studying. You don't want me to fail, do you?"

He tried relentlessly to get it out of me before Lowell came by to help me study. Pyre kept searching while Lowell and I studied, but he finally gave up on it.

I realized later that I forgot to tell him about the black rose. I was convinced it was Crystal trying to scare me, so I decided not to mention it. Pyre had agonized enough.

# Chapter 13
# Evil Pushes,
# Phoenix Pushes Back

We made it past the tests and I didn't experience another dream from Crystal. I figured she was saving her energy for the rebirth. The week before Valentine's Day came too fast for me. Even though I bought the phoenix dragon for Pyre, I wanted to do something more. I searched my brain long and hard for ideas and only ended up with a slight headache. I resolved not to think about it during classes.

"Students, since Valentine's Day is coming up, we're going to talk about Aphrodite, the Greek goddess of love."

*Joy. So much for not thinking about it during class.* As I took notes on the lecture, couples all around me flirted and giggled. *Make me sick.*

*What's making you sick?*

*These couples. They won't stop flirting.*

*Now aren't you glad I'm not that kind of flirter?*

*You're not a flirter at all.*

*Yes, I am.*

*You're idea of flirting is being rude.* There was a moment of silence.

*I didn't claim to be a good flirter.*

*And that's what I love about you.* I beamed to myself.

"Kira?" Luna whispered. I looked at her. "Where were you just now?"

"What do you mean?"

"You were making funny faces at your notebook."

"I was?" She nodded.

*Wow, Kira.* Pyre chortled.

*You be quiet.*

*Love you too. Lowell's chemistry class was canceled, so we're going to train. We'll be at Eira's if you need us. I'll take a break to walk you home after class.*

I started to object that he didn't need to, but I realized he'd only argue and worry. Class ended shortly after that. I tried to pack my stuff quickly to avoid the inevitable questions, but I wasn't fast enough.

"What are you and Pyre doing for Valentine's Day?" Luna inquired, keeping up with me as I attempted to escape.

"I don't know, he won't tell me."

"Is he the romantic type?" Stella asked.

"Not in the typical sense."

"What do you mean?" Luna asked. Lur caught up with us in the hall.

"It's hard to explain."

"It's okay to drop hints if there's something special you want." Stella suggested.

"You'll have to tell us all about it." Luna emitted a romantic sigh.

"Definitely don't skip the details." Lur said.

"I guess so. I'll see y'all later." *I can't wait to give him the dragon figurine. But I still need to come up with something else.* I waved at the girls and left the building.

Once outside, I walked past someone wearing a black ankle length hooded duster, but didn't pay attention to them otherwise.

"It's a beautiful campus." I stopped dead in my tracks at the sound of her voice. I slowly rotated to face Crystal. "I honestly thought the brochure I picked up at the airport was exaggerating but it is utterly beautiful. I can't wait to destroy it." She clapped her hands together like she was having fun, twirled around and stopped to face me. "You've been doing well." I noticed Lur, Luna, and Stella approaching us. "You're also trying to replace me." That made me laugh incredulously.

"No one could ever replace you, Crystal. You're way too crazy."

"That's true." She smiled the way she used to when we were friends.

"What's the point of all this, Crystal?"

"You'll see when the rebirth happens."

"When is the rebirth?"

"Soon." She waved and disappeared. Lur ran up to me.

"Kira, who was that? Where did she go? She just disappeared."

"That was the old friend Lowell mentioned. The three of you should stay together and stay away from Crystal. I'll explain more later, but right now I need to leave." I whirled around and walked away. *It won't be long now. I need to find Pyre and tell him.* I tried calling his name telepathically, but apparently he wasn't listening to my thoughts at the moment. *Of all the times for him not to be eavesdropping!* I started running to Eira's house.

*Please still be there.* When I got there, I ran inside without knocking.

"Hey, Kira, what's going on?" Eira asked as I entered the room.

"Where to begin. Is Pyre here?"

"He's in the back." Lowell's voice came from behind me. I turned to see Lowell without a shirt on, drenched in sweat. "We finished training a few minutes ago, but Pyre wanted to work out some more."

"Thanks." I ran to the back and heard Pyre grunting and yelling in the training room. I pounded loudly on the door and a sword flew through it, barely missing my head. Pyre opened the door.

"Kira? Oh my... Kira, are you hurt?" He rotated me all around, checking for injuries. "The sword didn't hit you, did it?"

"I'm okay." My voice was shaky and my whole body began to shake as well. "You missed."

"I'm so sorry." He laid his head on my shoulder. "I'll make it up to you. It'll never happen again, I promise. I'll take you to dinner."

"Pyre, I'm fine. Honestly I am. But why would you throw a sword at the door in the first place?"

"It was pure instinct. I was practicing my throwing and when I heard the knock, I threw toward the noise. We'll go out to dinner. I'll even dress up if you want. I swear I'll make it up to you somehow." He was obviously stricken about what nearly happened, cognizant that if I'd been hurt, it would have been by his hand. I didn't want him to agonize about being a danger to me again.

"You don't need to do that. I'm fine, you're fine,

it's all fine. Except the door."

"I know." He beamed with pride. I shook my head in exasperation, but then I realized he wasn't wearing a shirt. I stared appreciatively at his bare chest and his well-defined muscles. I didn't even mind the sweat.

*Fire demon or no fire demon, my boyfriend is ... it may be cliché, but he's definitely... hot.* I grew warm and fanned myself. I finally realized he was staring at me with a mischievous expression and a sly smile; the kind of smile that says the cat ate the canary, or in this case the fire demon who ate the cat that ate the canary. *Did he hear my thoughts?* "You'll take a shower first, right?"

"Of course. What brings you out here anyway? I told you I'd meet you when class ended." He kissed my forehead. "Your forehead is warm."

"Kira, are you feeling well?" Lowell asked, walking up to us.

"Yes. No. I don't know. I called for you, but you didn't answer. I ran all the way here." My head started to spin, so I held onto Pyre's arm.

"Why? What happened?"

"Class ended early. I walked outside, planning to call for you to tell you, but I was distracted with my thoughts and walked right past Crystal. She was there. Or maybe not, because when she left, she vanished. Poof. But Lur and the girls saw her too, so she was undoubtedly there." I started to ramble, my thoughts all in a jumble.

"Kira, take a deep breath and calm down, before you hyper-ventilate." Pyre rubbed my arms and back, trying to soothe me so I'd relax.

"Crystal said the rebirth will be soon, and she can't

wait to destroy the campus. I believe she's planning on the spring equinox. She accused me of replacing her with new friends. What if she does something to them? Lowell you need to watch out for Lur, all three of them. Promise me."

"I promise, Kit. Both of us will make certain nothing happens to them or to you."

Pyre pulled me into his arms and rubbed my back, still trying to get me to calm down. I abruptly felt fatigued and rested my head on Pyre's shoulder.

"Kira, you're obviously not well. You're forehead has gotten warmer too."

"The room is just warm. It got to me somewhat." I rubbed my eyes.

"Do you suppose it was the run from campus, or the adrenaline rush?" Lowell asked Pyre.

"Either that or something that witch has done. Kira gets unexplainably drained at random times when she was fully alert and energetic moments before. It's usually followed by one of those nightmares."

"So she might have one tonight? We need to figure out what's happening and how to handle it. I'll check with Vitas and come by later to tell you whether he discovered anything."

"Kira, how about I take you home? I'll cook dinner tonight instead. We'll go out some other night."

"Yes, please." I became aware that Lowell held onto my arms. "What're you doing?"

"He's preventing you from falling while I put on my shirt." Pyre explained while pulling his shirt on over his head.

"I'm not going to fall."

"Why are you leaning on me then?" Lowell asked. My eyes slowly traveled up to his face.

"I am?" He nodded and checked my forehead.

"You're not merely warm, you have a slight fever."

"Maybe I should take you to a doctor." Pyre clutched my hands.

"No, I'll be fine." I held my arms out to him. "Please, let's go home, and I'll let you cook dinner for me."

"Agreed, but if your forehead gets any warmer, I'm taking you to a hospital so you won't collapse."

"Whatever you say." Pyre wrapped his arms around me, looked over at Lowell and shrugged.

"You definitely have a fever or you wouldn't say that to me." He picked me up into his arms.

"Hmmm. You smell... hot." When we arrived at our apartment, he set me on the couch.

"I'm going to take a shower. Do not, get up from the couch under any circumstances."

"Yes, dear." He kissed my forehead to check my temperature, the way my mother used to do. He frowned at how warm I felt and left the room. He came back with some iced tea and a cold cloth and went to shower.

*I wonder why I'm so exhausted.*

*I don't know but you better be okay.*

*I'm okay. I only exerted myself more than I realized.*

*That better be the reason.*

*I'm sure it is. I hope Lowell finds out something.* I laid my head on the armrest and stared at the ceiling. *I wish I wasn't so drained. I don't want to fall asleep in case I do have another nightmare.* I felt fingers running through my hair. I arched my back to look at him.

"Try to clear your mind and focus on resting while I cook dinner." He checked my forehead again and went to the kitchen.

"What are you cooking?"

He stopped at the door and turned to look at me, smiling in his familiar way. "I haven't decided yet, but whatever it is, it will most definitely be... hot." I raised my head to glare and stuck my tongue out at him. "And by the way, it won't be feline. No cats in my diet." I hid my face behind a couch pillow and heard a satisfied guffaw from the kitchen. I ended up dozing off after a few minutes.

The dream I had was unlike the previous ones. I still reclined on the couch in the living room of our apartment. Vines appeared to grow all over the ceiling. The lights were off, which made the room appear even creepier.

"Kira, you need to give up. You will be much happier if you just give up." I heard Crystal's voice behind me. "These dream visits are increasingly tiring."

"You can stop the dream visits any time. Why are they so far apart anyway?" I responded while sitting upright.

"I must be meticulous and perform the sacrifices at precisely the right time. They are so exhausting I need to gather my strength between each one. They're also designed to remind you that I'm watching you. I'm going to all this effort for you, and you simply don't appreciate it." She walked around to stand in front of me. She held a cup of tea in her hand. "But don't worry about me. I'll be fine. I want to talk about this Pyre guy." She looked toward the kitchen door. My eyes followed her gaze to where Pyre stood in the kitchen.

"What about him?" Vines grew all over the couch and dirt formed around my feet. I had the impression that the earth wanted to swallow me. Branches reached for me and vines clawed at my arms and legs.

"You never were the type for a boyfriend. Why the change?"

"People change all the time. You're living proof of that." She put her tea on the table in front of me.

"Yes, but no one changes like you. Do you remember how you used to wear bright colors like me but switched to black and nothing else until you chose more earthy colors? When you change, you change more than your clothes or your style. You change intrinsically and in a dissimilar way from ordinary humans, Kira, because you are indisputably not a normal human. You are special and we need to show the world how special you are." I started to get irritated.

"I don't want to show the world how special I am, whatever that means. I am content with my life. I'm happy with Pyre and my new friends." The vines embraced me instead of pulling me down and I didn't need to struggle against the tug of the earth anymore. I also didn't feel threatened any longer. "You are no longer a friend of mine. These dream visits will stop now." As I stood up to face Crystal, flowers bloomed on the vines.

"Kira —"

"I said now!" The whole room shook, and the petals fell off the flowers and rained down upon us. My heart pounded forcefully in my chest and I sat back down. *D-did*

*I do that?* I looked at Crystal, confused by what happened. She had a creepy smile on her face immediately before she vanished. Pyre walked into the room, walking through her as her image faded and disappeared.

When I woke up, I was sitting on the couch. All the petals from the dream were laying all over the floor. Pyre stood in the middle of the room staring at the petals in complete shock.

"Pyre, you didn't by any chance do this, did you?"

"No, I'm pretty sure you did, and we need to figure out how." I glanced at the ceiling and realized the vines were still there. Crystal's cup of tea remained on the table, which meant she had definitely been there. If only I could figure out how to stop her from coming back.

# Chapter 14
# Special Days
# Bring Special Dreams

I sat on my bed and stared blankly at the comforter while hugging my knees to my chest. The events of the previous night tumbled through my mind. Pyre and I cleaned up the petals from the dream, and afterwards neither of us wanted to eat. We sat in the living room in silence, at separate ends of the couch, each of us lost in our own thoughts. Pyre eventually told me I should try to take a nap. I chose not to argue and simply nodded. He walked with me to my room and checked the closet and window. He offered to stay with me until I dozed off, but I told him it wasn't necessary. He started to say something but stopped himself. I laid there silently and watched him leave the room.

Sleep eluded me during the night. I was too afraid I'd have more dreams that would come to life. At least the fever broke after I had the dream in the living room. I heard the front door open. I got up and opened my door enough to listen to the conversation in the living room.

"How is she?" Lowell asked.

"She's extremely shaken. She didn't sleep at all last night. Neither did I to be honest. I'm scared, Lowell. I'm afraid I'm losing her to all of this, whatever it is."

"You won't, I promise you that. Were you checking up on her all night?"

"No, her mind did that for me."

I walked out into the hall to see them.

"How is Kira taking all of this?" Lowell studied the vines.

"How are you taking all of this?" Pyre turned to me and held out his hand.

"Not well." I walked over to Pyre and leaned against him. "Of course you're aware of that with how my mind kept racing last night." Pyre rubbed the back of my head. "Did I keep you awake?"

"No, I couldn't sleep either. I was extremely worried about you last night."

"What's happening to me? What if I'm the one creating the ice, the dirt, the tornado, or the vines?" Tears formed in my eyes as I spoke.

"What if it is you?" Pyre asked. "Wouldn't that be reassuring since it would mean Crystal isn't causing those things."

"Pyre, I'm attacking myself if that's the case."

"You just don't know how to control it yet. You need practice and—" He stopped when he realized he had become agitated and inhaled slowly. "Whether it's you or Crystal, we'll get through this together."

"Whether it's me or what Crystal is doing to me, what am I becoming? She keeps talking about a rebirth, and a transformation. It's obvious the rebirth is meant for me, and she's trying to change me into something that would potentially do these things. She's carrying on, moving forward, and apparently succeeding; and we still don't have any information about what's happening or how to stop her. It's not a mere growing phase, or something I can't control. People are dying, Pyre." I looked from Pyre to Lowell, who was deep in thought, trying to figure out how to get to the vines without a ladder.

"Whatever it is, we'll figure out what to do about it, reverse it. We will stop Crystal, I promise."

"How do we do that? We can't bring back the people who died." I watched Lowell climb on top of the couch to reach the ceiling.

"We'll... we would... Lowell any ideas?" Lowell looked down at us with a confused expression.

"What?" Lowell asked.

"Were you even listening?" Pyre asked.

"No, I stopped listening when you started ignoring me." Lowell returned his focus to the ceiling. I buried my face in Pyre's chest.

"If Kira is the one making all of this happen, we need to figure out how to help her to control it. If she's right, and Crystal's trying to change her into something else, it's imperative we stop her. We need to do something soon if Crystal's plans do involve the spring equinox, and we don't even know where to begin." He had grown agitated again and took several deep breaths to calm himself. "Whatever it is, we'll need to figure it out when she's awake."

"How are we supposed to do that when it only happens in her sleep?" Lowell asked. I struggled to suppress the nervous giggles which sprouted in my chest.

"That's what I need your help figuring out, Einstein. Did Vitas learn anything?"

"No, but he said he would keep trying. He uncovered some news though."

"I won't like this, will I?" I asked him apprehensively.

"There was a story about an airplane. It lost cabin pressure, and no one has determined why."

"Where did it crash?" I gripped onto Pyre's hand as I asked and anxiously awaited the answer.

"Here's the crazy part. It didn't. The plane arrived on time at its scheduled destination. Nobody onboard."

"No one? Not even a pilot?" Pyre asked incredulously.

"None. I should talk to Vitas again, now that the situation has changed."

"If it's Kira doing this, I don't want to bring him into it."

"Pyre, if it is Kira, Vitas is searching for the wrong solution."

They continued to argue, but I stopped listening. I finally decided I didn't want to remain in the room any longer and pulled away from Pyre.

"I'm going back to my room."

"I'll be right here if you need anything." Pyre rubbed my face. He seemed like he wanted to say more, or to kiss me to make it all go away, but I needed to be alone.

"Thanks, Pyre, and you too, Lowell." I couldn't watch them looking nervously at each other any longer, knowing it was about me. Even they were distressed by my latent metamorphosis. What if it was so terrible they had to... handle it. Surely Vitas wouldn't make them do it. He'd send someone else. If that happened, Pyre, and possibly Lowell, would undoubtedly kill Crystal, and whoever Vitas sent for me. They might even try to kill

Vitas himself. They'd be in a whole world of trouble, and then what would happen to them?

*I can't let that happen to them, and I can't think that way. I must stop Crystal or learn to control this somehow. That won't happen if I simply sit on my bed. Still, I need to stop brooding about it for now and give my mind a break. I need a distraction.* As if on cue, there was a knock on my door.

"Come in." Eira tentatively poked her head around the door.

"Kira, can I talk to you for a minute? That is, if you're up to it. Pyre said you had a rough night."

"Sure. I was thinking I need a distraction and homework would not be possible at the moment. What do you want to talk about?"

"I wondered if you might give me some advice."

"On what?"

"On what I should get Eros for Valentine's Day." I stared at her for a minute.

"Why ask me?"

"You've hung out with the guys and I thought he might've mentioned something to you about it."

"Not a word."

"Honestly? You'd tell me, right?" I nodded. "I hope he hasn't forgotten."

"Why don't you ask Gabby? She is his sister after all."

"I did, and she told me to make him take me to dinner and buy me flowers."

"That's no help. What about Laya? She's dating Caedmon, and he hangs out with Eros."

"She said they fight more than they talk."

"I can see that."

"Can you please help me?" She pouted, sounding desperate.

"What does he like?"

"He likes to fight."

"Besides that. He made me that beautiful frame for my birthday. Is he creative?"

"He's always making me stuff. He makes me lots of little boxes to put my jewelry in and he made a gorgeous trunk to hold the boxes."

"You could get him some tools to work with since he likes to carve things."

"I did that for Christmas." She waited expectantly as I scratched the back of my head and thought.

"Tell me about the day you met."

"Will it help?"

"It's worth a try." We sat down on the bed.

"It was in the middle of March last year. I moved here to keep an eye on Pyre for my parents. Pyre was angry, told me to go away, that he didn't need a babysitter. I wanted to stay to try and get closer to him. After a few days he introduced me to Lowell. I was drawn automatically to him, but the attraction wasn't mutual. The next day Lowell brought Caedmon and Eros by to meet me. Eros tried flirting with me, but I didn't like it. Finally I exploded and yelled at him to leave me alone. I learned later I had unintentionally hurt him.

"The next day, Eros stopped by and gave me the first box. He apologized and asked if we could be friends. I agreed and invited him inside to visit and get to know each other. We sat there and talked for hours. I asked him to stay for dinner. I planned to cook for him but we ended up cooking together instead. We cooked alfredo pasta with basal leaves and garlic bread. It was so delicious. We started dating after that." Eira's face lit up with the biggest and brightest smile as she spoke.

"That's what you should give him."

"What?" She was completely confused.

"Make the alfredo pasta and garlic bread, and give him that smile." Eira blushed as I continued. "Eros likes to carve things which means he pays close attention to details. Which also means he appreciates every little thing you do. I'll bet he also remembers every detail of that night, so you both share that vivid memory. He'll be gratified that you remember it as well as he does. Show him how much you appreciate him and remind him about how you feel about each other." She thanked me and we subsequently decided to go outside for some fresh air. *Now if I could work the same magic on myself. What should I do?*

*About what?* Pyre asked.

*There's something I want to do but I'm not sure what I'm going to do about it.*

*What is it?*

*Something important to me.*

*Which is?*

*She doesn't know what to get you for Valentine's Day.* Lowell interjected. I closed my eyes in embarrassment.

*Kira, is that true? You don't need to get me anything.*

*But I want to do something.* He appeared at my

side.

"Having you and your love is all I want and need." He rubbed my back. "Why are you so tense about it?"

"I've never celebrated Valentine's Day." I stared at the fountain in the yard.

"You've never had a boyfriend for Valentine's Day."

"I've also never had pleasant experiences on that day. I got picked on during my freshman year of high school because I didn't have a date for the Valentine's Day dance. I even punched a guy in the stomach before the day ended." Pyre beamed proudly at me. "I don't understand why we celebrate it as a day for love. It suggests that the rest of the days of the year aren't as important. Why should we only celebrate our love for each other one day out of the year when there are 365 days in a year for us to love each other?"

I looked up at Pyre's smiling face. He rubbed my face as I blushed and wrapped his arms around me. "You are most likely the only girl who has ever thought of it that way. I have an idea. How about we don't celebrate Valentine's Day?"

"What?" I felt relieved, but also moderately concerned. "What were you planning for Valentine's Day?"

"I hadn't quite figured it out yet. I do know I wanted it to be just you and me. We were going to enjoy our privacy and spend the day together."

"You didn't plan anything else?" He shook his head. "Promise?"

"Promise." He held me close and kissed the tip of

my nose.

"Let's do that, because I do want to celebrate, this being our first year together. But let's make it about us, and about how we feel for each other; not about a day on the calendar. I do have something I want to give you, and I don't want to wait. I'll be right back." I ran into my room, got the box, and ran back outside to Pyre.

"I told you that you don't need to get me a present."

"Yes, but I wanted to give you something." I held out the box.

"It's not a box of chocolates, is it?"

"No, silly." He opened the box and uncovered the dragon figurine.

"Kira, this is..." He pulled it out of the box.

"The same dragon you saw at the store the other day." He twirled the dragon around in his hand, and then spun me around, hugging me tight.

"I love it, thank you."

"You're welcome." He pulled out of the hug.

"I'm going to make you a romantic dinner tonight. Italiano?"

"I'll light some candles?"

"You can pick out any movie you want to watch."

"Or even just talking. Save the troubles for tomorrow."

"Sounds like heaven to me." He rubbed my back and pulled me in for a kiss. I heard someone giggling behind me. "Beat it, Wolf." Pyre mumbled while breaking off the kiss.

"I'm not the one who was giggling." Lowell gestured with his head toward Eira.

"What? I can't help it." She tried to sound innocent.

"You two need to get lost." Pyre said.

"I need to get ready for work." I laughed.

"You can call out if you want." Pyre rubbed my arms, imploring with his eyes.

"No, I need to get out of the apartment and away from the mess in the living room."

I was thankful work went well. I didn't fall or slip once, and my customers were all pleasant. When my shift ended, I walked outside to meet Pyre. He stood there holding a single red rose.

"Hello, my lovely lady."

"Hello yourself, but I shouldn't be seen speaking to you."

"Why not?" Pyre looked confused.

"I'm spoken for, and my boyfriend wouldn't like it."

"Oh, I see. Perhaps I could fight him for you."

"No, I think not."

"And why is that?"

"My boyfriend is strong and powerful. You could not defeat him."

"Perhaps I should try anyway. Your love would be worth the risk."

"But you see, it isn't simply that I'm spoken for, but that my love belongs to him. Even if you managed to defeat him, my love would not be yours."

"I could try to win you over."

"No, it simply wouldn't work. My love is not a prize to be won. It is only mine to give, and I have given it to another."

"In that case, would you grant me a kiss, a token to remember you by as I wile away my lonely hours."

"While I may sympathize with your plight, my kisses are for my love alone."

"And if I tried to give you a kiss instead?"

"That would require permission, which I do not grant. The consequences would be severe."

"This boyfriend of yours is quite a fortunate man."

"I feel I am the fortunate one."

"Then perchance you might favor this lonely fellow with..." Pyre paused to push a button on a music player he brought with him. "One slow dance." He bowed slightly and held his hand out to me as he'd done on New Year's Eve.

"I'm terrible at slow dances, but my boyfriend did teach me. One dance would be permissible." I placed my hand in his, and he twirled me once and pulled me close. We stared into each other's eyes as we moved to the music. We might have been in any other place in any other time. For that moment, there was only the two of us, and our love for each other. When the song ended, we kissed each other, softly and sweetly. I breathed in his subtle scent that invariably soothed me and made me feel like I was home.

"My Kira."

"I love you, Pyre."

"I love you. Let's go home."

When I walked in the door of the apartment, I was amazed at how wonderful the place looked. Pyre strung white lights along the ceiling to give the room a subtle glow. Soft music played in the background. The table was set beautifully with a white cover and matching cloth napkins, and full place settings and glassware. In the center of the table was a bouquet of lavender, rosemary and white roses, with two lavender candles in silver holders on each side. More candles were placed in various niches around the room. Small flames appeared on his hand as he walked around the room lighting the candles. When he pulled out my chair for me, I walked over to him. I touched my palm to his cheek and kissed him lightly before taking my seat.

"I'm surprised you did all this. The apartment is beautiful. Whatever you're cooking smells delicious. But didn't we say we weren't celebrating Valentine's Day?"

"This isn't for Valentine's Day. This is our day, to celebrate us and our love for each other, as we agreed. I hope you're hungry."

"I'm starving."

"Eccelente! Because tonight, as I feast my eyes on my lovely lady, we will be feasting on a full course of Italian cuisine, or cucina italiana."

"When you decide to be romantic, you pull out all the stops, don't you?"

"You inspire me." He bowed at the hip and raised my hand to his lips. I raised my face to his, in a silent request. He responded by kissing me so deeply, I grew light-headed, and was fortunate to be sitting. "We begin our meal with the antipasto, which is a caprese salad of tomato and mozzarella slices, with basil, drizzled lightly with olive oil and balsamic dressing, served with warm fresh bread."

The appetizer was so mouth-watering, I could have dined on that alone. But Pyre wasn't finished.

"The primo, our first course, is tagliolini con tartufo or tagliolini pasta with truffles and a butter and parmigiano cheese sauce."

I was hesitant about the truffles, since I hadn't eaten them before, but the pasta dish was superb. My hunger became satiated by that time, which was unfortunate, since there was more to come.

"The secondo, our second course, is spezzatino di manzo, basically a beef stew. This is served with the contorno, a vegetable side dish. Tonight's contorno is patate al forno, baked potatoes, with a garnish of grilled red peppers and black olives."

It looked too pretty to eat, but all the food was so delectable.

"Pyre, this meal was exceptional. I am thoroughly impressed with what a marvelous cook you are. Thank you for all of this."

"The meal isn't over yet."

"No? Pyre, honey, I'm so full, I can't eat anymore."

"A meal like this cannot end without the final course, the dolce. We conclude our meal with a wonderful dessert, tiramisu."

"But you can't eat dessert."

"That just means I can watch you enjoy it."

"Uh, no. I don't think so."

"Why not?"

"You are not going to sit there and watch me eat. I would be too self-conscious."

"I won't watch you eat in that case; instead, give me just one bite." He picked up a spoon and dipped a small bite of the creamy dessert. He held the spoon up in front of my mouth and I took the bite. When I tasted the light coffee dessert, I closed my eyes and savored it fully.

"Oh, my gosh, where has this been all my life?"

"You've never eaten tiramisu before tonight?"

"No, never. And you made the dessert, this whole meal, yourself?"

"Yes, for my Kira."

"You are a true romantic, much more than you ever admit to anyone."

"It's a secret. Don't tell anyone."

"Are you kidding? If I tell the other girls, I'll be forced to fight them in the yard every day to keep them away from you." He laughed.

"Somehow I doubt that. Are you finished eating?"

"Yes, I am so finished. I may not be able to eat again for a week. But everything was exquisite. You must have worked particularly hard on this dinner. Thank you so much for the wonderful meal."

"While I put everything away, why don't you pick out the movie you want to watch?"

"I could help you."

"No, I've got this. Go pick our movie, as sappy as you want." He flashed me his familiar smile.

I browsed through movies, but had a hard time deciding. *Should I choose the vampire-loves-human movie? No, that's too close to home. Maybe a romantic drama? No, those always make me cry. A romantic comedy? That has potential.* I came across "Grumpy Old Men." *No, that's too close to Pyre.* We needed a movie with romance, humor and action all in one. One of my favorite movies fit all three, "Romancing the Stone." We snuggled up on the couch to watch the movie. We laughed and kissed, and held each other close. At some point, the movie ended, the candles burned themselves out, and Pyre and I fell fast asleep.

While I slept in his arms, I had the most wonderful dream. I dreamed of finishing college, Pyre asking me to marry him, and a small trail that led to a cabin in the mountains. I saw Pyre walk up to the cabin door, and a woman, a slightly older version of myself, open the door for him, throwing her arms around him and kissing him. Pyre, looking slightly older himself, twirled her around, as he held her close to his heart. The woman gazed into his eyes and said one word, "Still?" Pyre answered her, "Always." Children ran out of the cabin and around the couple, a little boy and a little girl, looking so much alike. Pyre put the older me down and entered the cabin, followed by the two children.

The woman looked toward the trees where I was hidden. She walked over to me and said, "You look as young as I still feel. Pyre gave that to us, that openness, that realization of who we could be, and who we are. And I think we gave the same to him. He says I saved him, but in reality, we saved each other. Both of you are facing some critical times ahead. You worry about the future and what it holds, and about facing the coming dangers. I won't lie to you — it'll be hard, and scary. But when the time comes, you'll know what to do, and you'll face it head on. It's natural to be afraid, but let that fear give you strength. Let that strength give you hope. Let that hope shine the light in the darkness to show you the way. You were right when you said you're stronger together. In the end, love does indeed conquer all. Evil cannot truly love, or be loyal, or have faith and hope. Evil will perpetually fail when love stands its ground."

"I have buckets of questions. How do I stop Crystal? How can Pyre and I deal with the difference in aging? What will happen to Pyre, when...?"

"Well, here I am and here's what I know. Follow your heart and your instincts. Love when you can, and fight when you must, but stand together and never give up, not to the enemy, and not on each other. Crystal wants to change you into something evil. She can't change you into anything if it's not in you. Everything changes, and there's no denying that." The older me in my dream walked back toward the cabin, still speaking as she went. "But change isn't always bad, as long as you hold onto who you truly are, and hold onto each other. Dig deep within; everything you need exists within you. Keep taking it all one day at a time. When the time comes, don't be afraid to open the door, just make sure you choose the right one." And with that, she opened the door and went inside the cabin, shutting the door behind her.

The sound of the door shutting behind the Kira in my dream caused me to wake up instantly. I sat up and searched all around the room. Everything appeared exactly as it had when we started the movie. I glanced over at Pyre. He was wide awake and looking all around too.

"Pyre, are you okay?"

"I think so. I had a bizarre dream; a good dream, but surreal."

"So did I. What was your dream?"

"It was everything I've ever wanted and thought I would never attain until I met you."

"A cabin in the mountains?"

"Both of us, together, somewhat older." He looked at me and sounded as confused as I was.

"Children following you inside the cabin. Pyre, we dreamt the same dream. How did we dream the same dream?"

"It must be my telepathy. What does it mean?" He seemed moderately alarmed and uncertain about my reaction.

"I think it means we're going to be okay, we just have loads to do to get there, one day at a time. For now, tonight, and to be ready for whatever lies ahead, we need to sleep. As for me, tomorrow is another day at work."

# Chapter 15
# Demons at Work,
# Play and School

Time flew by, even with taking things one day at a time. March roared in like a lion. The wind seemed to blow harder with each passing day. According to the saying, the month should go out like a lamb. I only hoped I wasn't the lamb, being led to the sacrifice. We were convinced the rebirth intended to change me into something evil, and that it would occur on or about the spring equinox. That day approached with resolute speed. The stress and strain wore heavily on all of us as we mentally marked off the days. Pyre and I — along with Vitas, our friends, and Pyre's parents — tried desperately to come up with ideas and answers. What precisely were Crystal's plans? Where and how did she aim to put them in motion? What should we do to stop her? Everything we came up with only added more questions, with no solutions. I continued to train with Pyre and the boys. I understood that physical skill and strength would not measure up to her power for long, but hopefully it would hinder her enough to give us the chance to impede her final goal. Crystal hadn't contacted me again since she appeared in my living room. I hoped I behaved strong and confident enough that she had decided to let it go, but I realized deep down it was a fanciful notion. School and work offered welcome distractions from the stress and worry, if only temporarily. As we waited and watched with caution, life relentlessly marched onward.

"Have a pleasant day." Pyre encouraged me as he dropped me off at work.

"I'll try. No, scratch that, I will." I kissed his cheek and entered the building.

"Hello, Kira. Would you cut up some lemons and then restock the salad bar?" Franq said.

I nodded, clocked in and got right to work. The other servers arrived and helped with other tasks. The hostess assigned me a small section since I was still fairly new. Trina had car trouble, so we were slightly short-handed. We started getting busy and my section filled quickly. Clio approached me with a question as I carried food to one of my tables.

"Kira, can you pick up some additional tables?"

"No problem, which ones?" *I'm too busy as it is.*

"The tables in the last section."

"You don't mean all of them, do you?"

"Of course. All the tables in the section are now filled." She walked away.

*What I wouldn't give to be a demon right now.*

I ran the food to my tables and swiftly brought biscuits and apple butter to the other tables. After getting their drink and food orders, I rushed to put them into the computer. Wynne walked up behind me as I was making the drinks.

"Kira, can you help me? I need three sweet teas."

"Wynne, I'm kind of busy."

"Thanks, Kira." She had already walked away.

*I'm not making them.* I finished making my drinks and carried them to my customers. I rushed to the back when my name was called.

"Kira, where are my drinks?" Wynne stepped in front of me, but I walked around her.

"I didn't make them. I'm too busy to help you right now."

"We have a little thing here called team work. I guess people from Nashville don't practice it."

I stopped and turned to her. "Team work is when two people help each other. It is not when one person refuses to help others, but tells others to do something and expects them to do it no matter how busy they are. Now if you'll excuse me, one of my orders is sitting in the window." I walked into the kitchen and put my food on a tray.

"Kira, do you need help?" Franq asked.

"Please. I'd appreciate some help."

"You and I will split the section. I'll take the six top and four top. You can handle the two booths."

"That works. Thanks." I said as I lifted the tray.

With his help, the balance of the night went much smoother. I ended up making excellent money in tips.

Franq assigned side work, and I was stuck doing the dishes with Wynne. I washed the dishes while Wynne simply stood there.

"You know, Wynne, if you'd put the dishes away we'd get done faster." I said, putting more dishes in the machine.

"I don't do dishes." She leaned on the counter and filed her nails.

"I'm sure Franq won't mind staying until eleven o'clock."

"Why would I want to stay until eleven o'clock?" Franq walked up behind her.

"Kira's slacking on the dishes." Wynne said as she picked up some dishes.

"Then why is she soaking wet while you're dry as a bone?"

"I can fix that." I pointed the hose at her.

"Don't you dare." She walked around the wall to put the dishes away.

"Has she always been like that?" I asked Franq.

"No, when she first began working here, she was friendly and helpful. The owners loved her. Now we can't wait for the day she quits or gets fired."

"Do the owners realize how she acts?"

"No, whenever they come by she's an absolute angel."

"Of course she is." I sent the last of the dishes through the machine.

"Here let me help you." Franq walked over and helped me put the remaining dishes away.

"Are you already done?" Wynne walked back into the dish pit.

"We wouldn't want you to break a nail." I walked up front with Franq where the others were rolling silverware.

"Are the dishes done?" Dustin inquired.

"They are. I helped Kira finish them since Miss Wynne couldn't be bothered to lift a plate." Franq crossed his arms.

"Wynne should be the one to take out the trash in that case." Dustin stared at her insistently.

"I'm not doing it by myself." Wynne crossed her arms. "Kira's helping me."

I rolled my eyes. "Fine, but you're carrying the trash can." I walked back to the kitchen and waited by the back door. Wynne made faces at the trash and tried to keep it as far from her as possible.

"This is so gross." I watched her run to the dumpster with the trash. As soon as she tried to put it in the dumpster, the bag broke and spilled all over the place. I got the shovel and took it to her. "What am I supposed to do with that?"

"Shovel the trash into the dumpster." I pushed the shovel into her hand.

"Man, humans are totally disgusting." She scooped the trash and put it in the dumpster.

"It's not that bad."

"No, it's terrible. Where I come from used to be beautiful. Green trees, clear blue rivers, clean air. I could fly anywhere I wanted to, carefree and unrestricted."

*Fly? Don't tell me.* I rubbed my forehead.

"Once humans came in and built their factories, the air was so polluted, I couldn't breathe. Now I'm stuck here serving the vile creatures."

"If you don't like them, why are you waiting on them?" I stared desperately at the door.

"My mother thought it would be beneficial for me to work like a human so I can understand them. She wants me to learn more tolerance." She made an annoyed face and put an arm around my shoulder. "It's tough being a demon these days. Don't you think so?"

"Well, I..."

"I mean demons used to be on top. Now some are going extinct. And some are even breeding with humans. Can you imagine? How I miss the days when I could fly around without a care in the world." She floated off the ground as she raised her face to the sky. "Don't you?"

"I can't fly." I inched closer to the door.

"You must crave to swim in clean rivers."

"Not much of a swimmer."

"You miss the green earth then." She stared at me as if beginning to comprehend something.

"I haven't seen it any greener than it is in the spring or summer."

"Are you fire?" She put her feet back on the ground and slowly approached me.

"Not exactly."

"If you're not fire, earth, water, or wind, what kind of demon are you?" Her voice started to sound shrill.

"I'm... um..." My back hit the wall.

"You aren't telling me... are you human?" Her nails grew into claws.

"I..." I clutched the handle on the door. I barely managed to throw the door open and get inside before she lunged at me. I ran to the front to find everyone still rolling silverware. Dustin and Franq had transformed into demons. Dustin had become taller and more muscular with big claws and fur. Franq had grown scales, a long neck and black lines on his cheeks.

"Kira, you shouldn't run in here. It's too slippery." Franq remarked reproachfully and stuck his forked tongue out like a typical snake would, scenting the air. His reptilian eyes focused on me as he spoke.

271

"I... um..." I forced myself not to scream. *Did he have to be a snake?*

"Is something amiss, Kira?" Dustin walked up to me.

*Amiss? Is he kidding?* "I... just wanted... to tell you... I quit."

"Why?" Dustin sounded concerned.

"Where are you, you filthy little human scum?!" Wynne screamed from the kitchen.

"Health reasons." I replied.

"There you are." I spun around to see Wynne stalking closer to me. Her claws had become talons, and she had grown a beak. "You vile, home destroying, nature killing—" She raised her arm but Dustin got between us.

"What's going on, Wynne?"

"She's human!" Wynne screeched, pointing at me. The others whispered around us and I observed some of them now had pointed ears and fangs.

*They're all demons. Why did Pyre have to be right about this place?*

"You're only now figuring that out, Wynne?" Dustin crossed his arms.

"You were aware she's a human?" She kept trying to get past him. "You knew, and you still hired her?"

"Of course we knew. We wanted to see how differently humans work compared to demons; a sort of experiment to make things interesting. But we couldn't risk it with just any human and jeopardize our secret getting out around town. Since Kira knows about demons, she was a safe choice." Franq explained.

*They're worried about being safe? From a human?*

*How are they aware that I know about demons? On second thought, never mind.*

"And to our surprise," Ike walked into the room. "She's a better worker than half of you put together." As he spoke, I noticed he had also grown fangs; dangerously sharp fangs.

"She will never be a better worker than me." Wynne's voice sounded like nails on a chalkboard.

"She already is. Kira, I hope you'll reconsider quitting." Dustin's voice showed his annoyance with her.

"Yea, we enjoy having you here. It's entertaining working with a clumsy human." Franq nudged my shoulder, and I struggled not to flinch.

"You sincerely want me to stay?" I was relieved they didn't want me on the menu.

"Only if you want to stay." Dustin assured me.

"I don't know."

"I personally guarantee your safety. We do like you. You're respectful and a hard worker. Besides we don't want Vitas's boys coming after us. We're peaceable demons here. Most of us anyway." Ike said.

"No!" Wynne screeched. "I will not continue to work with her!" She lunged at me. Before I could blink, her head rolled past me.

"I'm so glad we're finally rid of her." Franq licked the blood off his hand.

"You're cleaning up this mess." Ike said as he walked back to the office.

"Kira, everything is done for the night. Shall we see you tomorrow?" Dustin eyed me hopefully.

I thought about it for a moment. *I've been weird my*

*whole life. Why should I imagine my first job would be anything close to conventional? My boyfriend and best friend are demons. What do I have to lose? Besides my head that is.* Still, they all seemed to like me. I made up my mind, while I still had the option, as well as the ability. "I'll be here." I clocked out and went outside to meet Pyre. *Pyre. He's not going to like this.*

"There's my angel. How was work?"

"I'll tell you later."

"Anything interesting happen?"

"A ton." I walked down the sidewalk, eager to get away from the restaurant.

"What's that supposed to mean?"

"Well..." I stopped to contemplate for a minute. *If I tell him everything, he won't let me work here anymore.*

"What happened?" He stepped in front of me.

*Forgot to block him. Again.*

"Indeed, you did. Now explain what happened."

"You won't like it." I spied Franq and the girls coming out of the restaurant, still in their demon forms.

"What won't I like?"

"Hey, Pyre, you've got quite the girlfriend." Franq walked by him like it was nothing unusual. Pyre stared at him and the girls as they all left.

"Good night, Kira. Can't wait to see what tomorrow holds. We're all glad you decided to stay." Dustin walked up behind Pyre.

"You're..." Pyre was flabbergasted and clearly angry. "You're a demon. Kira, how long have you known the manager was a demon?"

"I only found out tonight." I took hold of his hand.

"We need to talk. Wait a minute! He said you decided to stay. You didn't quit?" Pyre pulled me away from Dustin.

"Ike guaranteed her safety, and so do I, so Kira would be safe with us. We all like her. We won't do anything to hurt her, and we'd protect her if anyone ever tried to bother her." Dustin asserted.

"Like I'm going to take your word for it." Pyre pulled me over to a bench. "Kira, I don't trust him."

"You don't trust anyone."

"I especially don't trust a bear demon."

"Why not?"

"Past experience."

I didn't ask any more questions. "All the employees aren't demons." I tried another angle.

"No, they are. You're the only human." Dustin instantly corrected me.

*You're not helping.* I squeezed my eyes shut for a moment.

"I don't want you working here anymore."

"Good thing you're not my boss."

"Kira, I'm serious."

"I am too. You can't control me and you can't keep me from working where I want to work."

"I can when I'm concerned about your safety, and we had a deal." He eyed Dustin, weighing the potential threat.

"Our deal was that I'd quit at the first sign of trouble. The staff being demons doesn't qualify. My boyfriend's a demon. My best friend's a demon. Most of my friends are demons. According to you demons are everywhere, so why wouldn't my coworkers be demons? I understand and appreciate your concern for my safety. I respect that, so here's my compromise. Let me work tomorrow." He started to object, but I pulled on his hand. "If something happens tomorrow, I'll quit. If nothing out of the ordinary occurs, I'll continue working here; and at the first sign of trouble, I will quit."

He thought about it for a minute and kept glancing at Dustin. "That'll do, I guess."

"I assure you there won't be any more disturbances. The only trouble maker we had here got axed today." Dustin turned and left.

"What did he mean by 'any more disturbances', Kira?"

"You don't want to know."

"Oh, no you don't. What happened?"

"One of the waitresses, Wynne, was apparently some sort of bird demon because she was able to fly. She didn't realize I was a human at first. She didn't like humans, so when she found out about me, she tried to attack me."

"What?! I'll kill her!"

"You'd be too late for that."

"Meaning?"

"She sort of lost her head. Literally." Pyre rubbed his forehead. "Dustin promised I'd be safe, and they all seem to like me."

"I still don't trust them. You can come to work tomorrow. But I will be here. Any misgivings, any suspicions, even one little twitch of my doubt-o-meter, you're quitting. Agreed?"

"Agreed, I promise. Thanks, Pyre."

The next night Pyre and I were sitting in the living room when there came a rapid tapping on the door.

"Go away!" Pyre yelled at the door.

"Pyre!" I chastised him.

"What? I don't want 'em here." Lowell and Lur walked through the door anyway.

"Love you too, Pyre." Lowell said.

"Love is not what I feel for you. What do you want?"

"We came to see you." Lowell leaned against the armrest of the couch close to Pyre. Pyre moved away from him.

"We hoped you'd want to go on a double date with us tonight." Lur invited.

"You couldn't call?" Pyre ignored her and eyed Lowell.

"Could you be nice?" I asked.

"I don't wanna." Pyre stuck his chin out obstinately.

"Then, could you act your age?" He raised his eyebrow at me. Considering he's a demon, he would be extremely... "Hmm, never mind."

"Come on you guys, we want you to go out with us. It'll be fun." Lur tried her best coaxing, sugary sweet voice, always a mistake when trying to persuade Pyre of anything.

"In that case... No."

"Pyre!" I said.

"You're right. I mean, no, thank you. Now, get out!"

Lur leaned over to me and queried, "Is this a bad time?"

"Nope, he's usually like this. Except for when he's in a foul mood." He stared at me obstinately. I stuck out my tongue, and he rolled his eyes. I patted his knee. "It's okay, Pyre. If you don't want to go, you don't have to." He smiled smugly, believing he'd won. "I'll see you when I get home."

"Hey!" He tried to grab me but I stood up too fast.

"I'm just kidding, sort of. What did y'all have in mind for this double date?"

"We could go to dinner and a movie." Lur suggested.

"No, we do that all the time. If I'm going to go sit somewhere, I'd rather stay home." Pyre sounded bored.

"How about bowling?" Lowell suggested.

"Don't you remember the last time we tried to go bowling?" Pyre stared at Lowell.

"Oh... Oh, yea! Okay, no bowling." Realization dawned on Lowell's face.

"What happened?" I was instantly curious.

"We swore an oath never to speak of it, but Pyre can never go there again." Lowell chuckled.

"I'm liking the idea of spending the night with you less and less, Wolf!"

"I only asked you to go out. I didn't say anything about spending the night. I'm not that easy!" Lowell tossed his head and Lur and I laughed. Pyre looked to the ceiling for help, but found none. I decided I'd better get the conversation back on track.

"Okay, guys, that's enough. What else do you like

to do?"

"I love skating, or dancing. Do you want to go dancing?" Lur practically pleaded, doing a dance step.

"Pyre and skates, are a horrific combination." Lowell stated, and Pyre nodded in agreement. There was obviously another story there, but I didn't ask.

"Hmm, oh, I've got it! How about paintball or laser tag?" I looked over at Pyre, who was obviously intrigued.

"I could go for some of that." Pyre tried to fake casual interest.

"Yay, we finally decided on something to do!" Lur squealed.

"Only if you promise not to do that again" I joked.

When we arrived at the facility, there was another group of four who wanted to wage a laser tag battle against us. It sounded like fun, and we agreed. We suited up swiftly to get into the arena to allow our eyes to adjust to the low light and to find the best locations to begin the game. Lur was the first one to get hit. She squealed so loudly, that Pyre shot her again. At one point, I ran for Lowell's hiding place as a guy on the other team chased me. Lowell jumped up and blasted the guy, and gave me a high five. It left Lowell wide open for an attack by a girl from the other team. I dove for cover and crawled around to another spot. Several moments later, I watched as Pyre crept along, ducking cautiously. I detected that a guy from the other team had Pyre in his sights. I yelled at Pyre to roll to the side. As he rolled, I did a knee slide out and tagged the guy before he could get Pyre. I crawled hurriedly to safety and made it to Pyre.

"Where did you learn to do that?" Pyre asked.

"I took some dance lessons as a child."

"I see a light coming near us over there.  It might be... yes it is."  He jumped up and tagged the other player before she could sneak up on us.

"Nice shootin', Tex!  You're my hero."

"Aw, shucks, little lady."

Pyre was about to kiss me when Lowell and Lur walked over to us.

"Should we tell them the game has ended?"  Lur asked Lowell.

"Nah, let's see how long it takes them to realize the lights are on."

We went to check our score.  We beat the other team by one hundred points.

"That was fun.  I want to do it again.  Lowell, we should try to add some laser tag to our training sessions.  But now I'm hungry."

We all realized how hungry we were and decided to find a place to eat.  It was such a fun night.  Pyre was especially excited about it.  He acted like a small child, asking when we wanted to go again.

After we got home that night, Pyre kept looking at me, apparently with something on his mind.  I finally stared at him, waiting for him to spit it out.  "What's it like going to school?"

"Boring."

"Can I come with you to one of your classes?"

"Why?"  I wondered if I misunderstood him.

"I want to see what it's like."

"Didn't you go to school?"

"Nah, I was homeschooled.  I didn't play well with

the other kids." He had a mischievous expression on his face.

"That's hard to imagine." I replied sarcastically.

"So can I?" He was obviously hiding something.

"You're one hundred and eighty years old. What can you possibly learn?"

"I haven't learned art."

"And?"

"And what?"

"And the real reason you want to go?"

"To assure myself that you're safe."

"I knew it. You want to go because Crystal appeared on campus last month and the spring equinox is nearly here, right?"

"If she isn't reluctant to appear on campus, what might she be willing to do in one of your classes?"

"I doubt she would attack me in front of a whole class."

"You don't know that. Look at what she's done so far. She's crazy and I'm tormented by what she's willing to do." He pushed some hair out of my face. "I want to keep an eye on you."

"It's not enough that you stick around and sometimes talk to me through telepathy?"

"No." He stuck out his lip and tried to give me puppy dog eyes.

"You promise to behave and do everything I tell you to do?"

"If I have to." I mulled over my response. "I agree, against my better judgment."

"Yes!"

"But only if you're on your best behavior."

"I promise. I love you."

"I love you too." He kissed me good night and went to bed. He muttered to himself as he went down the hall, making some sort of list for the next day. *I'm already regretting this.* I shook my head and went to bed myself.

When I got up the next morning, Pyre was already in the living room with a backpack.

"I think I packed everything." He sounded incredibly excited.

"Everything?" I was apprehensive and wondered what all he had in there.

"I might've forgotten something. What all do I need to bring?"

"A couple of pens and a notebook."

He looked down at his backpack. "I guess I packed too much stuff." He took his bag to his room.

"How cute. He's like a little kid on his first day of school." I thought about it for a minute. "Now I understand somewhat how my mom felt on my first day of school." I went to the kitchen to make some coffee.

"Are you ready?" He stood in the doorway jumping up and down on his toes.

"Let me change and get a cup of coffee, and I'll be ready."

"Hurry up. We don't want to be late." He left the kitchen.

*What have I gotten myself into?* I rubbed my forehead.

After I made my cup of coffee and changed my clothes, we left for the campus.

Walking across the grounds to the first building, he saw a guy looking at me. He wasn't even looking at me, but at something in my general direction. Pyre wrapped his arm around my shoulders and yelled, "That's right, pal! She's with me. What? You don't have one!"

"He doesn't have one what, Pyre?"

"A girlfriend. Not one like you anyway."

I hid my face and practically ran for the door. We went straight to the art classroom. He stared everyone down in the room and they instantly became absorbed in their books. One girl grabbed her things and ran out of the room. I glared at him. "What? I didn't do anything."

"Hey, Kira," Lur greeted. "And... Pyre?"

"He wanted to see what it's like to go to school."

"Why doesn't he go to Lowell's classes?"

"He wants to be satisfied that I'm safe from Crystal since she wants to kill me soon."

"Why does he need to protect you? You're the toughest girl I've ever met."

"Crystal's probably a witch, definitely insane, and she's extremely powerful. As far as we know, I'm merely a normal human."

"You are anything but normal. And that's why I love you so much." Pyre declared.

"So whether I turned out to be a normal human or not, you'd still love me all the same?"

"Of course I would." He leaned his forehead against the side of my head.

"Aw, how cute." Lur teased. Pyre glared at her, but she wasn't intimidated by him at all, which of course irritated him even more.

"Hello, class, today we'll be learning a new technique." The professor walked in and noticed Pyre right away. "Who are you?"

"I'm Pyre."

"You're not one of my students, Pyre."

"He's here with me." I said.

"Why's he here?"

"He..." I looked over at him searching my brain for a reason.

"I considered taking classes next semester. Kira constantly talks about how much fun her classes are and I asked if I could tag along for the day."

"Very well." She seemed to buy it. "But do not disrupt my class."

"I won't."

Pyre took his seat next to me and we listened to the lesson for the day. We were supposed to draw a picture that represented a turning point or event that meant something to each of us. Pyre went to work on his paper, pausing occasionally to review what he'd done and sometimes erasing something he didn't like. When he finished, the professor came over to review his work. Whenever she would check our projects, she would show our work to the whole class so we would receive praise and helpful critiques. When she displayed Pyre's picture, some of the girls screamed. He drew a picture of himself, sword in hand, surrounded by bloody demon parts laying on the ground. The professor gave him a thumbs up for his first day, but expressed distress about what he had drawn. She finally proclaimed it was an excellent, though gruesome, portrayal of conquering one's own inner demons. Pyre started to contradict, but I stopped him in time. With his picture finished, he grew bored waiting for class to end. He got up and wandered around the room. He stopped by one student. "What's that supposed to be?" He moved on to another student and simply shook his head. At the third student, he muttered critically, "I was better than you when I was five. Give it up, man."

"Pyre! Come sit back down." I said.

His shoulders slumped, and he slunk back over to his seat. He sat, but he was still bored. He started drumming on everything with my drawing pencils. Until he broke them. He found tubes of paint on the shelves in the classroom, one of which he managed to squish all over my shirt. It was bright pink. Class finally ended and Lur ran ahead to meet Lowell, likely eager to report everything.

"I guess art isn't for me." Pyre hung his head as we left art class and headed for biology.

"Pyre, you did a great job on your drawing." I tried to cheer him up.

"Kira, I'm a demon. The picture was..." He looked down at the drawing in his hand.

"I like it." I squeezed his hand. "Come on. Biology might be more fun for you."

"I hope so."

Lur and Lowell were sitting at the desk flirting with each other when we got to the room. Luna mouthed the words 'help me' when we walked up to the desk.

"Gross! They flirt here too." Pyre acted like he was about to be sick.

"What is he doing here?" Lowell asked.

"Pyre felt lonely at home. I was concerned he'd be

destructive if left unattended, so I brought him to play with the other animals here at the zoo." Pyre made a face at me.

"I wanted to come to school and see how far I'd need to regress to be a big college boy like you." Pyre teased.

"What's the real reason?" Lowell wasn't amused.

"To protect me and watch out for Crystal." I said.

"Of course, I should've realized. Has he beaten anyone up yet?"

"Not yet, but it was this close." I held my hand up and pinched my thumb and finger together.

"That's only because I hadn't seen you yet, Wolf!" Pyre grumbled.

"After the way art class went, he'll be the one to get beaten up — by Kira." Lur quipped and Lowell laughed. Pyre glared at both of them, but they stared back.

"Not yet, but it was this close." I held my hand up and pinched my thumb and finger together. Pyre gave me his best stink eye, but it had no effect on me.

"What're you carrying, Pyre?" Luna queried, disturbed by the tension.

"My drawing from art class." Pyre tried to hide it behind his legs.

"Can I see it?" Luna tried to take it but Pyre moved it away from her.

"I don't think that's such a good idea."

"Pyre, it's a great picture." I rubbed his arm. "Isn't it, Lur?"

"Oh yea, it's great." She didn't sound convincing. "As long as you don't have a weak stomach."

"Come on, Pyre, let us see it." Lowell entreated.

"I'll let you see it, but no one else." Pyre kept an eye on Lur as he walked over to Lowell. Lowell took the drawing and lifted the cover sheet.

"Aw, man, Pyre. This is exceptional. Very realistic." Lowell had an amazed expression on his face. "Is this the day we—"

"Yep, it was the first thing that came to my mind." Pyre now felt moderately better about the picture. I walked over to the boys.

"The day you what? What did you boys do?"

"This was the day you two met for the first time." Lowell said.

"You mean when we went to the park? This was that day?" I scrutinized the drawing.

"The professor told us to draw something symbolic of a turning point in our lives, and I chose that day, because that's when I first met you."

"Who says you're not romantic?" I wrapped my arms around his neck.

"You should hang it in the living room." Lowell handed the picture back to Pyre.

"That's romantic? Kira, you really are weird." Lur sounded incredulous. I chose to ignore her.

"That's an outstanding idea. Let's hang it as soon as we get home." I said.

"Okay." Pyre blushed and tried to hide his huge grin. The professor walked in at that moment.

"Students, sit down, eyes up front." She noticed Pyre immediately. "Hold on here. Who are you and why are you in my classroom?" She pointed at Pyre.

"Well, I'm—"

"I don't care; just take a seat."

"Pyre, come sit here." I pulled an empty seat over for him.

During the rest of the class, the professor and Pyre got into arguments. While working on the experiment for the day, Pyre spilled liquid all over the desk. While I worked to clean it up, he tripped over his chair and knocked the blue dye out of Lur's hand. The whole class laughed when it landed and spilled all over my head. Luna and I rushed over to the restroom to try to get it out before it stained permanently. The dye stained most of my hair and neck, but I only had a few blue dots on my face after all the scrubbing. With pink on my shirt and blue in my hair, I looked like a cotton candy machine had erupted on me. When we went back to the classroom, we found Pyre sitting outside the door with a sad expression on his face.

"The mean lady kicked me out of the classroom."

"The professor kicked you out?"

"No, Lur did."

"It's okay, Pyre." I rubbed his face and kissed his forehead. "It was an accident. I have at times wanted to color my hair."

"You didn't want to dye it blue."

"True, but compared to some of the other students, no one will even notice. Let's go back inside. Biology is nearly finished. There won't be anything to spill or break in mythology class."

We all went back into the room. Pyre snuck in behind me and sat in his chair. He sat completely still and didn't touch anything else until the class ended. He tried looking at Lur with a smug face, but she only glared at him.

When biology ended, we headed for mythology.

"I wish I knew what my problem was." Pyre was still dismayed over the dye. "I ruined your shirt and dyed your hair all in the same day. I don't remember ever being this clumsy."

"Don't worry about it. You're just nervous and on edge because this is all new for you. The paint will wash off and the dye will eventually wash or grow out of my hair." I looped my arm through his. We walked by some vending machines.

"Wait, I want to get a soda." He walked back to the vending machines and chose what he wanted. He didn't have any change, though, so he hit one of them. It didn't do anything, so he hit it again. I walked over and put a dollar in and handed him his drink. "Thanks. I hope I'm done being clumsy." He opened his soda, and it spewed in my face. I stared into space with a frustrated expression as I pulled a tissue out of my bag. "Sorry."

"It could happen to anyone. But mostly to me. Let's just head to class now."

We walked the rest of the way to class and sat next to Stella and Luna.

"Hey, Pyre, what're you planning to do to Crystal?" Stella asked.

"I'm not sure yet." He put his bag on the desk. "Haven't decided if I want to maim and mangle or go straight for the kill."

"Man, I hope I'm there to watch. I love a good fight."

"Seriously, Stella?" I was appalled she would encourage him like that. She simply beamed at me, at first.

"Luna told me what happened in bio, but it's way worse than I imagined." Stella laughed when she got a good look at me. To say she loudly cackled or guffawed would be more accurate. I sat down and didn't say anything, refusing to acknowledge or look at any of them.

The professor arrived and introduced the lesson for the day. "Today we're going to discuss Hermes, the Greek god of messengers." That's when he spotted Pyre. He stared at Pyre for a few minutes, walked over to Pyre's desk and asked, "Who are you?"

"Pyre."

"Pyre, great name. You haven't been in my class before today. Are you a student here?"

"No. I'm visiting the campus today."

"Fascinating. You should have someone show you around who is familiar with the whole campus. I've been here for a while and could show you all the best spots." I stared at my lap and covered my face.

"Thanks for the offer. I'm here with Kira, so she can show it to me."

"Oh, well, some girls have all the luck." The professor was obviously disappointed. He didn't pay me any attention, and I was thankful.

Pyre leaned over and whispered, "Kira? Was he hitting on me?"

"No... no, I would say probably not. He's just overly proud of the campus." I glanced over at Stella and Luna who were desperately trying to control themselves.

The rest of the class was fairly uneventful until the end. One of the male students came over to us and asked, "I wasn't here for the last class. Can one of you share your notes with me?"

"Kira invariably takes excellent notes. If you want you could study with us sometime." Stella tried to flirt with him, but he only stared at me.

"I'd like that."

Pyre was out of his seat before I could respond. "What's that supposed to mean?"

"It means I'd like to study with them. What's your problem?"

"You're my problem, Joe College. She's not available. Got it?"

"Kira, who is this guy?"

"I'm her boyfriend."

"Then she has my sympathies."

"You're gonna need the sympathy when I get done with you." Before I realized what was going to happen or could do anything to stop it, Pyre was on the guy. They fell over desks, knocked things over, and knocked over other students, while the professor stood there watching, enjoying the spectacle. And I thought there wouldn't be anything to spill or break in mythology class.

Finally I yelled, "Pyre! That is enough. Break it up!" But he didn't listen or pay any attention, I had no idea which. Some of the other guys in the class came over to try to break up the fight, and some of them ended up being dragged into it too. At one point I tried to get Pyre's attention and grabbed his arm. Another student shoved him and he fell right into me. I stumbled into Stella and Luna, and we all fell down on each other in a pile. Pyre was up immediately, launching himself at the guy who shoved him. The girls and I sat there for a moment until I got up and helped them to stand. I observed the melee for a moment and finally yelled, "That's it! That is it! I have had enough for one day. I'm going home." I grabbed my things and stomped out of the classroom. Pyre looked up and yelled my name as I went through the door. I didn't stop or look back. I walked outside to where we intended to meet Lowell and Lur.

"Kira, are you okay?" Lowell was immediately concerned when he saw me.

"No, I am not okay. I am so totally not okay. I'm going home, in case anyone asks."

Pyre ran through the door and caught up to us. "Kira? Where are you going?" I walked away and didn't answer. He turned to Lowell in confusion. "But the day just got interesting."

I was steamed all the way home. Lowell said bye to Lur, and he and Pyre trailed along behind me. They didn't dare to try to speak to me. They didn't even speak to each other unless they did it telepathically. When we got home, I walked into the apartment and headed straight for my room.

"Kira, I'm sorry." Pyre said behind me. I was about to open the door to my room but Pyre got in front of me. "Kira, please." He had my focused attention now. I set my sights on his face and glared.

"Pyre, you're in the doghouse. You're forced to wait for her to let you out of it." Lowell still stood at the door. Pyre stepped aside without looking at me.

"Lowell, would you give us some privacy?" I continued to glare at Pyre. Lowell left without saying a word, but he looked at Pyre sympathetically as if to say,

"Dead man walking." Pyre waved at him and turned to face me. The expression on his face was too cute. It was hard to stay mad when he looked like that. But not impossible.

"Kira, don't be mad, please? I'm sorry. I didn't mean it."

"You didn't mean it when you squirted paint on my shirt. You didn't mean it when you broke my drawing pencils. You didn't mean it when you spilled blue dye on my head. When you attacked another student in the middle of the classroom simply for talking to me, you meant it!"

"He was coming on to you."

"Maybe. Maybe not. And if he was, I could've handled it myself, without turning it into a huge brawl and tearing up the entire classroom."

"The professor liked it."

"Seriously, Pyre?"

He walked over to my bed and sat down, looking dejected. "I guess it was a bad idea for me to go to class with you."

"No, it wasn't a bad idea. It was just a bad day. And I'm not angry, at least not anymore. Pyre, you can't go around attacking every guy who looks my way. Let 'em look. It doesn't matter, and do you know why?"

"Why?"

"Because I'm with you. I'm not looking at them. I'm looking at you, and no one looks at me the way you do. No one makes me feel the way you do. Ignore them and trust me, and everything else will work itself out."

"I can do that. I think. I trust you anyway."

"Good enough. Now, where's your drawing? Let's

go hang it on the wall."

# Chapter 16
# Burned, Buried, Reborn

I walked through the campus in the middle of the night. I knew night classes were scheduled, but there were no people anywhere. Everything was eerily still and quiet. My footsteps echoed off the surrounding buildings in the silence as I approached the dorm where I stayed last semester. The building stood cold and dark and appeared to be abandoned. I proceeded toward the center of the campus. Along the way, I spotted a sign on a building that read, 'Welcome Kira.' A chill running up my spine warned me not to go in there. A light came on through the doors. I continued to stare at the building, as all the lights came on inside, one by one.

"I've seen this movie. I die as soon as I go through those doors. I'm going this way." I saw a welcome sign on every building I passed but I kept walking. As I walked by each one, the lights came on in an orderly fashion like in the first building. When I got to the center of the campus, there was no one there. "I'm done with this. Pyre!" I waited for a response. "Pyre, are you there? I need you!"

"He's not coming." I whirled around to face Crystal. "I'm finally here. The campus truly is beautiful, and this stroll has been fun, but we have somewhere else to be. Why won't you come to your welcome party? Everyone's waiting for you." We were instantaneously back in front of my old dorm. "Come on, Kira." She walked inside, but I stood still for a moment.

"Yep, I'm gonna die." I followed Crystal inside the building. I saw which room she entered and walked to the door, but didn't proceed further.

"Come on, Kira, Pyre's over here." Crystal motioned for me to come forward and pointed toward one of the walls. I stayed where I stood but leaned to get a glimpse of him. He was chained to the wall with blood dripping down his face. I stopped myself from running to him. "Kira, he's been waiting for hours for you to get here. Why won't you go to him?"

"This is only a dream. None of this is real." Tears filled my eyes and trailed down my cheeks.

"What a clever girl you are." The room and Pyre instantly disappeared. Only the two of us remained, standing in the building's hallway now in some sort of spotlight, surrounded by eerie darkness. "I'm here, Kira. That is real."

"Why did you have to come here? Why won't you leave me alone? What is the point of this rebirth and what am I to be reborn into exactly?"

"So, you figured it out; score two for Kira. It's so you'll be like me! Soon, you'll view the world like I do, and we can be friends again!"

"That'll never happen."

"We'll see. Gotta go. So many preparations for the big event, so little time. I'll leave you with this." She threw back her head, raised her arms and disappeared as I was surrounded rapidly by fire.

"PYRE!" I screamed, as the flames reached for me.

I woke up in my room and sat up in bed. Ashes floated around my room. I watched as one drifted down through the air and landed lightly on my hand. Pyre and Lowell ran into the room.

"Kira, baby, are you hurt?" Pyre ran to me, pulled me up off the bed and embraced me. I buried my face into his shirt. "Kira?"

"Kit, what's wrong?" Lowell asked as he checked me all over for burns or injuries.

"She's still coming. She wants me to be like her." Pyre tightened his grip around me. I pushed against his chest as an urgent need gripped me. "I need to see something. We have to go to the campus, right now!"

When the three of us arrived at the campus, we approached a group of people crowding around my old dorm.

"What's going on?" Pyre asked. My heart pounded in my chest. "Kira?"

*Please no.* I ran over to the group, needing to discover what had happened.

"Kira!" Pyre yelled, running after me. I pushed through the people and stopped in front of the building. Pyre wrapped his arms around me and attempted to pull me back as I continued to push forward. "Kira, you don't need to see this."

"Pyre, she did this. I didn't do this. It was her. It had to be her!"

"I know, Kira, but you shouldn't see this. Come away with me, now. Please." He pulled me away from the building.

"Pyre, someone might've gotten hurt in there, and if they did, it's my fault. What if it was me?" I broke down into tears.

297

"No, Kira, it's not your fault. Like you said, you didn't do this, you wouldn't. It was Crystal." He stood in front of me shaking my shoulders. "Listen to me, none of this is your fault." Lowell and Lur ran over to us.

"Pyre, is she okay?" Lowell asked.

"Crystal caused the building fire last night, but Kira is blaming herself. I think she may be hysterical or in shock." He tried to pull me close, but I pushed against him.

"Someone got hurt because of me!" I screamed as I closed my eyes.

"No, Kira, no one was in the building when it caught on fire." Lur tried to console me. I didn't respond and merely shook my head as my eyes wandered wildly around the area. I was sure she had only said what I wanted to hear. "Lowell overheard the firemen say that no bodies or remains were discovered in the building. I stood nearby and heard it too."

"When we got here, I went over to find out what happened and ran into Lur. When we heard what the firemen said, we rushed over to tell you." Lowell rubbed my face. Lowell and Pyre exchanged worried glances.

"See, Kira, no one got hurt and even if someone did, it wouldn't have been your fault. It's not in you to do something like that." He gripped my hands, warming them with his own. "Come on, baby, listen to me. Please." Pyre didn't take his eyes off mine the whole time.

"No one got hurt?" What they were saying finally registered, and I looked hopefully up at each of them. "You're not just saying that?"

"No, Kit, no one got hurt. Like we said, they didn't find any bodies." Lowell affirmed.

"They're certain? Ashes, human ashes, nothing like that? What if the bodies were entirely incinerated, or cremated?" I hoped they were right, but I was so afraid they were wrong.

"I can go check for you." Pyre offered and started to pull away.

"No," I frantically reached for his hands. "Please don't go in there."

"I won't if you don't want me to."

"Kira, it's okay. They didn't find any evidence of humans in the building." Lur still tried to help even though she didn't fully understand the situation.

"Can I go back to the apartment?"

"If that's what you want." Pyre took me in his arms, preparing to take me away from the scene.

"We'll inform your professors." Lur said.

"Don't leave her alone for any reason, Pyre." Lowell suggested with a furrowed brow.

"I won't. Trust me, I won't." We got to the apartment in no time. "Are you hungry?" He set me down on the couch.

"No."

"Can I get you anything?" I shook my head. "You want to just sit here then?"

"Stay with me, please?" I clenched his hand. I didn't want him out of my sight. What if they were mistaken? What if someone did get hurt in the building? What if Crystal chose to show up again now? What if Pyre was hurt because of me?

"Of course." He sat down with his back against the armrest at the other end of the couch. "Come here." He held out his hands to me and I crawled over to him. I laid down with my head against his chest and he rubbed my head.

"How are we supposed to stop her?" I played with the laces on his hood.

"I'm not certain, but we'll figure out a solution. Did the metaphysics professor ever come up with any more information?"

"No, he told me all he knew. He was convinced it was only dreams and nothing to worry about, but we know he's wrong. We're out of time, and I am worried and scared. Pyre, in my last dream, she had hurt you. You were bleeding and chained to the wall." I sat up and searched his face.

"I won't let that happen."

"But what if it does happen?"

"If it does, Lowell will be there to save me."

"And if he can't?" Tears formed in my eyes and I started to panic again.

"If he can't, my angel will." He wiped my face.

"But what if—"

"Kira, no matter what happens, we'll get through it. You're becoming adept at using a sword."

"I almost killed that one guy who was my training partner."

"That's why I took over being your training buddy. Not to mention I was ready to kill him myself. You should've seen the way he was eyeing you."

"Your point?"

"My point is if something does happen to me, I'm confident you'll be there to save me." Pyre pushed my hair out of my face. "Just like I save you." He leaned forward and kissed my lips. I wrapped my arms around his neck. "I won't let anything happen. Not to you, to me, our friends, even the oaf." I realized he wanted to cheer me up. "The lowlife who used to be your training buddy. Who am I forgetting?"

"Stop it." I half-heartedly punched his arm. I finally started to recover control.

"And all those other people I don't like."

"Well, that's everybody." I glanced up at him and finally smiled.

"There's my girl." He hugged me close, and we sat there cuddling until I sat up and looked intently into his eyes.

"Pyre, let's go over to Eira's."

"We can go if you want, but why?" He brushed some of my hair out of my face.

"I want to be with all our friends right now." He appeared concerned about my intentions. "I'm worried about Crystal."

"I won't let her hurt you."

"I'm more worried about her hurting you or the others. I've been thinking. No bodies were found in the dorm, but the fire sacrifice might still have been made."

"Might? Why do you say might?"

"In the ice sacrifice, the people were frozen. In the earth sacrifice, a sand storm in the building caused everyone to disappear without a trace. There weren't any people on the airplane after the wind sacrifice was made. What if the reason they didn't find any bodies in the dorm was that there weren't any after the fire?"

He seemed to be processing what I said. "The spring equinox is here too, so we need to prepare immediately for Crystal." He stood up and started to pace.

I grabbed his hand and stood up too. "I want to go to Eira's place and be with our friends."

"But, Kira, we—"

"Our friends can help us prepare. We need to all be together right now, safety in numbers, and her place is bigger than our apartment." I wrapped my arms around his waist. "Please, Pyre."

He reached over to the phone and made a call. "Everyone meets at Eira's." He put the phone down and picked me up gently in his arms. I buried my face in Pyre's chest on the way to Eira's house.

"Pyre, what's wrong?" Eira asked.

"Everyone's coming here. We're getting ready for Crystal." Pyre rubbed the back of my head.

"I'll make some tea."

Footsteps exited the room as others entered. Lowell's familiar hand touched my shoulder.

"It'll be okay, Kit." Lowell whispered in my ear.

Everyone was talking around me, but I wasn't listening. My mind raced and images flew through my head — images from my nightmares, growing up with Crystal, the friends I made since moving to Russellville, and being with Pyre. As I thought about my days with Pyre, the image of fire burned into my mind. The image brought to mind Crystal's car accident.

*How did she change into what she is without the sacrifices?*

"Vitas might know the answer." Pyre snapped me

out of my thoughts.

As if on cue, Vitas walked through the door.

"Any news on the dorm fire?" Lowell inquired. I took a good look at everyone there in the room. Lowell sat in a chair with Lur sitting on the armrest. Luna and Stella stood next to a window talking. Eira and the girls sat on the couch with Caedmon and Eros standing behind it. All the people in the room were my friends, my family, and they were all in danger now.

"Yes, and it's... to be honest, it's horrific." He held a file in his hands. "There were people in the dorm. About thirty people to be exact."

"But they didn't find any evidence of people being in the dorm during the fire." Eros said.

Vitas looked me in the eyes as we said in unison, "That's because there was no evidence to be found."

"You were right." Pyre rubbed my face.

"Then, what, they disappeared? How?" Caedmon inquired.

"The fire didn't burn them. It consumed them." Vitas replied.

"Consumed?" Iris asked.

"Like an animal consumes food?" Lowell questioned skeptically.

"How could the fire consume something and not leave any trace?" Laya inquired.

I shook my head vehemently. "No, you're wrong."

"What?" Vitas asked.

"It didn't consume them. They became the fire."

"Became the fire? Kira, that isn't possible." Vitas sat down in front of me.

"It is if you're a witch. Think about what happened to the people in the other nightmares. The ice nightmare is the only one where physical bodies remained in the location. They all disappeared in the others." Pyre explained.

Everyone started talking all at once, which gave me a slight headache.

"I'm going to the restroom." I looked at Pyre.

"Are you okay?" He touched my forehead.

"I just need a moment."

"We'll be right here."

I walked into the restroom and locked the door behind me. I leaned over the sink and looked in the mirror.

*At least my friends are safe.* I bent over and washed my face. As I raised up I was startled by branches coming toward me. They grew out of the walls and came through the window. I tried to step back, but I slipped on the rug and fell backwards. As I was falling, it seemed like I would never hit the floor. Trees grew around me and the ceiling was replaced by the afternoon sky. As I hit the ground, chains appeared and held me in place. I looked all around and discovered I was in a cemetery.

"Pyre!" I yelled as I frantically pulled against the chains.

"He won't hear you." I looked to my left and saw Crystal. "We're miles away from Russellville."

"Let me go, Crystal."

"I can't, Kira. You must be reborn."

"Why, Crystal?"

"I told you. So you can be like me, and we can save sister earth."

"The earth doesn't need us to save her."

"That's where you're mistaken. She does need us. Between the humans and demons it's a wonder she hasn't been destroyed yet." She gazed up at the sky. "We can do it. We can save her, but first you need to be reborn. As the earth is reborn in the spring, you will be reborn on this very night."

"Crystal, don't."

"It will all be over soon." She began chanting and roots sprang from the ground.

"Crystal, stop! Please!" I screamed. "Somebody, please help!" The roots started to pull me under the ground. "Pyre!" I screamed Pyre's name several times. I fought against the chains but the roots gave them extra support. I fought with difficulty to remain alert, but everything went black as I was dragged into the earth.

I heard children laughing. I opened my eyes and saw the playground where Crystal and I used to play.

"Kira, let's save the world!" I recognized the two little girls as Crystal and me.

"How will we do that, Crystal?" The five year old me asked.

"We'll use the earth. We'll learn how to make plants grow big to stop our enemies and we'll protect sister earth." Crystal was proud of her plan.

"Don't you mean mother earth?"

"No, 'cause we already have mommies but we don't have sisters."

"I don't know, Crystal. We're only kids." I kicked at the dirt.

"We can do it when we're older."

"Can I think about it?"

"Sure." She was dissatisfied with my answer.

The scene disappeared and there was nothing to be seen for miles.

*Am I dead?* I moved my arms and stood on my feet. *Where are the chains, the dirt and the roots? I was dragged into the earth, wasn't I?*

"Kira, are you coming?" I turned to find Pyre and the others hanging out in the park. He took my hand and pulled me over to the others. "Everyone's been waiting for you."

"Why?"

"They want to help us celebrate, silly." He behaved outlandishly, entirely unlike Pyre.

"Celebrate what?" I backed away slowly.

"You know what." He had an abnormally large smile on his face. Lowell walked up to us.

"Hey, beautiful." Lowell waved wildly.

"Lowell?" I stared at him in doubt and confusion.

"Are you healthy? You look a wee bit pale." Lowell tried to touch my forehead.

"Um... I'm fine, I guess, but I don't understand." I retreated from his hand. I looked around at everyone. *What's going on? This is like a horror movie.*

"You seem perfectly fit to me. Come with us, Kira." Eira bounced up to us. "We've finished preparing the area."

I looked behind her and saw they had made a picnic with leaves, twigs, and bugs as the meals.

"Sweetheart, please come join us now." Pyre motioned for me. I looked up at him and was horrified.

His face was completely made of dirt. I backed away from him.

"Kira, you need a succulent meal. We prepared everything for you." Lowell stepped behind me. I spun around and saw he was made of dirt with grass growing on top of his head. Everyone else transformed into trees and their arms became branches that reached out for me. Pyre tried to come near me but I ran away.

*This is just a dream.* I ran through the trees. *Crystal's doing this. She has to be. That's the only explanation.* "You won't get to me, Crystal!" I stopped next to a boulder to catch my breath. "I need to get out of here." I screamed for Pyre while searching around the forest for a solution.

"Kira, I'm right here." I turned to see the Pyre made of dirt with mushrooms growing all over him. "Why did you run away?"

"You're not Pyre. Pyre isn't made of dirt. Pyre isn't overly polite." *And Pyre isn't here.* Tears filled my eyes, but I willed myself not to cry or panic.

"But Crystal told me what he was like and that after the rebirth you'd be happier with a better Pyre."

"I want to get one thing straight." I clenched my fists and walked toward him. "There is no replacing Pyre. From his temper to his kind heart, there's no replacing him." I wiped my face.

"But Crystal said—"

"I said no!" The leaves on the trees began to fall around us. "If Crystal wants this rebirth, she's going to get it." I stomped away, determined to find a way out, or confront her if necessary. "Crystal, this is the worst mistake you will ever make." I marched up a hill. "Do you hear me Crystal? You will regret this!" I continued to search the area. *How do I get out of here?*

The wind started blowing around me, and she instantly appeared a short distance away. "Poor, deluded little Kira. Do give up now, won't you? You can't beat me. No one can."

"I will beat you, Crystal. You will not change me into anything close to whatever you are. Because I am like the earth, Crystal. I possess roots in this world. There may not be any blood family remaining in my life, but I have Pyre, and my friends. They're my family now. And we watch out for each other. I have more in this world than you could ever imagine."

"How sweet. I might even cry." She mocked me, but I continued.

"You are like the wind. No form or substance. You can never have anything or hold onto anything. You can blow all you want, but the earth remains long after you're done."

"But if the wind is strong enough, like a tornado or a hurricane, everything else gets blown away. The tree will try to stand strong against the wind, but it loses its leaves and branches; it bends and eventually breaks."

"What about your mother, Crystal? Do you even care about what this is doing to her?"

"My mother? My mother! Who preferred you over me? Why would I care what she thinks of me or anything I do? I wanted to kill her the night you came to move your things. I was surprised to find there was a small shred of humanity left in me and I couldn't do it. I decided it might be more fun to keep her alive anyway."

"I realized you were insane, but I didn't comprehend to what extent. You're completely demented."

"And once again, little Kira states the obvious, ladies and gentlemen." The trees behind her, or what appeared to be trees, all laughed. Their laughter was unnatural, eerie and unnerving. Crystal clapped her hands together a few times for attention. "Enough chatter. It's getting late and I must perform one last ritual. Be a good girl and come along now."

The trees behind Crystal moved forward. *I want out of here. If this rebirth is supposed to change me and give me the same abilities as Crystal, why can't I use them? I made the leaves fall, didn't I? Perhaps I can control the earth.* I looked down at my hand, at the ring Pyre gave me for Christmas. He said it was a promise ring, and he'd be with me wherever I go. *Then a part of him is here with me now. I need to remember everything he's taught me. I can do this. I can hold her off and give him time to find me. I'm not defenseless, and maybe I'm not powerless either.* I clenched my fist and held the ring to my heart. I reached out to him telepathically, holding the image of the cemetery in my head, followed by the memory of being pulled into the earth. I reached into my pocket and pulled out the triquetra Lur gave me. I held it tightly in my hand and stared down at the earth. "You brought me into this, now get me out of here!" I yelled at the ground. The wind blew harder, threatening to knock me over. "I will not bend or be broken, Crystal!" The earth rumbled beneath my feet, moving me along, away from Crystal.

"Kira!" I heard Pyre calling my name.

*It's probably the dirt Pyre.*

"Kira!" Pyre's voice sounded louder.

"Pyre!" I yelled. "Pyre, please be you!" I started running again, ducking under branches, the earth moving beneath me giving me more speed. As I ran, I tripped on a root sticking out of the ground, hit my head on a rock, and passed out again.

"She's okay," I vaguely discerned Pyre's voice through the haze in my head. "She'll be okay, right?"

"She'll be fine, Pyre." Lowell tried to calm him down. "Come on, let's finish digging her out before that witch shows herself."

I slowly opened my eyes and Pyre was the first thing I saw. He was covered in sweat and dirt, and never looked so good as he did in that moment.

"I'm going to make Crystal pay for this." Pyre pledged.

"Get in line." I said. They both looked startled, only now realizing that I was awake.

"Kira, you're okay." Pyre kissed my face and hugged me tight.

"And you're squishing me."

"I was so worried about you." He closed his eyes, breathed deeply, and brushed my hair out of my face.

"Worried. More like frantic." Lowell snorted.

"Like you weren't? Are you done digging out Kira's legs yet?" Pyre eyed him menacingly.

"Working on it." Lowell went back to digging.

"Let's hurry and get you back home." Pyre let go and helped Lowell with the digging. I witnessed Crystal sneaking up with a knife. She looked at me with a demented smile and put her finger to her mouth to indicate shushing.

"Behind you!" I screamed holding out a hand. Plants surrounded her and pulled her back. Pyre faced her with a defensive stance.

"You won this round, Kira, but we're not done. I'll be back."

Pyre was about to respond, but I interrupted him. "If you have any brains or sanity at all, you won't. Because I'll be here, and I'll be ready."

"Ooh, scary." Crystal imitated shivers, snapped her fingers and disappeared.

Pyre stared at me in surprise and then turned to Lowell. "You timed that too close, don't you think?"

"Sorry, but I didn't realize she was there until Kira yelled."

"Your hearing is better than mine, and you didn't hear her?"

"You didn't sense her thoughts?"

I looked at the plants with disappointment and sighed. *I wasn't the one who controlled the plants. But if it wasn't me, why am I bothered about it? Shouldn't I be thankful it wasn't me?*

"Kira?" Lowell brought me out of my thoughts. "What's the matter?"

"I just realized that I wasn't the one who controlled the plants."

"That upsets you?" Pyre stared at me with a furrowed brow. Lowell returned his attention to my legs, finally pulling them out of the ground.

"I honestly don't know." I looked down at my

hands. The ring was intact, and I still held onto the triquetra. I said a thankful prayer that I had them with me and hadn't lost them as I slipped the triquetra back into my pocket.

"Let's get you home and we can talk some more." When Pyre picked me up, I gripped tightly onto his shirt. "Do you need anything?" Pyre held me close and brushed my hair off my face.

"Nothing. My feet are made of clay, made of clay, don't you know?" I yawned. Pyre looked at me in confusion, and then at Lowell like he would panic again.

"Well... um... take a nap, we'll be back home soon." He kissed my forehead as I dozed off.

I woke up in my bed. I sat up and spotted Pyre sitting in a chair next to the door napping with his chin on his chest. Eros walked up to the door.

"How do you feel?" He whispered.

"I'm all right." Eros nudged Pyre awake.

"What do you want?" Pyre asked, rubbing his eyes.

"I thought I should inform you that Kira's awake." Eros pointed in my direction. Pyre looked over at me and exhaled a huge sigh of relief.

"Thanks."

"Anytime." Eros headed for the living room.

"How are you doing?" Pyre walked over to me.

"I'm all right. Other than being covered in dirt. How about you?"

"Much better now." He sat down next to me and wrapped his arms gently around me. I leaned my head on his shoulder and stroked his arm.

"How long was I out?"

"All night." He started twitching in his familiar way.

"What is it?"

"Will you ever stop nearly dying on me?"

"I'm working on it. I'm not exactly a big strong demon." I looked up at him, disconcerted. "I guess I'm not exactly a puny human either."

"I know, and we'll figure out everything. But no matter what, you'll always be my Kira." He pushed my hair out of my face. "Make me a promise? After we've stopped Crystal, you and I will move some place where only our friends and family can find us. No more enemies or psychotic friends, and we'll live a happy life without a care in the world."

"Sounds heavenly. Where would we go?"

"Anywhere. The mountains, the middle of the forest, but not the beach."

"What's wrong with the beach?"

"Water plus fire demon equals bad combination."

"Can't you swim?"

"Like a fish, but it's not a good idea for me. If I go swimming, my fire goes out."

"Cel mentioned something about that. When you say out, do you mean permanently out or out like after you dry off you're fine?"

"I'm fine after a few days but only if another fire demon helps by keeping a fire around me at all times."

"But you can take showers?" I was thoroughly confused.

"Not like a human. Since fire demons can't be in the water, we use other methods to get clean."

"How?"

"We basically burn off the dirt and oil that builds on our skin and hair."

An image of Pyre surrounded totally by fire popped in my head. His chuckling brought me out of the image.

"Not quite like that. It's kind of like the fire is a sort of soap. It'll be easier if I show you." He held out a hand and made little flames appear. "All I do is rub it all over my skin and the dirt and oil are gone."

I thought about it for a minute. "I like the mountains."

"The mountains it is; maybe a cabin among the trees." We held each other's gazes, remembering the dream we had shared.

"Are you two coming?" We looked up to see Lowell. He threw his hands up as if to defend himself. "Everyone wants to see how Kira is doing."

"And they will soon enough." Pyre growled loudly.

"I'm sorry I walked in, but it was either me or Eros."

"Apology accepted." Pyre replied.

"Did I miss something?" I asked, looking at Pyre.

"Nothing." Pyre had a strange expression on his face.

"He called me mean names through telepathy." Lowell pretended to pout.

"Pyre, why did you call him mean names?"

"Because." Pyre sounded like a little kid.

"Because why?" I smiled at their familiar antics.

"Because he made me mad." He pouted.

"My big, scary fire demon." I kissed his cheek.

"You know it." He started to kiss me back but realized Lowell still stood there. "We're coming." Pyre growled as he picked me up in his arms.

"Can't I walk?"

"Nope."

"Why not?"

"I said so."

"You're not the boss of me."

"I am when you're in danger."

"I'm regularly in danger."

"And?"

"You're mean." I pouted.

"I'm not mean. I love you too much."

He took me to the living room and sat down with me in his lap.

"Kira, when we found you, you were unconscious and talking. Were you dreaming?" Lowell asked.

"I was, I guess. I think it was a dream anyway."

"What were you dreaming about?" Pyre asked.

"First, I was dreaming about a memory of Crystal and me. We were talking about saving the world. After that, I was in a field with you and the others where everyone had made a picnic area. That's when I noticed all of you were made of dirt with things growing out of your bodies. I ran into a forest but the fake you followed me."

"Fake me?"

"It was a dream made by Crystal so the people in the dream weren't real. The fake you was polite to everyone and even offered to replace you after the rebirth was done."

"What did you tell him?"

"There's no replacing you." I wrapped my arms around his neck and kissed him tenderly on the lips.

"Kira, are you sure that... Ow!" Eros rubbed his arm while Eira gave him a steady stare.

"You like it when I'm rude to everyone?" Pyre asked, ignoring Eros.

"No, but I don't like you overly nice, either."

"Is that even possible?" Pyre asked; Eros snickered but didn't say a word.

"I have no clue. I do prefer for you to be yourself, though, because I love you for who you are."

"When we found you, you said something strange. You were basically out of it and falling asleep. You said your feet were made of clay. What did that mean?" Lowell asked.

"I said my feet were made of clay?" I puzzled it over in my head for a moment. "I'm not sure exactly. The only thing I can recall is this old movie I used to watch with my mother called 'The Philadelphia Story'. Katherine Hepburn starred in it and toward the end she'd nearly passed out and said something like, 'My feet are made of clay, made of clay.' It's apparently also a Biblical reference, when Daniel interprets the dream of Nebuchadnezzar. I must have thought of it because I told Crystal that I was like the earth, with roots in this world, but that she was like the wind. I later yelled at the earth to get me out, and the ground started moving underneath my feet. I wondered for a second if I was becoming part of the earth, or if it was becoming part of me."

"Kira, why did Crystal do that to you?" Laya touched my arm in concern.

"She wants me to be like her."

"She wants you to be a witch?" Caedmon asked.

"You're way too sweet to be a witch." Eros answered.

"You're not earning any points." Pyre muttered. I looked at Pyre in confusion. "Don't ask."

"Why did she try to bury you?" Iris asked.

"She thought it would change me, like she did. She hoped I would be reborn."

"Reborn?" Gabby asked.

"Into something else, something like her, supposedly to save the earth from the humans and demons." I stared at the floor.

"I think you would've changed in a different way." Lowell asserted. Everyone appeared to be concerned, uncertain what to think. "From the beginning you've been down to earth and from what you've told us, Crystal was more in the clouds. Her accident may have brought her back to earth so fast that it affected her worse than a typical person."

"But I didn't change, did I? I mean we're still not certain I wasn't the one causing all of those things to happen while I was asleep. I realize I'm not the one who controlled the plants last night to attack Crystal, but that doesn't mean I can't. In the dream, I made leaves fall off the trees, and I tried to control the earth to help me escape."

"I think you succeeded to an extent." Pyre said hesitantly.

"What do you mean?"

"We heard the commotion in the bathroom. We unlocked the door and saw the branches and vines. You

317

were gone, and I had no clue what to do or how to find you. At first I couldn't sense you at all until I inexplicably got an image in my head of an old cemetery. I recognized it as the cemetery at Scofield. I also saw an image of you being pulled into the ground. We traveled there at once. I hoped it was the right place, but I was so afraid it was misdirection or that I was wrong in my recognition of the cemetery."

"I did that. I remembered what you said when you gave me the ring. I held it close to my heart and thought of the cemetery, trying to send it to you telepathically."

"It worked, brilliantly. Once we got there, I sensed your presence, but I couldn't find you. I called your name repeatedly, hoping for some kind of sign or reaction. The ground abruptly opened up and dirt and rocks erupted out like a pot boiling over. Roots crawled through the dirt, and then we saw you. It appeared as if the earth was pushing you out of itself. We grabbed you and started pulling and digging."

"It pushed me out, like I was being born from the earth? What if there is something that's been inside me all this time, but I never realized it? What if it only needs to be awakened? Crystal was affected so intensely by her accident that she was able to control things over night. If I can, I can only do it while sleeping, at least up to now. What makes her unlike me?"

"I found a possible answer to that." Vitas said as he entered the room. "Crystal has demon ancestors. When she had her accident, she died for a few seconds but was revived. She experienced a sort of rebirth of her own, but she came back all wrong."

"That would explain a lot. Caedmon and Eros have demon ancestors. That's how they acquired their abilities. That would explain Crystal too. And it would explain why they aren't like Crystal." Pyre continued.

"Could Kira have demon ancestors?" Eros asked.

"I'll research it." And with that, Vitas was gone.

"It's even more important now to find out what my dad knows, if anything."

"Kira might be like us." Caedmon said.

"But Crystal wants Kira to be like her." Laya added.

"Is there a way to stop it?" Iris asked.

"As long as Kira doesn't have demon ancestors, we won't need to worry." Lowell stated.

"What if she does?" Eros asked.

"It doesn't change anything. Even if Kira acquires abilities due to her bloodline, she'll still be Kira." Eira said vehemently.

"There's the potential for good and evil in all creatures. Demons and witches too. Kira is unfailingly kind-hearted. It sounds like Crystal has always had some of her crazy plans in her head. Kira would still be Kira, just with powers." Pyre added with conviction.

"She'll be like Caedmon and me." Eros grinned until he saw Pyre's face.

"It would take a lot to change Kira." Lowell agreed.

"And we won't let that happen." Pyre gazed at me. "You're unusually quiet. What's on your mind?"

*I'm scared of what she'll do next.*

*I won't let anything happen.*

*She wasn't happy when you saved me. She probably thinks you stopped the ritual.*

*Let her attack me. She won't hurt you ever again.* He wrapped his arms around my waist as I wrapped mine around his neck. *I love you, Kira.*

*I love you too, Pyre.* As he hugged me close, I looked out the window and saw Crystal standing on the fire escape. She had a creepy smile on her face, and a black rose in her hand. I was about to tell Pyre but she waved and disappeared. *I think she just accepted your challenge.*

# Find Me Online

If you liked this book, I hope you will consider recommending it to your friends and reviewing it online at Amazon, Barnes and Noble, Smashwords or your favorite retailer.

Please visit my website for updates, contests and promotions at
https://www.alexecarey.com
My website's contact page will be updated with all places I can be found online.
Consult my events and news page for information on book signings and other events.

I invite you to like the Facebook page for the Elemental Series for updates, contests and freebies.
https://www.facebook.com/elementalcarey

You may tweet me at
Alex@ESeries5
or search by ElementalSeries5@gmail.com

You can also find me at
Google+, LinkedIn, Pinterest and Goodreads

# Fire's Love

## The first novel in the Elemental Series

Readers praise excerpts

for Alex E. Carey and Fire's Love:

"Great read!" * "Entertaining" * "Exciting"

"Couldn't put it down!"

"Can't wait for the next book."

# Water's Reflection

## The third novel in the Elemental Series

## Watch for it - Coming soon!

The tides are changing for Kira as her life becomes not only more dangerous but more confusing.  As Kira confronts her father and her past, her boyfriend Pyre asks questions about his own past and finds trouble when a water demon attacks.  Kira must learn to control her new abilities or risk losing the love of her life.  The past helps the present as the present threatens to fall apart.  Will they succeed or will they drown in Water's Reflection.